THE SEASHELL PROMISE

A Women's Fiction Mystery, Nantucket
Point Book 3

JESSIE NEWTON

feel good fiction

LIANA JOHNSON

ISBN-13: 978-1-63876-120-4

Chapter 1

Annie Mason sighed over the side of the ferry, wishing she'd stayed in the car the way her daughter had. Paige was not happy to be coming to Nantucket for the holidays, and Annie hadn't the heart to tell her it was either the Point and Aunt Julia's cooking, or an empty house with an empty fridge at her father's.

Donovan, her ex-husband, hadn't told anyone he and his partner had decided to leave Chatham. Annie had found out quite by mistake, actually when she'd called him on the way to his house with Brianne, and he'd blurted out that he lived in Vermont now.

An entirely different state.

"Guess he doesn't want to be as involved as he claimed," she said into the wind.

"What?" Bri asked, and Annie turned toward her, putting a false smile on her face.

"Nothing, dear." She lifted her arm and put it around her youngest daughter. Bri hadn't given her any trouble about coming to Nantucket for Thanksgiving, but she didn't have a boyfriend she had to leave for six whole days.

Six days. Annie rolled her eyes toward the sky, glad she stood taller than Bri so her daughter couldn't see. Annie herself, as a mother, had learned to see everything around her, and she knew Logan and Paige were *not* just friends.

Just like she'd known that Donovan had stopped loving her right about the time Bri turned ten years old. He'd stayed for a year or two, but in the end, he'd embraced a whole different part of himself, one he said had been suppressed for too long.

She didn't fault him for that. She wouldn't want to be untrue to who she really was. She simply wanted to be communicated with, and having the father of her children leave the state of Massachusetts without telling any of them had opened wounds she'd thought she'd stitched closed.

"Aunt Julia says Maddy is the best cook on the island, and she's already been baking for a week."

"Pumpkin pie?" Bri asked, a big smile on her face.

"And apple," Annie said, returning the smile. "Rolls, tarts, and I got a text this morning that she's even prepared the breakfast casserole already. Apparently, it has to sit overnight."

"I can't wait," Bri said.

Annie turned her face into the wind, because she was looking forward to five days where she didn't have to take care of things. Someone else could make breakfast, lunch, and dinner. Someone else would make her bed once she left. Life away from home, with someone who would tell her where to sit, what time to get up, all of it, was exactly what Annie needed right now.

Her stomach tightened at the thought of spending the holidays with a half-sister she barely knew. She'd met Janey a few times now, and they got along just fine. She didn't really *know* her, though, and something buzzed in Annie's blood.

She couldn't decide if she wanted to know her half-sister better or not.

What she wanted felt completely out of her control. She wanted the sense of stability she'd once had. She wanted to be able to talk to her daughters without it turning into an argument or hearing the words, "You just don't get it, Mom."

She wasn't so out of touch that she didn't know what the world was like for teenagers, though that was how Paige made her feel.

She wanted to feel happy again. Not just the brief kind of happiness she experienced when her daughters brought home good report cards or one of her patients got to check-out of the hospital early.

But true happiness. The kind that a person woke

with deep down in their soul. The kind that made simple things like a child playing in a fountain bring a smile to her face and the general feeling that all was well in the world. The kind that told her she was good enough, just as she was.

Her phone rang, and she almost didn't want to check it. It would either be her shift boss, her mother, or Julia. At the moment, Annie didn't particularly want to speak to any of them.

She couldn't just ignore her phone, and she lifted it to check the screen. *Mom* sat there, and out of the three, she was the worst one.

"Don't answer it," Bri said. She even reached over and took the phone from Annie before she could blink. "She'll just say something to make you mad or feel guilty." She silenced the phone and stuck it in her back pocket. She glanced at Annie, who blinked at her in pure surprise. Her daughter looked out over the water too, and Annie took a few seconds of silence to figure out what to say.

"She's going through a hard time," she finally said.

"We all have things," Bri said without looking at her. "And I don't feel that bad for her."

"Bri," Annie chastised. "She…" She didn't have adequate words for her mother. A few months ago, they'd all found out about Janey Forsythe, a woman the same age as Julia, her oldest sister.

The only problem was, Janey wasn't Annie's full

sibling. She only had her father's DNA running through her veins. Proven with a paternity test.

At some point in the past, he'd been unfaithful to her mother, and Annie didn't want to judge her mom's reaction and then subsequent actions.

She'd first gone to Toronto, where her family hailed from. She'd stayed there with her mother and sister for a few weeks before returning to the huge house in Southampton where Annie had grown up with her two siblings.

Then she'd asked Dad to move out, but he'd refused. They'd been living in the house, but barely speaking. Annie had witnessed it first-hand when she'd gone to visit in October. She'd never felt such tension in her life, not even when she and Donovan had sat down with the girls to lay things out for them.

Her mother was supposed to be hosting Thanksgiving dinner, but Annie had adequately warned Julia and Eric, her brother, and they'd all made alternate plans. Because of everything going on, Mom hadn't invited anyone until last week, and it had been easy to say they'd already made arrangements for the holidays.

"She's being childish," Bri said. "Grandpa has explained everything a thousand times over."

"It's hard to know what really goes on behind closed doors, honey." She gave her daughter a closed-mouth smile.

"It's just...you've been through hard things." Bri

met her eye, some measure of strength in hers. "I didn't see you shrink up and run away."

Annie's shock reverberated through her again. "What did you see?" she asked, wanting to watch herself through her daughter's eyes.

"You told us the truth," Bri said. "And you didn't sit around feeling sorry for yourself. You went from part-time to full-time to support us, and you didn't even break stride with anything. I even saw you pack boxes for Dad, Mom."

Annie swallowed, her chest so tight. "We all handle things in different ways," she said. She had worked incredibly hard to maintain the sense of normalcy for her girls. She'd been working part-time as a nurse when she and Donovan had started the divorce process.

By the end of it, and through the grace of God, Annie had been able to move into a rare full-time position in the radiology department—a coveted job that didn't come up very often.

One layer of tension heating her muscles released, and Annie had the distinct thought that she needed to be better about acknowledging the things she'd been blessed with.

She also couldn't give up the job in Chatham, though Julia had been needling her to come to Nantucket and work at the hospital there. "Or any of the doctor's offices, Annie," she'd said. "They have a need here."

She'd been tempted by the job boards in Nantucket, Annie could admit that. It would be nice to be closer to Julia, who'd been going through her own divorce and major life changes. *Now that Donovan was gone…*

Annie cut off the thought and put her arm around her daughter. "I love you girls."

"I know." Bri leaned into her side, and Annie loved the weight of it.

Annie blew out her breath, letting more of her dread and tension go with it. "Now," she said. "What are we going to do about Paige this weekend?"

"There's a trick with Paige," Bri said.

"Oh, yeah? Do tell."

"Let her talk, and then agree with her before you try to give any opinion." Bri grinned up at her mom. "I think she just wants to feel heard, and with you especially, she doesn't."

Annie's first reaction was to say how unreasonable Paige could be. She held her tongue and let her younger daughter's words swirl through her mind. "That's why she gets so loud."

"Exactly," Bri said. "It would be great if we didn't have to scream at each other over Thanksgiving."

"It would be great," Annie agreed with a smile. "I'll work on that."

"Mom," Paige said from behind her. Annie turned that way and opened her other arm for her eldest.

"Hey, bug. You left the car."

"Grandma called," Paige said, stepping into her side. Annie took that as a major win, though her heart had dropped to the soles of her shoes.

"Why? What did she want?" Annie looked at Paige, and she really was a gorgeous girl. Nearly jet-black hair, with long eyelashes, and eyes the navy color of deep midnight. They could glint like the moon off still water when she was happy and shine like gold in a dark cave when she had something up her sleeve.

Of course, Annie had also seen the hard-as-nails flint in them when she wasn't pleased. She told herself to let Paige talk and to actually listen before she said anything.

"She wanted to know if Aunt Janey would be at the inn," Paige said. "I told her I assumed she'd be, yes. Isn't she bringing her kids?"

"Yes," Annie said with a sigh. "I've already told Grandma all of that."

"She asked if she and Grandpa could come. I had no idea what to say."

"What *did* you say?"

"I told her to call Aunt Julia. She's the one who knows how many people they have coming for Thanksgiving dinner."

Annie's pulse stormed through her veins, cracks of

lightning bolting out every few seconds, making her fingers twitch and her eyes blink rapidly.

"Can you imagine?" she asked, her voice barely louder than the wind. "Grandma and Grandpa...in the same room with Janey?"

"Janey's cool," Bri said.

Annie said nothing, because she knew more about Janey Forsythe than the girls. She knew the woman had been in a psychiatric unit and that she'd been to visit their father three times now. Dad had gone to Nantucket once, without Mom.

Why in the world would her mother even *want* to come to The Lighthouse Inn for Thanksgiving? It made no sense, and Annie fought the urge to drop her arms and demand Bri give back her phone. She needed to call Julia and warn her, then call her mother and tell her in no uncertain terms to stay home.

She didn't need to blow up this holiday for anyone, least of all Annie. If she wanted her family around, she should've planned better and sooner.

The ferry continued on toward Nantucket, completely unaware of the turmoil brewing inside Annie Mason. She didn't know how to exhale it out or release it into the atmosphere, and she didn't ask for her phone. It was as if someone had encased her in ice, and she was slowly going numb.

They reached the dock, and people began to move

toward the exits. They'd brought their car, so they had to return to it and wait their turn to depart.

"Let's go," she said quietly to the girls, and the three of them made their way toward the lower decks, where the cars drove on and off the ferry.

"Can I have my phone, Bri?" She held out her palm, and Bri gave her the device. Annie waited until she sat behind the steering wheel, seat-buckled in, waiting to get off the ferry, before she looked at it.

Julia had texted, and she went to that message string first. *Look what I found in the storage room at Maddy's father's house!*

She'd sent a picture with the words, and a book sat there. An old, tattered book with a pink, purple, and blue cover. Black lettering ran across the front of it that said *The Seashell Promise.*

No author name accompanied the title, and Annie frowned. Was she was supposed to know what this was?

Another message sat below the picture. *I wrote this in college, and Maddy and I want to do it while everyone is here.*

"Do what?" Annie asked as she typed out the letters. She sent the message, then started another one. *Did you talk to Mom?*

The ferry lurched, signaling they'd been tied and secured, and Annie looked up and out the windshield. They wouldn't be first to exit, as she'd barely made it onto this ferry. Everything seemed to take forever these days, including packing and getting the girls out the door for their vacation.

Her phone vibrated, and she looked at it. *I did,* Julia said. *I didn't know how to tell her no. They're only coming for dinner and one night.*

Oh boy, Annie said.

Yeah, Julia sent back. *Now I just have to figure out how to tell Janey...*

Chapter 2

Janey Forsythe stood on the dock, watching the ferry come toward her. Her anticipation climbed as she'd been waiting for weeks for her children to arrive.

Both Rachel and Cole should be on this ferry, as they'd both texted on the family thread that they were. Her heartbeat pounded the same way the rain hit her heavy-duty umbrella, and she wished it wasn't raining so hard today.

A microburst had just arrived on the island of Nantucket, along with the ferry.

"Do you see them?" she asked Sean, who held the oversized umbrella above them.

"They don't even have it tied yet." He chuckled, but Janey pressed her fingertips together, trying to get her thoughts to align across her brainstem. Her therapist had taught her the exercise, and Janey often crossed sides of her body to try to quiet her thoughts.

She felt so much better than she had in months—probably since her mother had died last spring. She hadn't quite mastered everything at her job at the law firm where she worked, but she had a comfortable role there. It helped that her boyfriend was her boss and very forgiving. Sean had been willing to teach her any technical, lawyerly terms she'd needed to know, and Janey had enjoyed getting to know a lot of the permanent residents on Nantucket.

"Have you thought any more about moving in with me?" he asked now, startling Janey.

She dropped her hands and tucked them into the pockets of her windbreaker. "Of course I'm thinking about it, Sean," she said. "I don't think now is the best time to bring it up."

"Okay," he said. "It's just been a few weeks, and I thought of it, because both of your kids live with their partners."

As if Janey didn't know. Rachel and Travis had gotten engaged a couple of months ago, and Janey had spent quite a bit of her off-the-clock time talking to her daughter about wedding plans.

Rachel wanted to get married in the tulip gardens at Holland Hollow, one of the largest flower fields and greenhouses in New Jersey. Janey hadn't been surprised by that in the least, because she'd taken her kids to Holland Hollow every year as they grew up.

She hadn't been a super-great mom, but she'd tried. Married and divorced twice, and then quite the stretch of being single now. She'd had boyfriends on and off, sometimes more than one at a time.

Those days were behind her, as she'd learned so many things in the past several months. About herself. About others. About how to have a healthy relationship.

Cole and his girlfriend, McKenna, had been together for years. Janey had no idea if they'd talked about marriage or not. They lived in Atlantic City, where Cole worked at a private marina, helping to guide the yachts and boats of the rich and famous into place.

He then detailed the vessels while their owners dined at the luxurious, seaside restaurants, or went to the nearby spas, or simply took their children to the private beach.

Her son made quite a bit of money with the work, and he'd said the tips were unbelievable. Janey knew he made enough to keep him in Atlantic City and at the job for the longest he'd ever kept the same one.

Her son hadn't excelled in high school, and college had intimidated him to no end. He'd entered the work force as an assistant to a chef, and he'd liked it. But something had happened that he still hadn't told her about entirely, and he'd left that job after only eight months. Janey had a suspicion that he'd been fired, but he'd never admitted it. Sometimes her son was still a mystery to her.

"There she is," Janey said, almost darting out into the weather. The ferry station had a covered walkway from the watercraft to the building where one could buy tickets. She and Sean could've waited indoors, but she wanted to see her children the moment she could.

"Rachel," she called, lifting her hand high above her head. Her daughter shielded her face from the driving rain, the path soaking wet as the wind pushed it under the covering.

Behind her, her boyfriend, Travis, towed a rolling suitcase and wore a backpack. Janey's heart expanded at the sight of them, love thrumming through her with every step they took.

"Mom." Rachel ran the last few steps to her, and Janey flung her arms around her daughter. She was rail-thin, with long, almost white-blonde hair. She usually wore it in waves that spilled over her shoulders, but today, it had been pulled back into a messy ponytail.

They clung to one another, and Janey only released Rachel in order to hug Travis. "Can you believe your flight was delayed so much that you're on the same ferry as Cole?"

"We sat forever at the airport," Travis said, his hug strong and sure.

Janey stepped back, a sting pricking her stomach as the warmth of Sean's body reminded her that he hadn't met anyone yet. "Rachel, Travis." She cleared her throat. "This is my boyfriend, Sean Masterson. He owns the law firm where I work. Sean, my daughter Rachel, and her boyfriend Travis."

"Fiancé, Mom." Rachel grinned.

Janey sucked in a breath. "I can't believe I didn't get that right." She shook her head, embarrassment streaming through her. "We've been talking about the wedding every day for two months."

She looked at Travis. "I'm sorry, Travis."

He chuckled and tugged his suitcase out of the way as people kept streaming by. "It's fine, Janey. You have a lot going on."

"Not that much," she said just as a man called her name. She turned back toward the ferry, spotting her tall, thin son easily.

Her mother-heart had never been so full of joy, and she took a few steps toward Cole. "My goodness," she said. "You cut your hair."

"He earns more in tips now," McKenna said, stepping into Janey at the same time Cole did. The trio embraced, and Janey held them so tight, one under each arm.

She breathed in and out, and said, "Oh, I missed you guys so much."

"Miss you too, Momma," Cole said, and McKenna echoed him.

She stepped back and looked at them both with adoration. McKenna had pulled her dark hair back on the sides, and her wide, brown eyes glinted with happiness. She wore a nose ring and false eyelashes, and Janey thought she was simply perfect for her free-spirited son.

"How's the jewelry-making?" she asked. "Did you sell out at the early holiday fair?"

"I have four pieces left," McKenna said. "It was unbelievable. I told Cole I'm doing that fair every single year." She glanced behind her, and Janey returned to Sean's side.

"Guys, this is Sean Masterson, my boyfriend. Sean, Cole and McKenna." This time, she didn't include any qualifiers. She didn't need to. She'd told Sean all about her kids.

Cole wore a wary look in his eye, and Janey didn't blame him. She'd put that anxiety in his attitude, and she hated herself for it. She hoped this holiday weekend would be good for all of them, and she hoped to be able to speak to her children one-on-one in order to heal any cracks, crevices, or crannies that existed between them.

Mostly, she needed to make sure she had done

everything she could to heal herself, and her therapist had encouraged her to go through a similar program that alcoholics did. She needed to face herself and the things she'd done wrong, then try to make them right.

"Are we ready?" Cole asked after shaking Sean's hand. "It's pouring, and I'm freezing."

"You need to add some body fat to your frame," Janey said, grinning at him. She turned and laced her fingers through Sean's, glancing up at him. He wore a smile too, and he never seemed to get ruffled by anything.

The six of them headed for the van Janey had rented when she'd learned they'd be on the same ferry, and everyone loaded their luggage into the back of it.

Cole gave an audible sigh when he got in the back seat, and Janey flipped on the windshield wipers before pulling out of the parking lot and heading toward the Point.

"I hope the rain lets up," Rachel said. "I want to see all the things you've told me about."

"Let's see what the weather will be," Sean said, swiping on his phone.

"Looks like rain today and tomorrow," Cole said from behind her, and Janey glanced in the rearview mirror to see him checking his phone too.

Sean lowered his without saying anything, and the tension in the van skyrocketed, at least for Janey. It suddenly felt like Cole was going to compete with Sean for everything, and Janey wanted to diffuse the situation.

She didn't know how, and it wouldn't help anyway. Sean looked out his window, and Janey put a smile on her face. "Did you figure out the cake, Rach?"

"Did you not get the pictures I sent?"

"No," Janey said, meeting her eye in the mirror before focusing on the road again. Water sluiced off of it, and she too wished it wasn't raining quite so hard. There was so much to see from downtown Nantucket to the Point, and she wanted to show her kids the magic of this place.

She wanted them to have a fantastic experience here, the way she always had.

"I'll resend them," she said.

Janey wouldn't be able to see them right away, but it didn't matter. She'd gush over them at the cottage.

"Aunt Tessa made Gramma's clam chowder for your welcome meal," she said.

"Is Matt coming?" Cole asked.

Janey shook her head, a twinge of sadness pulling through her. "No," she said. "He's been dating this woman, and Aunt Tessa said it's gotten pretty serious. They're going to her parents' for Thanksgiving."

Cole nodded and looked out his window. Janey and Tessa had gotten their kids together as they grew up, but she hadn't anticipated Cole to ask about Matt, his only cousin. They hadn't exactly been best friends, especially for the past several years as they'd graduated and moved out of the house. She'd be sure to tell Tessa, as it would probably make her happy.

Tessa had really been searching for a way to be happy, especially now that her divorce was final. She'd struggled with that more than she'd anticipated, and Janey had assured her that her emotions and reactions were normal. Expected. Worth feeling and experiencing and examining.

Janey swallowed, because these next few days should be filled with festivities and fun. They would be, if she knew Julia and Maddy, who were hosting dinner at The Lighthouse Inn. Tessa also had plenty of food planned, as did Helen, who would be catering brunch on Friday morning from the bakery she owned.

She hadn't told her children about her half-siblings. They didn't know that the man they'd called Grampa wasn't bound to them by blood.

At least Ryan wasn't coming for the holiday. She had pictures of her with him, and she'd tell her kids before they left on Sunday morning. They would have to decide what to do with the information, the same way she had. The same way Ryan Harper had.

She reminded herself that both Rachel and Cole were adults now, and they had to learn how to deal with adult situations.

She'd just pulled up to the bright blue cottage that

bordered the beach when her phone rang. Cole opened his door to get out, and everyone followed him.

Janey reached for her phone and saw Julia's name on the screen. She hesitated, but her children had busied themselves with their luggage. Even Sean had gotten out to help the kids, and Janey swiped on the call.

"Hey," she said, keeping her voice low but hoping it came out bright enough too.

"Hey, hi," Julia said, which was Janey's first clue that something was amiss. Julia spoke in doubles whenever she was nervous. Janey hadn't known her long, but they had been spending more and more time together, getting to know one another. Julia had shared quite a few stories of her childhood, and Janey had too.

They'd both had good lives, and Janey hadn't felt like she'd missed out on something by not knowing that Ryan Harper was her biological father.

"Where are you?" Julia asked.

"I just picked up my kids," Janey said, watching Rachel make a dash for the steps that would lead to shelter and safety. "We just got to the cottage."

"Okay, good. They made it okay?"

"Finally," Janey said. "Rachel and Travis's flight had some major delays. I had to rent a van since they all came in at the same time."

"A van is a good idea for the weekend," Julia said.

Surely she hadn't called to talk about this. "Yeah," Janey said. "What's up, Julia?"

She exhaled, another tell of her nerves. "Okay, I better just spit it out."

Yes, she better. Janey said nothing, because Julia could derail at any moment, for any reason.

"My mother and father are coming for dinner on Thursday," she said, her voice even and polished, like a newly laid hardwood floor. "It's one night. A few hours. I didn't know how to tell them no."

Janey's mind raced. She opened her mouth, but her brain didn't provide any words to her vocal cords.

"I'm sorry, Janey. You and your kids are still welcome, of course. I spoke to my mother, who *asked* to come. I couldn't tell her no. I've been texting Dad, and he said we should let you decide how you want it to be handled."

How she wanted it to be handled? She had no idea what that even meant.

"So…" Julia let the word hang there. "How do you want to handle it? Do you want to tell your kids? Just have me say they're my parents? I mean, they *are* my parents…"

Janey stared out the windshield, the scene in front of her blurry and warped because of the rain. She felt like everything wavered the way it did through the rivulets on the glass, and nothing in the world would ever be solid again.

"Janey?"

"I don't know," Janey said. "I've got a couple of days, right?" She flinched as Cole slammed the back of the van and hurried toward the cottage too. Janey was now alone, and she thought about what Helen had said about finding new strings to keep her tethered.

She'd really been trying to do that, but it suddenly felt fruitless, like a fight she'd have to endure every single day and she'd never be able to win.

"Sure, yeah," Julia said, using the doubles again. "Let me know."

"I will." Janey lowered the phone and let her half-sister hang up. She stayed in the silent van, two options in front of her.

She could start up the vehicle and drive away. Just go around the whole island and ignore her phone until she knew what to do.

Or, she could go inside and blow up everything by making a couple of announcements.

She took a deep breath, her mind flowing through several scenarios.

Then she got out of the van and headed for the door.

Chapter 3

Tessa Simmons couldn't stop hugging Rachel. She'd
seen her and talked to her via phone and video, but for
some reason, the girl radiated light that Tessa desperately needed. She finally stepped back, and Rachel's
smile still existed on her face. Nothing ever seemed to
bother her, and Tessa wished she could be more like
that.

"It's just so good to see you," she gushed at her
niece. She then took Travis Newman in her arms and
practically cried into his shoulder too. He was as thin
as Rachel, and they'd probably have children who'd
disappear when they turned sideways.

Having people her son's age in her presence made
Tessa miss Matt all the more. She understood why he
hadn't come, though she'd invited him well in advance.
He was pretty serious with a woman named Kimberly

Bird, and they were visiting her parents this holiday weekend. She hailed from Virginia, so they wouldn't be able to come to Nantucket.

Tessa wiped her eyes as she stepped away from Travis. "Do you guys want to get changed? It's been raining so hard." She caught sight of Cole as he entered the house at a run, and she darted around Rachel and Travis to go help him and McKenna. Everyone dripped all over the floor, but Tessa didn't care. Janey had put in the expensive bamboo floors that mopped up easily.

She'd been mad when her sister had first done it, but now, she didn't mind at all. Sean came inside as well, and Tessa hugged McKenna first, her radiance also filling the house. She made jewelry for a living and had a real spiritual connection with Buddha. Tessa didn't really understand that, but if she saw something she could stand to put on her fingers or in her ears, she tried to support McKenna.

She stepped away from her and took a good look at her nephew. "Your hair looks wonderful, dear," she said, as if she were her mother paying a compliment. A stab of missing and grief pulled through her at the thought. Her mother. She'd literally just spoken like her, and the way she was teary over everyone coming for a simple meal told Tessa how very much like her mother she really was.

"Where's Janey?" she asked as she met Sean's eye

over Cole's shoulder. He gave the tightest, best hugs, but sometimes they went on just a smidge too long. He finally stepped back, his smile huge too.

"Outside, I guess," Sean said just as the door got whipped open again. He jumped out of the way and the storm—and Janey—came barreling inside. Together, they managed to get the door closed, and Tessa pulled her cardigan tighter around herself.

"My goodness," Janey said, slicking the rain out of her hair. "It's insane out there." She looked around at everyone. "We might not be able to get to Wainscott."

Tessa would gladly host them all here at the cottage, but she'd have to put people on couches and blow up air mattresses to do it.

"The rain is only supposed to last until about nine," Sean said. It had been dark all day, and as evening fell, it would only get more and more black. "It's not snowing yet."

Tessa shivered at the thought. It did snow in Nantucket, but usually not until Christmastime at least. He looked back at her, and it was clearly her show. "Yes," she said. "Everyone get into dry clothes if you need to. There's a bathroom down the hall here. If you go up the steps, there's another one. You can leave your bags wherever. I have the tables set for all of us."

She bustled into the kitchen—or tried to. Janey stopped her by darting in front of her, her hazel eyes

27

darker than Tessa had seen them in a while. This wasn't good.

"I actually have an announcement first," she said, her expression now pleading with Tessa for help. "Is that okay?"

Tessa swallowed, as she had a very good idea what this announcement would be. "Of course," she said as diplomatically as she could. She pulled her sweater again and moved to Janey's side. She'd always been at her sister's side, and she'd never truly minded it. Lately, though, everything her sister did rubbed at Tessa the wrong way.

Janey was the fun sister. The one who always dressed hip and cool. The one who experimented with hair color and piercings, who went to the fancy restaurants, and who dated more than one man at a time.

Since she'd come to Nantucket, she'd only been dating Sean. She'd broken up with everyone else, and Tessa could see so many changes in her. A great many —some of which were vital to having and keeping her sister in her life.

"All right." Janey clasped her hands together in front of her. "I wasn't going to say anything until later, but things have changed." She looked at Tessa again, but surprise moved through her. She wasn't aware of any changes.

Janey tucked her hair behind her ear, and Tessa noted the dark blue streak was gone. "It's for the kids."

She turned slightly to face them. "Aunt Tessa and Sean already know this."

Tessa relaxed, and she wondered if this would be the first time she'd see Rachel be upset.

"Guys," Janey said. "So when I was here with Aunt Tessa this summer, we learned a lot about our mother." She cast a look over her shoulder to Tessa, who moved back to her side. "And our father. Or *my* father." She exhaled and drew in another big breath. "My dad and Tessa's dad aren't the same. We're half-sisters biologically." Her hand slipped into Tessa's, and she gave her a beautiful smile. The type which wasn't covered up by anything false or fake. Nothing being hidden behind the gesture. It was a pure smile, filled with love and understanding, and Tessa found herself forgiving Janey for all the craziness that had happened in the past few months.

Gunshots and accusations. So many secrets and misunderstandings.

"Of course, we're still bonded as sisters," Janey said, looking back to her kids. "But my father is Ryan Harper, and well, it's been a wild few months." She gave a light laugh. "Another of his daughters also lives here on Nantucket, and she runs The Lighthouse Inn."

"We're eating there on Thanksgiving, right?" Rachel asked. She wasn't smiling, but she didn't seem too tense. She did cast a look around at Travis, Cole, and McKenna.

"Yes, dear," Janey said. "Julia and I are about six months apart, and we're also half-sisters. So you have another aunt."

"Two of them, actually," Tessa said, her voice a tad rusty. "Annie got in this morning too." She looked at Janey, who nodded.

"And another uncle," Janey said. "But Eric isn't coming for the holidays."

"Thank goodness," Cole said dryly. "I can't even keep up with what you're saying."

Tessa gave him a smile, because he was clearly joking.

"That's just the beginning," Janey said, ducking her head. Tessa hated it when she did that, because it truly did mean she was about to deliver something bad. "Julia and Annie are great. They're my age, with children close to yours or a little younger. It's…well, Julia's parents are coming to Thanksgiving dinner too."

Silence draped the house, almost like someone had pushed mute on their lives just inside that cottage. Then Tessa took a big breath, and several people— including her—spoke at once.

"Why are they coming?" Sean asked.

"What are you going to do?" Tessa wanted to know.

"So we'll have to meet our real grandfather?" Cole asked.

"No," Janey said, looking at him. "No, the word

isn't 'real.' Your grandfather was your *real* grandfather."
She wore a blazing look of determination that he know
this fact. "This man's name is Ryan Harper, and yes,
we have his blood in our veins. But that doesn't make
someone a father or a grandfather."

"You do visit him," Tessa said gently.

Janey whipped her attention to her. "Yes," she said,
her eyes searching Tessa's. She hadn't meant anything
bad by it, but she knew Janey went to see Ryan Harper.
He'd come here too. Janey didn't talk to her about it a
lot, but Tessa *knew*.

She was trying not to live her life in such isolation
anymore, and that included confiding in Julia and
Maddy, who had become good friends. It meant calling
Janey just to find out what she'd done that day and
how she was feeling. It meant she told Janey the ways
she suffered over her divorce and the feelings of loss
that came with it.

Janey looked back at her children. "He's a nice
man, and he'll be here on Thursday with his wife." She
swallowed, and Tessa read the body language. "I'm not
sure what to do."

"To do?" Sean asked, taking a step forward. "What
is there to do?"

Janey looked at her boyfriend. "Julia said she
wanted to know what we wanted to do." She met
Tessa's eyes. "I told her we had a couple of days, and I
would decide."

"Are you thinking we won't eat at the inn?" Tessa asked. Yes, she'd lumped herself in with Janey and her children. They were her family, all she had here on Nantucket, and she wanted to spend this first Thanksgiving without Mom with them.

"I don't want to do that to Julia and Maddy," Janey said quietly. "But it's an option."

Tessa refrained from starting her next sentence with "You should." She'd hated that with a passion when Ron, her ex-husband, said it to her, and Janey wouldn't appreciate it either. She wanted to tell her she should let Julia know sooner rather than later if *seven* of them wouldn't be showing up for dinner. With Julia's parents, that would leave only eight people for dinner, and surely Maddy wouldn't have to make three turkeys —her plan as of right now.

Viola Martin, the older woman Janey lived with, was planning to come to the meal, but if Janey wouldn't go to The Lighthouse Inn, she'd cancel too. Maddy would have her father there with her, and Julia, and then her parents. With Julia's sister and her girls, that would make eight.

In her pocket, her phone chimed, and Tessa hurried to release her sister's hand to silence it. She didn't want Janey to hear that specific sound, and she couldn't believe she'd left her notifications up so loud. The *bloopety-bloop* sounded again as she pulled the phone from her slacks, and she hurried to silence it while seeing Abraham's name next to the bright white heart in the upper notification bar.

Please don't let Janey see that, she thought, and she quickly shoved her phone back into her pocket. She looked at Janey, and her sister's attention was swinging back to her kids.

"I'll think about it tonight," she said. "Okay?"

Tessa's phone continued to buzz, but she only knew because she felt it against her thigh. No sound met her ear, and she ignored the messages from Engage, the dating app she'd started using earlier this month. She'd "met" Abraham Sanders through the app, which catered to singles above the age of forty-five, and they'd been talking for the past several days.

She'd looked at a few other dating apps, but she'd decided on Engage, because it was as much about being social with locals—engaging with others who lived nearby—as it was about dating. She'd had conversations with women here on Nantucket about what to serve to her family tonight. She'd learned about a holiday concert on Sunday night from a minister at a church in downtown Nantucket.

Then, she'd met Abe. They'd been talking, and he hadn't asked her to meet face-to-face yet. After their first few conversations, Tessa had been crippled with guilt. Was she moving too fast after her divorce? Was she ready to date again? She wasn't Janey; she didn't just dive into something new the moment something else ended.

She shook the thoughts out of her head. Abe lived in downtown Nantucket, according to his profile and what he'd told her, and she'd resisted the urge to go by his specialty meat shop when she'd gone for groceries yesterday. It wasn't in downtown Nantucket; he just lived there. His shop was in the same area as where Janey lived—Wainscott. The ritzy, higher-end shore of Nantucket in the southeast. He did well there, and apparently, he'd been working at the shop with his father and brother for decades.

It all sounded so small-town-cute and quaint, and Tessa had really liked the idea of meeting him, being utterly charmed, and falling in love on the first date. Then she'd remember she was almost forty-six years old, and that didn't happen to women her age.

"Tess," Janey said, breaking into her thoughts once more. "The timer is going off. Do you want Rachel to take that out?"

Tessa flew into action. "I've got it. Thanks." She busied herself in the kitchen while the others went to change, as she'd suggested before Janey's announcement. By the time they all returned, Tessa had the soup ready to serve, with the short ribs resting under a heap of aluminum foil.

"Can I help?" Janey asked.

"Nope." Tessa gave her a smile, but Janey was sort

34

of a disaster in the kitchen. She thought she could cook, and she did an okay job—if one wanted to chew on their pork loin for a half-hour. Without gravy.

Tessa wasn't one of those people, so she preferred to cook if it came down to her or Janey. "Just go sit. It's ready."

Rachel and Travis already sat at the table, both of them looking at a single device, their heads bent together. Cole and McKenna giggled from somewhere down the hall, and Janey yelled, "Time to eat, guys!" to get them to come join the fun in the kitchen.

Tessa had set up a card table and set it next to the four-person table that stood in the eat-in dining room full-time. She'd covered everything with two gorgeous blue cloths she'd found at Holiday House, then set white plates rimmed with silver in each spot. Her mother's good silverware adorned every spot, and Tessa had purchased silver napkins to go with the dishware and tablecloths, again from Holiday House.

"Our first course is soup," she said as Sean sat next to Janey and put his arm around her. Cole and McKenna sat in the two spots across from them, leaving the single end spot open for Tessa. "It's a kale and chicken sausage soup, with potatoes and white beans." It was a new recipe she'd gotten from Helen Ivy, an older woman who owned the bakery around the corner. "Anyone not want any?"

"I can't wait," Rachel said, and she actually picked

up her spoon.

Tessa gave her a warm smile and started to serve the soup. She sat down last and took a moment to gaze down the table at the six people there with her. Her heart expanded with love for her sister and her children, and it might've just been the holidays, but Tessa sure did feel like she belonged here with them. They belonged with her.

"Happy Thanksgiving," she said almost under her breath, but no one heard her, because Janey had just taken a sip of her soup.

"Tessa," she moaned. "This is the best thing I've ever eaten." She took another bite, her face filled with joy. "I once made a soup like this, but it didn't have kale."

"No," Cole said quickly. "Mom, I love you, but no. You've never made a soup that tastes like this." Broth dripped from his spoon he'd loaded it so full. He put the whole thing in his mouth as Janey protested. Tessa silently cheered, because even Mom had deemed Janey a better cook than her when she'd been alive.

It wasn't true, and hearing it from Janey's son made everything inside Tessa warm. Around her, the conversation continued, and she felt like she'd fallen into one of those movies where everything was perfect, everyone got along, and the holidays brought love, joy, and happiness.

As she got up to finally serve dessert—a gorgeous

lemon curd cheesecake—she caught sight of her half-reflection in the dark front windows. *Something wicked this way comes*, she thought as she turned away to get the plates set.

She knew better than most that a morning always dawned after a terrible night. She also knew that good times didn't last forever, that a storm always came after days and days of sunshine and blue sky.

It had been raining physically here in Nantucket today, and Tessa couldn't help feeling like they'd had quite a few days of rest mentally, emotionally, and spiritually, and that yes, a new type of storm would be making landfall soon enough.

For right now, she served the cheesecake, accepted the praise, and laughed with her sister and her family. She'd need the emotional strength of these times when the harder ones came, she knew that.

⊏══⊐

LATER THAT NIGHT, after Janey had left with everyone she'd brought, Tessa locked the door and made sure the dishwasher was humming before she wandered down the hall to her bedroom. She changed into her pajamas and snuggled into her comforter, a happy sigh slipping through her lips as she turned on her phone.

It had been a few hours since Abe's messages, but

he knew she was entertaining her family tonight. He'd probably been hoping to catch her before they arrived, despite everything being delayed due to the rain.

She smiled to herself as she started reading his messages.

Closed up for the night and thinking about you, he'd sent. Warmth filled her, because it was nice to be thought about.

His bright smile looked out at her from his profile picture as she read. *I know you're busy this week with your family. I am too.*

I hope it goes well.

I've been thinking…

How do you feel about meeting after everything this week? Dinner next week?

If you wanted to start off easier, we could get coffee or go to lunch. Something low key.

All right, I'll stop spamming you.

Fine, one more message.

She laughed quietly when he sent four more after that. He liked to send short sentences in single messages, whereas she usually typed paragraphs with many thoughts before hitting the arrow to send it all to him.

I think you're beautiful.

I like talking to you.

If it's too fast, just say so, and I'll wait. We can keep talking and getting to know one another.

38

But I'd love to ENGAGE with you off the app, in person. Let me know.

He'd ended the last message with a heart, and the app had made the word *ENGAGE* in all caps. It was their signature item. If two people wanted to meet because of the app, that was the language they used. It had only taken Tessa a single day to learn that, as she'd had a man send her that as his very first message and it had been in all caps.

She'd thought he'd been shouting at her until she did a bit more research into the app.

What woman didn't want to hear she was beautiful and worth talking to? Tessa had spent so much of her life feeling exactly the opposite of that, and Abe made her feel like a million bucks.

She still had a warning voice in her ears telling her to *go slow, be cautious.* She didn't need to run out and meet him tonight, at close to eleven o'clock at night, in a storm.

She did send, *Dinner sounds lovely. It's late, so I'm headed to bed right now. I hope you have an amazing day tomorrow, and let's set something up when we're both on again.*

Then she plugged in her phone and collapsed back into her pile of pillows, the happiest she'd been in years. Again, she got the foreboding sense that something huge, hulking, and harrowing was coming…but for now, she fell asleep quickly and dreamt of a fantastic first date with a handsome man.

Chapter 4

Julia Harper hurried into the kitchen at The Lighthouse Inn, the scent of coffee strong in her nose. Thankfully. "Maddy," she said, not even looking for the woman. "Olive Rune just said there are no more cheese danishes." She reached for the coffee pot but frowned at how empty it was.

She looked up and around the cavernous kitchen. She and Maddy had worked like dogs to get The Lighthouse Inn open in only a couple of months, and their reviews had been strong and steady since. They'd been open less than a month, but their rooms—the inn only had five—had booked quickly, and they currently didn't have any reservations until springtime available.

"Maddy?"

She wasn't in the kitchen, which was odd for breakfast service. Huffing, Julia spotted the cheese danish pastries on the stainless steel counter, grabbed them, and took them with whatever coffee was left in the pot. It would have to do.

Her sister came into the dining room just as Julia did, and her smile came instantly to her face. "Annie," she said pleasantly, though her nerves pounced down her throat. "Find a spot. The breakfast buffet is a hot bar this morning."

Julia put the tray of danishes on the bar, nodded to them for Olive, and then proceeded to go around the table to fill coffee mugs. She ran back into the kitchen to brew more coffee and find out where the devil Maddy had gone, only to find her standing at the stove.

"There you are. We're out of coffee, and the bacon is getting dangerously low. Trust me, we don't want the Thompson twins to run out of bacon."

"More right there," Maddy said, indicating the serving container of it sitting on the counter. "Sorry, Kyle called."

"Hmm." She gave Maddy a cocked-eyebrow glare. "By 'Kyle,' do you mean 'Ben'?"

"No," Maddy said, but she wore a grin the size of Texas. "Ben's on the ship until noon. He's leaving this afternoon."

Julia needed to get the bacon out to the dining room, but she decided she could risk her life just this once. Six-year-olds couldn't tear her limb from limb before their parents interceded, could they? "And how are you feeling about him going to see his family without you?"

"Fine," Maddy said, turning back to the stovetop. She lifted the huge pan where she scrambled eggs. "We've only been seeing each other for a few months." She poured the eggs into an identical serving dish and nudged it closer to Julia. "We're not super serious. He doesn't get much time off, and his mother has had pneumonia for the past three weeks."

If anyone understood the health crisis of a parent, it was Maddy. Her father lived here in Nantucket, and she tended to him daily.

"Okay," Julia said. "Is he taking you out before he leaves, at least?"

Maddy grinned at her and picked up the eggs. "He'll be here at three on his motorcycle." She giggled, and Julia joined in.

She grabbed the bacon and followed Maddy toward the dining room. "Wait. I thought you said tonight would work to go over *The Seashell Promise*." Julia wasn't sure she wanted to drag the past into the present, but Maddy had seemed so excited about The Seashell Promise when she'd discovered it.

"It does." She hipped her way out into the dining room. "After dinner."

They'd gotten permission to have a catered dinner brought in tonight and tomorrow as Maddy prepared to serve a downhome, traditional American turkey feast on Thursday evening.

"Okay," she said. "Janey and Tessa are coming and everything." She shot Maddy a look that told her not to be late, but Maddy's attention got shifted to an older gentleman who said, "Ah, more eggs. Thank you, darling."

Maddy giggled, which earned them a few dollars in tips, and she let Mister Hunsaker twirl her around the buffet. He was here with his brother, each of them in a separate room, for the holidays. Both of them had lost their wives that year, and they hadn't wanted to spend Thanksgiving in such familiar surroundings.

This older of the two had taken a real shine to Maddy, and she encouraged him by dancing with him and chatting about old records, bands, and long-gone-by pop culture. Julia could only smile and shake her head. Everything Maddy had said and done with Tyler Hunsaker was just…Maddy. It spoke true to who she was. She loved vintage everything, and she loved dancing, and she drew people to her like insects to honey.

She was kind and personable, and everything Julia lacked at the inn, Maddy made up for. They'd started here as enemies, but now, Julia wouldn't want anyone else at her side. They ran The Lighthouse Inn and all the activities and meals as a seamless team, and Julia really loved her new life on Nantucket.

She could've done without finding a body of a decades-missing little girl in the upper balcony, but once that had been handled, life had settled and gone back to normal. As normal as normal could be, at least.

Julia hadn't found herself a hot military boyfriend the way Maddy had, but again, that was so Maddy. She wasn't surprised at all that Maddy had found Benjamin Downs, a Coast Guard captain stationed here on the island, after injuring herself on their maiden voyage of the yacht they did tours with now. The two had started out fairly slow, and if Julia believed Maddy, they were still on that track.

She swept crumbs from the buffet and then surveyed it to see what else they needed. Not much. Several of the guests had eaten already, and those that hadn't were in the dining room. She could probably make one more pass with fresh coffee and then join her sister for breakfast.

She did just that, sinking into the high-backed chair beside Annie several minutes later. Bri sat on her other side, but Julia didn't see Paige at all. "No Paige this morning?" she asked, watching her younger sister for her reaction.

Julia had cried the moment she'd seen Annie, and she wasn't even sure why. She loved being here in Nantucket, but she supposed she did feel a little isolated. A short ferry ride separated her from the mainland, but sometimes, when all one saw was water, they felt a bit…alone.

Alone was a great word to describe how Julia felt. Even surrounded by guests, busyness, new friends just down the beach, and Maddy, she still felt alone. Her father didn't live here; everything surrounding her father brought so many feelings to the surface, and Julia couldn't sort through them fast enough.

She and Annie had stayed up late talking last night, and even she hadn't helped Julia come to any conclusions. She felt like she'd tossed seventeen breakable plates into the air, and as they came tumbling down, she needed to catch all of them simultaneously. There was no way to do it, and a keen sense of overwhelm hit her even as she lifted her coffee mug to her lips.

"Ew." She got up and retrieved a couple of sugar packets and a little container of cream.

Annie smiled at her as she sat back down. "You never did like black coffee."

"No, I did not." She emptied the sugar and cream into the coffee and stirred. She took a breath to ask Annie about Paige again, because she hadn't answered. Julia knew her sister's oldest had been causing some problems, mostly over boys, and she wanted to support Annie if she could.

"She's still in bed," Annie said before Julia could ask. "I told her breakfast went until nine, and she groaned, rolled over, and started snoring again. So."

She lifted one shoulder and then her mug to her lips. "Not my problem if she's starving later."

It would be her problem, and they both knew it. Paige would *make* it her problem. Luckily, Julia could get her niece something to eat any old time, and there were a couple of restaurants along the row of businesses here where The Lighthouse Inn sat.

"The rain is gone," Julia said next. "Perhaps the girls could go to the beach today."

"I want to go to the beach," Bri said, leaning forward to see past her mother. She looked at Julia with hope, then switched her gaze to her mom. "Can we, Mom?"

"If there's time," she said. "This afternoon, when it's warmer. I want to take you and Paige to that shop downtown."

"I hate shopping with Paige," Bri complained, and Annie didn't argue with her. Julia reached over and patted her sister's hand. She'd raised three boys, and she didn't envy her sister's stage of life, with teenagers and all their hormones, their concerns, and the seemingly constant whining about school, friends, grades, sports, and more.

She'd gotten lucky with her sons, she knew, and she'd loved being their mother. Of course, she was still their mother, though they were all grown and out of the house now. A sharp tang of her old life, in the gorgeous Brownstone in Manhattan, touched her tongue, and she quickly raised her mug to swallow down the sweeter coffee.

"I want to go shopping," Julia said. "How about I go with Paige, and you take Bri?"

Annie swung her gaze to Julia. "Can you? Don't you have tours today?"

"Only one," Julia said. "It's right here at the inn too, so we'll be done at ten-thirty. If you can wait until then, I can drive us downtown." She smiled at Annie and Bri, who looked so hopeful. She nodded to her slightly, and Bri went back to looking at her phone while occasionally scooping up a bite of scrambled eggs.

"Anything from Janey?" Annie asked, asking the question out of the corner of her mouth as she shielded the words with her mug.

Julia shook her head, the moment turning more tense. Sober. "I told her. She said she'd let me know."

"She doesn't have much time." Annie frowned. "If they're not coming, that's a significantly less number of people."

Julia was aware. She didn't need to hash it out with Annie. Again. "I'm going to go help Maddy in the kitchen." She plucked a pinch of muffin from the top of her sister's blueberry delicacy, ate it, and called that —along with her coffee—breakfast. "Everything's okay with your room?"

She'd had to cram Annie and both girls into a

single room, as the inn was booked solid. Paige hadn't been happy about that, but Annie said she wasn't happy about anything these days. Julia understood the feeling, and she wanted her niece to feel like someone cared about her. That for one shining moment—or a morning or an afternoon of shopping—she'd had fun.

Paige entered the dining room as Julia left it, and she quickly changed her course. However, trying to turn around while still moving forward didn't work. Unfortunately, she was boxed in by the doorway too, and the swinging gray door that separated the kitchen from the dining room.

It swung forward and hit her backside, bumping her forward when she wanted to go the other direction. She grunted, groaned, and saw herself falling to her knees in slow motion. It happened that way too, and then Maddy crouched in front of her, concern shooting from her bright blue eyes.

"I fell," Julia said stupidly. Pain rushed through her legs and arms, flying from her fingertips. She wasn't even sure why, or what had been injured. Tears sprang to her eyes, and she looked down at herself. She wore the white blouse with tawny feathers on it. She'd tucked it smartly into a pair of gray slacks, and all seemed well on her torso. No gushing of blood, at least.

"You're okay," Maddy said. "Let's get you up." Behind her, no one said anything, but she had the distinct impression a slew of people stood there. She took Maddy's hand and helped her to her feet. She placed one palm against the stainless steel countertop and took a peek behind her.

Yep, the guests from breakfast stood crowded into the doorway, including Annie, Bri, and Paige. Her sister took a stutter-step forward, but Julia must've lasered her back with her eyes, because she didn't come forward.

She worked out the kinks in her knees, realizing she'd lost a pump. "My shoe," she said, apparently only able to string together two words to make a sentence. Embarrassment heated her face as she thought about what the guests behind her might've seen.

Annie appeared at her side, her heel in her hand. "Here you go, Jules. Are you okay?" She too wore concern in her eyes, and Julia nodded.

Maddy said, "She's okay, everyone. Go back to breakfast, okay?" She sounded completely pleasant, but Julia still didn't dare turn to look. She heard the plastic door swing closed, and some of the apprehension left her shoulders.

"Yes," she said, taking the shoe and slipping her foot back into it. "I'm okay. I just saw Paige, and I wanted to talk to her, but I was already committed to going through the door."

"The last thing we need is a hospital trip." Maddy

gave her a sharp look. "I was there with Daddy last week, and I'm not keen to go again."

"It's not like I wanted to fall down in front of everyone," Julia said, frowning at her back. She turned and walked out of the kitchen just as the clock struck nine, and that was her cue to start pulling down breakfast.

Her niece stood at the bar, filling a plate with eggs and fruit, so Julia went that way. "Paige," she said, her voice a bit on the sugary side. She tried to tame it, because her sons had not liked it when she spoke like that to them.

The seventeen-year-old looked up at her. "Hey, Aunt Julia." A smile even touched her mouth. "The room is great. Thank you."

Surprise darted through Julia, but she concealed it with a smile. "Of course. Your mom said you guys were going shopping today, and I proposed that you come with me, and she can take Bri." She touched Paige's bicep like she was pushing a button. "What do you think? I know the *best* place to get those ripped jeans you like." She leaned closer as she said it, almost as if she and Paige couldn't let Annie know what they were talking about.

"Really?" Paige asked.

"Yes," Julia said, smiling.

"Yeah, sure." Paige hugged her with one arm, her smile truly broadcasting happiness. "Thanks, Aunt

Julia." She turned and went to join her mom and sister, and Annie nodded to Julia in gratitude.

Finally, she felt useful to her sister, who'd been through so much the past few years. She then picked up the half-empty platter of danishes and then the bowl of fruit and took it into the kitchen.

LATER THAT EVENING, she clutched the tattered book in her hand and watched the front entrance to the inn. Maddy was late. Annie didn't seem concerned, but Julia's stomach buzzed. She didn't like it when people didn't return when they said they would. First, it had been her husband, as he claimed to be staying later and later at work.

Then, when everything had happened with that missing girl... No, Julia didn't like it when someone didn't show up when expected. She went over to the glass door, which she locked at ten p.m. Guests could access the inn with their keycards after that.

Dinner had ended thirty minutes ago, but Julia had handled it with Annie so Maddy could go out with Ben. He was supposed to be leaving to go see his family, and Julia stared out at the darkness beyond the glass. The outside lights lit up the sidewalk, but she didn't see Maddy. She couldn't see anything beyond the halo of light.

She hated that feeling, and she squinted and strained into the darkness, trying to see past where the light fell. Of course, she couldn't. Secrets often felt like this, like she was trying to see something that wasn't there. Then her mind would conjure up all kinds of scenarios and disasters, and she simply didn't like not being able to see what she wanted to see.

"Mom says they'll be fine to find a hotel," Annie said from behind her, and Julia turned. She almost dropped the book she'd written in college—a silly tome about friendship and the promises made between twenty-somethings who didn't know any better. Who didn't have life experience and hadn't experienced true heartache, nor the more difficult situations in life, like infidelity, crippling debt, or absolute self-doubt.

Julia suddenly hoped Maddy didn't show up. Then they wouldn't have to go through the book.

"They aren't going to find anything," Tessa said, looking up from her phone. She'd been extraordinarily consumed inside it since she'd arrived ten minutes ago. "The whole island is booked for Thanksgiving."

Julia nodded, the anxiety eating away at her stomach. "I told them that. I think my mother assumes because I run this inn that I'll magically be able to pull a room out of a wall for her." She shook her head, a touch of irritation seeping into her voice. She wished she were a bit stronger and had been able to tell her mother no, she couldn't come to Thanksgiving dinner at The Lighthouse Inn.

They simply didn't have room, and the last thing Julia wanted to referee was a meetup between Janey and her mom.

"Doesn't Janey's boyfriend have a standing hotel room somewhere?" Julia asked, turning back to the glass door.

"Oh, that's a good idea," Tessa said. "Let me text her."

"Why isn't she coming?" Annie asked.

Julia kept quiet. She wouldn't want to show up to a get-together with three of her half-sisters, two of whom she'd only known about for a few months, and go over friendship promises. Janey still had a lot of personal issues of her own she had to work through, and Julia hadn't been surprised when she'd canceled on them all tonight.

She'd said the weather was so nice, and she wanted to take her kids to see the Floating Lights while it wasn't raining. Julia couldn't begrudge her that, and Annie had almost taken her girls too. If Maddy would ever show up, she still might be able to make it to at least the last half.

Bri and Paige weren't hanging out in the lobby with Julia, Annie, and Tessa, but they'd opted to stay back in the room. They had gone to the beach that afternoon, and just because it was wintertime didn't mean the sun didn't burn. The wind could exhaust a person in only a few minutes as well.

"I'm going to call her," Julia said at the same time Tessa said, "Janey says Sean isn't using that room. He's calling Harbor House right now."

The air rushed out of Julia's lungs. "It would be fantastic if they could stay there." Harbor House was downtown, which meant a twenty-minute buffer. She'd tell her father he had to put on his pin, and then she'd set it to ding whenever it moved. Then she'd know when they were coming, and she could prepare.

What, she wasn't sure. Her mental attitude? Perhaps some restraints should her mother get a little out of control. She'd simply make sure she spoke to both of them before the big meal tomorrow, and she'd restrict her mother's alcohol intake. Just the fact that Julia needed a plan for Thanksgiving dinner of this magnitude irritated her. The holidays should be a light, carefree, joyful time.

This was the opposite of that.

Seconds passed, and probably piled up into a minute. Tessa looked up and said, "Sean says they can have the room. He just confirmed with the Harbor House."

"Praise the heavens," Julia said, sinking into the wingback beside Tessa. "Thanks, Tess. You're a lifesaver."

"He's Janey's boyfriend," Tessa said, slipping her

phone under her thigh. She looked over to Julia. "Are you okay?"

"Just stressed about my parents coming." Julia reached over and squeezed Tessa's hand. "Janey hasn't canceled yet."

"Janey is…unpredictable," Tessa said.

Julia nodded, because that was putting it mildly.

"She'll probably come," Tessa said. "But she'll be late, and she'll probably have eaten already." She offered Julia a kind, sympathetic smile. "I've learned with her to have no expectations. Then I'm not disappointed."

Julia nodded again, but she didn't like what Tessa had said. She appreciated Annie all the more in that moment, and she needed to get this show on the road or she was going to lose Annie back to her girls.

She picked up her phone and dialed Maddy, already rehearsing the lecture in her head. The line rang, and rang, and rang.

Chapter 5

Madeline Lancaster knew the person calling her would be Julia. She pulled away from Ben with some difficulty and said, "I'm late, Ben."

"So am I." He kissed her again, and Maddy melted into his touch. She could admit it was exciting to ride on the back of his motorcycle, listen to him talk about boarding vessels and making arrests, and then sneak around behind the barracks to kiss him. He was a decade younger than her, and everything about him felt so...exciting.

"I really have to go," she said. He still had to drive her back to the inn, and then he'd want to kiss her again. Julia would likely be standing guard at the entrance, peering through the glass for the first hint of headlights. So there'd be no kissing back at the inn.

That thought alone had her touching her lips to his again.

His chest rumbled as he laughed. "I thought you had to go," he whispered, his lips moving along her neck.

"I do," she said. The wind shook the building around them, but she felt utterly safe and cared for within the circle of his arms. Darkness had fallen a couple of hours ago, and that made riding the bike even more thrilling. Ben had purchased a helmet just for her, and everything he did made her feel so special.

His phone shrilled out a sound, and he sighed as he stepped back. "That's my mother."

"Busted," she teased though she was probably too old to use words like that. She kept her back pressed into the building behind her so the wind and cold couldn't sneak down her coat while Ben answered his mom's call.

"Yes, Mother," he said, his voice hinting at irritation. "I'm leaving in five minutes." He caught Maddy's eye, and the two of them smiled. "I'm sure the highway will be open." He rolled his eyes, and some of the fog that had started to settle over the island obscured him from Maddy's view.

She didn't like the fog on Nantucket. It came often in the winter, and she shivered, suddenly wanting to be back at The Lighthouse Inn, where everything would smell like roses and be brightly lit. She stepped away from the building and took Ben's hand in hers. They walked toward his motorcycle while he continued to assure his mother that he would indeed be in Montreal by midnight.

Maddy didn't think so, but she stayed silent. Maybe if he'd left on time, but he hadn't. The windswept, chilly ride back to the inn left her legs and lungs cold, and Ben kissed her again though Julia actually came out onto the sidewalk, The Seashell Promise booklet clutched in her hand.

"Call me when you get there," she said.

"Yes, ma'am." Ben grinned at her, saluted Julia, and buzzed off into the mist. Maddy watched him, a sigh escaping her lips. She felt Julia approach, and she turned into her once-again best friend as she arrived at her side.

"He is trouble," Julia murmured. "Bringing you home late like this. Did you see the way he saluted me?" She clicked her tongue the way Maddy's disapproving mother once had. The way *Maddy* once had for her own daughter when Chelsea had snuck out to meet a boy.

She glanced over to Julia, who had her arms folded and her eyebrows drawn down in complete disgust. She started to giggle, and she linked her arm through Julia's when the other woman turned to glare at her. "Come on," she said. "We can't stand out in the fog."

"You like him too much." Julia stumbled as if her legs were wooden and didn't bend right.

"I do not," Maddy said, tossing her long, blonde hair over her shoulder. "I'm being perfectly level-headed about the whole thing."

Julia scoffed. "You are not. You've kept us all waiting for thirty minutes, and your lipstick is smeared halfway across your face." She tugged her arm away from Maddy's, who reached up to fix her makeup. "Take a moment, because Helen came over, and I'd hate for you to scandalize a woman in her seventies." She marched away, the book swinging in her hand now.

Embarrassment moved through Maddy, but she turned her back on the inn and quickly fixed her face. No need to bring further humiliation to herself if it wasn't necessary. Everyone would know anyway. She was thirty minutes late after spending the afternoon with her boyfriend.

When she pulled open the door and went inside, every eye moved to her. Julia glared; Annie gave her a small smile; Tessa's grin could've lit the whole island; Helen frowned.

"I'm sorry I'm late," Maddy said as diplomatically as possible. "Did we want coffee or cookies?" She shrugged out of her coat and hung it on the rack near the door. No guests used it, but along with Julia and Vivian—the woman from the Historical Society who signed her checks—Maddy had decided that she and Julia could hang their personal items there. It made the inn feel more homey, more lived in, and less of a place people stayed for one or two nights before moving on.

She'd been thinking about that a lot. The Lighthouse Inn had only been open for a few weeks, but the number of people she'd met and interacted with was already astronomical. At first, she'd wanted to make a connection with everyone. She and Julia had painstakingly gone through the photo albums they'd found to make antique art pieces on the wall that also told the history of the inn.

She wanted that same type of connection that had existed in the scrapbooks. She wasn't getting it, and she'd started to think of people as nameless, faceless. She didn't like that, which was why she'd been so excited about The Seashell Promise when she and Julia had found it in storage in her father's house.

"We don't have time for cookies," Julia complained.

"It'll take three minutes to get them in the oven," Maddy shot back. "You guys go get set up in the dining room, and I'll be right out."

Instead of doing that, the four women followed her into the kitchen. Julia put the book, which looked like a fourteen-year-old obsessed with unicorns had created it, on the stainless steel counter and admired it. Julia had loved bright colors in her youth—she still did.

"All right," Maddy said as she turned to get out the cookie dough she'd already made. "Twenty minutes."

Helen busied herself with making coffee, and when everything was bubbling or baking, they all gathered around the book. Maddy reached out to open it, because it seemed like no one else wanted to. "Janey's not coming?" she asked.

"The weather was good today," Tessa said. "She and the kids stayed at the beach late, and then they had a family dinner planned." Her words sounded true, but Maddy recognized them as a thin excuse for her sister.

Maddy didn't mind, because she understood. She'd made plenty of thinly-veiled excuses for her husband in the past. She'd always put a smile on her face, the way Tessa was right now, and she always did her best to charm the guests Chris was supposed to.

She'd succeeded for quite a long time too. That part of her life felt so far away, when it had once been so close. She wondered what had changed, and as she flipped open the book, she realized *she* had changed. Since coming to Nantucket only a few short months ago—she'd changed a lot.

"Do you remember writing it?" she asked Julia.

"Vaguely," she said. "It was a checklist of things friends should share with each other, grow closer, and thus become best friends. I remember wanting charms and necklaces once the list was complete." She smiled around at the group, and Maddy truly regretted making her stress and wait.

She opened the book, and a drawing of a pair of holding hands met Maddy's eyes. She smiled at the artistic lines, the way they almost seemed abstract, though the lines of the fingers could clearly be distinguished. She reached out and traced her fingertip along one of them. "I forgot how much you loved to draw."

"Mm." Julia stared at the book, her long lashes blinking faster than normal. "My parents didn't think art was a worthy pursuit." She drew a deep breath, and that seemed to break whatever trance she'd fallen into. She flipped the page, and on the back of the first page sat the number one.

"Tell each other a secret," she read aloud. She surveyed the group, her eyes wide. Maddy's heart pounded a couple of times before settling back into a regular beat, and she wasn't even sure why. She'd kept and told plenty of secrets in her life. Some she'd wanted to keep and hadn't been able to. Some she'd kept for so long, and later, she wished she hadn't.

"I just told one of mine," Julia said, smiling. She didn't relax though, and in fact, the tension seemed to skyrocket as the other women looked around at one another.

Tessa lifted her chin and held up her phone. "I've joined a social media dating app, and I've been talking to a man named Abe. We're meeting for dinner next week."

Silence filled the whole kitchen, and then Julia squealed. She flung her arms around Tessa, who shone like a star on the darkest of nights. She could've easily cut through the fog handing over the island, and Maddy reached over and squeezed her hand once Julia had released her.

"Good for you," Helen said once the excitement had died down. "I guess my secret is that I'm a closet romance reader."

Maddy scoffed, the sound turning into a giggle. "What does that mean?"

"That's not a secret," Annie said. "You read books?" She too made a noise of disbelief and looked around at everyone. Maddy didn't know her extremely well, but she had the same dark eyes and earth-colored hair as Julia. She seemed less nervous and more in control of her emotions, but she was clearly struggling with aspects of raising her girls. Being a single mom of two teenagers was probably the hardest thing anyone ever had to do, and Maddy reminded herself that she didn't know the road Annie trod, and therefore, couldn't judge her.

"That's my secret," Helen said, waving one wrinkled hand toward the book with a deep frown between her eyes. "Next person."

Maddy looked at Annie, and Annie looked back at her. "Pass," Annie said.

"No," Julia said, slapping her palm over the book. "You have to tell a secret."

"What if I don't want to be part of the Seashell Promise?" Annie challenged. "I'm just here for Thanksgiving dinner, Jules." She held up both hands, her face turning pinker and pinker by the moment.

"She shouldn't have to," Maddy said, and once again all eyes came to her. "We can't expect for everyone to be ready to share a secret right out of the gate." She gestured between herself and Annie. "For instance, I barely know Annie. Maybe I don't want her to know something super personal to me right now."

"Exactly," Annie said. "No offense." She looked around at everyone. "But I don't know any of you. Not really."

Julia put her arm around Annie, and they leaned into one another. Maddy smiled at the pair of them, missing her son and daughter powerfully in that moment. Those emotions could come so swiftly and without any warning. Sometimes the sight of an empty cereal bowl in the morning would remind her of Kyle and how her boy seriously couldn't pick up after himself. She thought of his girlfriend, Bea, and how they were getting married in just a couple of months, and then Maddy would be a grandmother soon after that.

The kids had chosen to stay in the city and celebrate the holidays with their father and his parents. Maddy had not been invited, of course.

"My secret," she said, her voice barely above a whisper. "Is that I'm still hurting from the loss of my family." Her chin shook as she tried to form her lips into a smile. "But that I know for maybe the first time, that I'm going to survive this." She nodded and looked around at the group of women who she did feel close to.

They'd been through a lot in a short amount of time. She'd gotten to know Tessa and Janey, and she'd forgiven Julia. They worked together, and they'd grieved together, and they'd helped one another through easy times and hard. It didn't matter that it hadn't happened over a lengthy period of time. Some things brought women together and bonded them instantly, and Maddy could say she felt connected to each woman standing the kitchen with her.

The timer on the oven went off, breaking the mood. She sniffled and turned away, already reaching for the oven mitts. "All right, Tess," she said as he strode toward the oven. "I think you have the best secret, so you have to give more details."

"No," Tessa said, but her protests got overridden by Annie, Julia, and Helen.

Maddy smiled to herself as she checked the cookies, deemed them crisp on the edges and ooey-gooey in the middle, and pulled them from the oven. She took them right over to the counter and lifted them over Julia's head to place in the middle of all of them. "They're hot. Let me get forks."

"Forks?" Tessa asked.

Maddy only smiled as she retrieved a fistful of forks. She placed them next to the cookie sheet, and Helen wasted no time picking up a utensil. She went right into the middle of the chocolate chip cookie nearest to her, saying, "They're best right from the tray, right from the oven."

The chocolate peaked as she pulled up her fork, and Maddy's mouth watered. She reached for a fork too. "Really, Tessa. Tell us more about Abe. Does he live here in Nantucket?"

"Yes." She watched as the others picked up forks and started tasting the cookies. She chose last, and her eyes rolled back into her head on the first bite. "He owns a specialty meat shop down in Wainscott."

"Abraham Sanders?" Helen asked, her bright blue eyes blazing now. "Oh, honey, hold onto him."

"What does that mean?" Julia asked, giggling.

Maddy took another bite of her cookie, wondering why chocolate brought out the looser tongues, as if it were alcohol. Even Annie grinned now, though, and with enough sugar, Maddy would bet she'd spill a secret.

"One of my bakery assistants dated him a year or

two ago," Helen said, her expression full of mischief now. "She said he's the best kisser she's ever dated."

Annie and Julia started to laugh and tease Tessa, whose face turned bright red. She shoved bite after bite of dessert into her mouth, and Maddy finally reached across the table and took her fork.

"Hey," Tessa said.

"Just give us something," Maddy said, wagging her fork in front of her.

"I don't have anything to give," Tessa said, lunging for her fork. She caught it too and took it back from Maddy. "Besides, it sounds like you should be quizzing Helen. She seems to know more about him than I do." She gave Helen a glare and certainly didn't seem happy about that. She stabbed her fork around at each one of them. "And I haven't told Janey anything yet, so this stays between us."

"Oh, yes," Julia said, bringing the book back to front and center. "Anything talked about while the book is open stays with the people present. That's all."

Tessa nodded like this sparkly book would be the binding tape on their secrets. Maddy had no reason to tell Janey, so she'd keep her mouth shut.

"So," Julia said next, and Maddy looked at her, the warm chocolate and crispy cookie in her mouth making her so, so happy. "Helen, tell us about one of your novels." The all erupted into giggles again,

Helen's permafrown and Grumpy-Grandmother attitude notwithstanding.

Maddy enjoyed her time with her friends, as she
didn't feel quite so alone when gathered with others.
Not just anyone. Not someone who was here now and
would be gone tomorrow. But people she could confide
in. Women she could trust. Friends she saw every day
and who knew her and understood her.

"Mom," a girl said, and Maddy spun toward the
doorway as if they'd been caught pilfering from their
parents' liquor cabinets.

One of Annie's daughters stood there, and she
tossed her fork onto the cookie sheet. "Thanks for the
treats, Maddy." Annie went toward her daughter, easily
sliding her arm around her shoulders and guiding her
out of the kitchen.

The mood had sobered, but Maddy didn't mind so
much. She started cleaning up the kitchen, and little by
little, everything got done. Julia left at some point with
the others, then came back so it was just the two of
them.

Maddy hung the dishtowel from the rack and
looked at her. "I'm really sorry I was late. This was
fun." She nodded to the book still lying on the table.

"We're re-convening tomorrow after breakfast."
She scooped the book into her arms and paused. "I'm
sorry I was rude about Ben."

"Maybe I'm not handling it as perfectly level-headed...ly as I think I am."

"Perfectly level-headedly." Julia grinned like she'd just caught Maddy in a compromising situation. "I don't think those are words, Mads."

She shook her head and half rolled her eyes. "Come on. I'm tired, and we have to be up to start breakfast pretty early."

They left the kitchen together, went down the few steps to the lobby, and then continued down another flight to their rooms in the basement. Julia didn't look back as she veered right toward her room. Maddy's sat around the corner to the left, the door out of sight.

"Good night," she said to Julia, who twisted back to her. Something passed between them, and Julia nodded.

"'Night, Maddy."

Securely in her own room—the Blue Room it had once been named—Maddy sighed. She had no one to call and check in with. No texts to be sent. She sank onto the bed, a keen sense of loneliness filling her. She fought against it, but it was like trying to stop the tide from coming ashore.

She finally reached for her phone and called her father, just so she'd have someone to talk to. After they'd chatted for a few minutes, she felt more content, and she plugged in her phone and changed into her pajamas.

Once in bed, with only the lamplight surrounding her, Maddy whispered, "I'm ready now. I am. I'm ready for a change." Whenever she'd manifested things like this before, they'd eventually come true. Satisfied that she'd put her will out into the universe, she reached over and snapped off the lamp.

In those first few moments of darkness, Maddy always shivered. Her mind ran away from her, and she thought of the little girl who'd died here. Then her rational mind took over, and she settled into her pillow, ready for whatever change was coming next.

Chapter 6

Annie pointed, though her parents weren't hard to see. "There they are." Both Bri and Paige had accompanied her to the ferry dock that morning to greet them. Thankfully, they'd had to leave immediately following breakfast, so she hadn't been able to stay for another session of The Seashell Promise book.

She barely knew Maddy, Helen, and Tessa. There was no way she was going to reveal her secrets to them. No way. She'd spent the evening fuming in her room, and she hadn't been able to calm down until she'd texted everything out to Julia.

How dare you put me in that situation? had been one of the texts. *I'm not comfortable with this was another.*

Both were true.

She wasn't prepared to spend the day with her parents and her girls either, but there she stood, a false smile plastered to her face as she waited for the ferry to come to a complete stop. The wind blew, and the sun shone weakly through the seemingly ever-present haze, and Annie knew why people called Nantucket the Grey Lady.

The fog definitely carried a dark hue to it, and when she'd gotten up for a run along the beach that morning, all she'd been able to see in every direction was gray. Gray, gray, gray.

Her mother seemed to have the color hovering around her too, but Annie opened her arms and hugged her she and Dad finally made it off the ferry. Dad wore a backpack on his back, and he was all smiles for Annie, Paige, and Bri.

Mom, on the other hand, wore a large pair of sunglasses as if she were an A-list celebrity, and she carried an oversized tote bag for her purse and towed along a carry-on-sized piece of luggage.

"Mom," Annie said, tapping the strap on her purse. "What all did you bring? Aren't you just staying for one night?"

"We'll see," Mom said evasively. She lifted her sunglasses and squinted into the distance. "Are those scones? Ryan, I adore scones."

Annie worked hard to refrain from rolling her eyes. She exchanged a look with her girls, and she gestured at them to follow their grandmother toward the scone hut.

"After this," she said. "We'll stop by Harbor House and drop off your luggage. Then the girls want to show you this amazing shop they found yesterday. Paige thinks she found the perfect bracelet for you." Annie didn't like how chipper and upbeat she sounded, but she had to at least pretend. She didn't want the spotlight on her, and if she could escape this weekend without too many questions coming her way, she'd be grateful forever.

"A bracelet?" Mom asked, peering at Paige now.

"Yeah, Grandma. You're going to love it." Paige painted a bright smile on her face, but Annie hated how she had to pretend for her grandma. Shouldn't her mother be the one pretending to be happy today? She was the one causing the problems, and Annie wiped her hand across her forehead.

As the younger daughter, she'd always let Julia handle their mother. She hadn't fought with her much growing up, because Julia had worn her down, worn her out, and taught her which battles to fight and which ones not to. Annie had worn a strapless gown to her senior prom no problem, but only because Julia had endured three weeks of fighting with their mother over her gown a few years earlier.

Annie wanted to say something to her mom, but she didn't know how. She trailed behind everyone as they made their way across the parking lot to the scone shack, and she waved off her dad's offer to buy her something. She'd eaten at the inn. Bri and Paige had too, but they both got a scone while Annie hugged herself against the tension and the wind.

"Let's get your luggage over to the hotel," she said. The sky above them darkened as the sun moved behind a bank of clouds Annie would've testified in court hadn't been there a few moments ago. Didn't matter. They were there now, and she practically started shoving everyone down the cobblestone streets toward Harbor House.

With the luggage dropped off, she breathed a sigh of relief. Her parents would have somewhere to stay tonight after the four o'clock turkey feast, and all she had to do was keep them entertained for another couple of hours.

"Let's go over to Pier and Piedmont," she said, giving Bri a meaningful look. They left the hotel and started down the street.

"They aren't open," her daughter said.

"What do you mean? We looked online." Panic clawed at Annie's throat. They had to be open. If they weren't open, she didn't know where to take her mother and father. *Lunch* popped into her head, but she wasn't hungry, and Mom literally still carried part of her blueberry scone.

Bri shrugged. "I noticed the sign was on closed when we went by to bring the luggage."

"Let's go see." With every step Annie took, she

prayed. Could she take them to a movie? A bowling alley? Out on a tour? Something. Anything.

Her brain spun, because she couldn't take them back to The Lighthouse Inn this early. Julia had begged her to keep them occupied while she dealt with guests and food, and Annie had promised.

Not a seashell promise, she told herself. She couldn't control the operating hours of a retail establishment. It wouldn't be her fault if she had to take them back to The Lighthouse Inn a little early.

Overhead, thunder crashed, and she yelped. A loud sound filled the sky, and her blood ran cold. She'd lived in Massachusetts for a long time. Before that, Southhampton She knew what she was hearing—a warning siren.

"Come on!" she yelled, grabbing onto Paige's hand. "Grab Bri. Everyone hold hands! We have to find somewhere to shelter!" She looked around, her first instinct telling her to go back to Harbor House. They'd be able to duck into the kitchen there. Something.

They'd come further than she thought, and she didn't think they'd make it back to the hotel. The sky foamed with black clouds, and she pulled her daughter toward the only thing she could see through the thickening fog.

A market.

The lights beamed out into the darkness, and they

weren't the only ones running for it. The siren screamed; rain pelted Annie's face; her heart panicked in her chest.

"Wait!" she screamed as a man came outside in a black apron. He started to pull the grates closed. "Wait!"

He heard her that time and looked her way. He gestured for them to move faster, but Annie was going as quickly as she could. She heard someone crying behind her. Probably Bri. She kept moving, and she steamrolled into the market.

The man did pull the grates closed after them. The doors slid closed, and he locked those too. Three other workers came forward with huge boards, and they made quick work of covering the windows and glass door.

"To the back of the store!" he bellowed. "Every-one. Now!"

Annie's chest hitched, and her lungs begged her not to move. They just needed a moment to recover. It wasn't going to be here, and she wrapped one arm around Paige and the other around Bri and strode toward the back of the store. "Good job, Annie," her dad said, panting, from behind her. "Come on, dear. It's not much farther."

Sniffling came from her mother, and it ignited an angry fire inside Annie's head. She literally saw red, and she took a deep breath in through her nose in an attempt to calm herself. Four breaths later, she didn't think she'd whirl on her mom and tell her to grow up.

A couple dozen people huddled near the dairy cases, and Annie moved right into the midst of them. She found an elderly couple sitting on the floor, and she pushed Bri down next to them. "Can we sit by you?" she asked.

The older woman smiled up at her. "Sure, dear."

Annie groaned as she got on the ground. The building around them shook, and a few people in the store sent up cries. Her heartbeat throbbed against her ribcage, but she managed to keep her voice quiet. "Do you live here?"

"Yes." The old woman patted Bri's leg. "Don't you worry. We get these squalls all the time. They pass, and we'll go outside, and the sky will be the most beautiful shade of blue." She smiled encouragingly, and Annie appreciated her so much.

She looked up at Paige and nodded to the floor. To her surprise, Paige sat down and leaned her head against Annie's shoulder. All of her motherly instincts kicked in then, and Annie was reminded that while Paige wanted to be seen as an adult, she wasn't one. She was still a child, and she still needed her mother.

She stroked her hair and said, "Thank you for grabbing Grandma."

"She almost fell," Paige whispered. "She would've dragged me with her."

"She didn't."

"Grandpa caught her."

Annie looked over to the pair of them. She hadn't known her father had been unfaithful to her mother until a month or so ago. There had been no indication of it during her childhood, her teens years, her young adult years, nothing. Ever. He'd been devoted to her. He showed up to family functions on time. He didn't stay late at work. He was a good man, and a good father, yet she'd seen Janey's paternity test.

Did something he'd chosen to do almost fifty years ago get to vilify him now? Mom had thought so, at least for a little while. She'd run to Toronto and her mother and sister for a few weeks. Annie had enough of her own problems, and she'd never been one to gossip, even within her own family.

Her father caught her eye and offered her a smile. She returned it, and he came closer to her, bringing Mom with him. "At least we'll have food if we have to stay here for very long," he said.

"It won't be that long," the older gentleman said. "I'm Justin. This is Gertrude. Who are you, and where are you from?" He gave them a kind, grandfatherly smile, and Annie appreciated the kindness and good-ness of others.

"I'm Annie," she said. "These are my daughters, and we're from Chatham."

He nodded, his pale gray eyes almost bordering on

blue. "I used to do some business out of Chatham," he said, glancing over to his wife. "Not for a while, though."

She patted his leg. "You've been retired for twenty years, dear. That's more than a while."

Annie laughed lightly with them, then her father introduced himself and Mom. She refused to sit on the ground and instead perched on the lip of the refrigerator case, packages of hot dogs and bacon at her back.

The chatter in the store picked up, and Annie looked at her phone. No service. No way to get in touch with Julia, and no way to receive messages. Justin had said the sheltering wouldn't last long, but at least an hour passed before the workers removed the boards and opened the doors.

Gertrude had been right at least—the sun did shine outside. As Annie walked from the store to the great outdoors, she marveled at how different it was than the last time she'd stood in that exact spot. It felt like a whole new world, where everything had been turned upside down and inside out.

She'd felt like this before too—when Donovan had told her he needed a divorce. She'd endured the curveballs, the twists, the turns, the ups, and the downs life had thrown at her. She'd never seen the sky look so different. She'd never felt like she'd escaped something truly life-threatening...until this very moment.

"Let's go back to Harbor House," Dad suggested,

and since Annie hadn't wanted to spend any of this holiday in charge of anything or anyone, she nodded. She walked side-by-side with both of her daughters, with Mom and Dad in front of them. No one spoke, and she wondered if they were marveling at the newness of the world too.

"This isn't good," Dad said, and Annie tore her gaze from the cobbled street. He'd slowed to a stop, and she did too. The Harbor House sat only a stone's throw from them, on the other side of the street.

It looked like a very large animal had prowled between it and the building next to it—a seafood restaurant. While running by, the animal had thrown out its claws and dug them into and through the Harbor House.

Long gashes of siding were simply gone. Shingles hung like loose threads. A thin line of smoke rose from the far side of the hotel.

Mom began to cry, and Annie admitted only to herself that she wanted to do the same. Her phone chose that moment to emit a series of beeps, and her adrenaline spiked as she mistook the notifications for the sheltering siren.

She hastened to pull out her phone. Julia had texted several times, each becoming more panicked than the last. Annie stabbed at the phone to call her sister, and she said to Paige, "Stay right here. I'm calling your aunt."

Annie put a couple of paces between her and her family so she could have an honest conversation with Julia. "Pick up, Jules," she muttered as the line continued to ring.

"There you are," Julia finally said. "I've been so worried, but there hasn't been any service on the island."

"We sheltered in the market," she said, still watching that tiny trail of smoke as it appeared, lifted, and then disappeared. "No service, so I couldn't get a text off."

"Are Mom and Dad with you?"

"Yes." Annie blinked, her inner well of strength solidifying and rising through her the way that smoke continued to do. "I don't think they're going to be staying at Harbor House, Jules."

"Why not?" Julia sounded more panicked about this than she had about not knowing if Annie, her girls, and their parents were okay. "What's going on over there?"

"A lady in the store said it was a squall," Annie said, hearing the words come out of her mouth in an even monotone. She felt numb from head to toe, and she commanded herself to snap out of it. As a nurse, she'd seen a lot of trauma and terrible things in the past. She didn't get to go into this zone.

She blinked, and the world rushed at her again. "The Harbor House got hit hard," she said, making a decision. "We'll get their luggage from the front desk, and we'll be at the inn within the hour."

"You can't bring them to the inn," Julia hissed. "We're moments away from serving our first Thanksgiving meal, and there are no rooms here."

"There is no room *here*," Annie snapped at her sister. "They can have my room. I'll sleep on your floor. I don't care. But they can't stay here!" She took a calming breath and turned away from the sight of the ruined Harbor House. Everyone watched her, and she took another long breath in through her nose.

"Get ready," she said to Julia. The sheltering siren didn't go off again, but it might as well have. Everyone at The Lighthouse Inn needed to hunker down for the storm that was Sandy Harper. "We'll be there within the hour."

Chapter 7

Tessa had just taken the last sip of her tea, which was now cold, as the sun disappeared behind a cloud. She got to her feet, her teacup still in her hand and watched a blackish-bluish-green wall of clouds come straight for the island.

Nantucket Point sat on the far eastern side of the island, and the beach she'd frequented since moving here had shallow, warm water and easy waves most of the year, due to it being in a little inlet.

"My goodness." She headed for the corner of the house, her goal to get inside as quickly as possible. Thankfully, there weren't very many people on the beach, and those that were had already started coming in.

Tessa could shelter anyone who needed it, and she dashed to the top of the steps and started waving her arms. Everyone went toward The Lighthouse Inn, which sat a jog to the east, around the swell of sand dunes separating her house from it.

Fine by her. As long as everyone got inside.

She checked the beach one last time, didn't see anyone, and spun toward her front door. She darted inside and locked the door just as a horrific sound of thunder filled the sky. Tessa yelped, some unknown response to the noise making her jump, and dropped her tea cup.

It shattered on the floor, and Tessa backed away from it, her hands covering her ears. A steady, increasing sound—that of rain lashing the windows, the roof, the porch—filled her senses, and panic built within Tessa.

She didn't like that sound. It reminded her…of something. Something where she hadn't been able to move. Somewhere her mind hadn't worked properly.

Like a light switch being flipped, the memory shouted in her mind.

She'd been kidnapped not that long ago, and the rain and wind sounded like the water against the sides of the boat where she'd been held captive. She cried, tears streaming down her face, utterly perplexed as to why this storm had trigger that post-traumatic stress inside her. It wasn't the same situation at all.

She sank down, her left leg hitting the couch. She stumbled but managed to land on the sofa instead of the hard floor, and she curled into herself, her eyes closed, and waited for the storm to pass.

⊏▭⊐

SOMETIME LATER, Tessa opened her eyes to the sound of knocking. Was that inside her head or out of it?

"Anyone here?" a woman yelled. "Help!"

Tessa got to her feet faster than she knew possible, her maternal instincts kicking in. She strode to the door and unlocked it. She pulled it into the house, the wind giving it a mighty push as if she couldn't do it alone.

A woman stood there, dressed in a pair of jeans with a black coat over them which fell almost all the way to the ground. Her dark hair lay in plastered strands to her face and head, and she shivered violently. "Help," she said weakly, and Tessa barely had time to open her arms before the woman fell into them.

She grunted, but Tessa managed to hold her upright and get her in the house. She once again didn't worry about the water and mess accumulating on the floor, though it had taken her an hour to sweep and mop after the family dinner a couple of nights ago.

"How long have you been out there?" she asked.

"A while," the woman said. "No one's home."

"It's winter," Tessa said, like that was a perfectly reasonable explanation. It kind of was. Nantucket was a summer island, and a lot of people only lived here seasonally.

She got the woman onto the couch and hurried back to the door to close and lock it. She faced her again, feeling the chill and wetness that had seeped into her clothes from the woman's start to make her skin turn to gooseflesh.

"I'll make some tea," she said. The woman on the couch didn't stir. She lay back, her eyes closed and her legs straight out in front of her. Water continued to drip from everywhere, and her chest kept rising and falling, so Tessa decided to let her have a few minutes to just breathe.

"I'll see if I have some dry clothes for you," she said, though the woman had to be a size or two smaller than her.

She hesitated to leave her there, alone in the living room, and a chill ran down Tessa's back. She went past the still woman, giving her as much of a berth as she could, and into the kitchen. The tea got made while Tessa kept one eye on the stranger, and then she hurried down the hall to her bedroom.

For a reason she couldn't name, she closed the door behind her and locked it. Her phone showed she didn't have service, but she sent a text to Janey anyway. *A woman showed up during the storm, needing a place to stay. Hope you're safe.*

She sent the same thing to Julia and Maddy, satisfied that now three people knew she was with a stranger. If they didn't hear from her after the storm, well, hopefully they'd come check on her.

She dug through the bottom drawer in the dresser, because she'd kept some of her mother's things there. Mom had been a bit smaller than Tessa her whole life, and she managed to find a pair of loose beachcomber pants in black, and a sweatshirt in plain heather gray.

Something hit the window, and Tessa cried out again. She stumbled away from the dresser as she looked toward the glass, but she didn't see anything there but darkness. And rain. Her heartbeat lashed against her ribs much the same way the wind did the house, and it took several long seconds for her to get a decent breath.

She hated feeling so jumpy, and yet she couldn't help it. She didn't know how to control the adrenaline. She couldn't make her body stop reacting to every sound and creak, and her mind kept conjuring up terrible stories about what was going to happen to her.

Once she'd calmed, she scooped her phone from the bed where she'd dropped it and put it in her pocket. She picked up the clothes she'd likewise thrown when the phantom had knocked on the window and faced the door.

"You have to go back out there," she told herself. She didn't want to. Somewhere, an alarm shrieked, and Tessa couldn't be entirely sure it wasn't only inside her head. "You'll keep distance between you," she told herself. "You're wearing shoes. You can run."

In a storm? she argued with herself. And not just any storm. That had been a squall wall, and Tessa knew it. No one should be caught outside in a squall, and she might not survive if she had to go sprinting from the house.

The Lighthouse Inn wasn't that far away—*it's across open sand*, her mind reminded her—and she took a steeling breath, and then another.

That woman could be no one. Someone who happened to be leaving the bakery at the wrong time and couldn't get back in. Someone who'd made a wrong turn when they'd meant to go to The Glass Dolphin, which was serving Thanksgiving dinner from noon to eight p.m. today.

Tessa's mind spun, and she finally forced herself to take the first step. *You're strong*, she told herself. *You survived a kidnapping. You swam to shore alone. You have done so much this year.*

Surviving a divorce after learning her husband had been cheating on her.

Putting up with Janey—who she'd also learned was only her half-sister, not a full blood relative—and her lies, her half-truths, and her eventual psychiatric break.

Moving from the only home she'd known as an adult and settling here, in her mother's old beach house on Nantucket.

Facing a man she'd believed to have murdered his sister. Then learning he really hadn't.

Tessa could certainly go out into the main area of her own house and face a drenched, nearly drowned woman. She could.

She did, though she paused in the hallway where it met the kitchen. She didn't see anyone in the kitchen, at the table, or the living room. "Hello?" she asked, wondering if the woman had gone down the hall to the bathroom and would be behind her.

The thought terrified her. She didn't like it to this day when someone stood behind her, and she knew that came from the kidnapping for sure. She had the distinct thought that perhaps Janey wasn't the only one out of the two of them who should be seeing a counselor.

"Hello," the woman said, and she rose from the couch in the living room, right where Tessa had left her. "Sorry, I am just so tired from running through the storm."

Tessa committed to taking a step into her kitchen. She held up the clothes. "I found some old things of my mother's."

The woman pushed her hair back, and though it wasn't very well lit inside the house, Tessa saw a flash of gray along the woman's hairline. She suddenly realized she was probably ten or fifteen years older than she was, though she'd assumed her to be close to the same age when she'd seen her on the porch.

She relaxed further, but only for a moment. Hadn't Bobbie Friedman been a generation older than her? Yes, yes, she had.

She'd still kidnapped Tessa and tried to hurt Janey, all for money.

The woman came toward her, limping, and Tessa asked, "What's your name?"

"Caroline," she said. "Caroline Fyfe." She smiled and continued to rake her fingers through her hair. She twisted it up into a bun she secured by just tying the hair around itself, which revealed her neck. The skin there was wrinkled and saggy, very much like an older woman's would be. Maybe twenty or twenty-five years older than Tessa.

She shook the fact from her mind, not sure why she was so fixated on this woman's age.

"And you are?"

"Tessa," she said, leaving off her last name. She held the clothes out in front of her like a shield and passed them to Caroline.

"Thank you," she said, her smile quite bright now. "Thank you for letting me take refuge here. I'll be right back."

Tessa nodded and retreated to the kitchen, where

the electric tea kettle she used to heat water had already switched itself off. The water steamed, so it had boiled and would still be plenty hot. She got out two cups as Caroline went through the kitchen and down the hall, and she watched as she went into the bathroom at the very end of it. That room didn't go into any other rooms, and Tessa relaxed.

She made two cups of tea and sat at the dining room table facing the hallway. Caroline's footsteps came closer only a couple of minutes later, and she looked over to Tessa. Another smile, and it felt just too happy. Or maybe Tessa was really just not right in her head yet. She certainly didn't feel level-headed or clear at the moment.

She did nod to the tea. "It should be ready."

"Thank you, dear," Caroline said, and she pulled out the chair across from Tessa and sat down. "Oh, it's black tea." She looked up, her eyes a dark shade of blue now that she stood a bit closer. "I love black tea."

"It's Refined Arts," she said. "They're a local brand right here on the island." She forced herself to take a sip. "Are you from Nantucket, Caroline?"

She stirred her tea and shook her head. "No, just visiting." She looked up, and Tessa looked away, unable to hold her gaze. She wasn't sure why. She'd worked at a library in Pennsylvania, and she worked as a docent in the Nautical Museum here now. She spoke to strangers all day long.

Yet, she couldn't think of another question to ask Caroline, and she seemed content to stir and stare for the time being. She finally did lift her teacup to her lips, and as she set it back down, she said, "I found some porcelain in my shoes. I must've stepped on something outside while I was running."

Tessa remembered dropping her teacup from the porch. She twisted to look at the front door, but of course, she couldn't see it from here. "Oh, I think I dropped a cup by the door when I came in," she said, turning back to Caroline.

She still smiled, but it held a Cheshire Cat quality now. Almost creepy and definitely too big given the circumstances. "I can help you clean it up."

"Oh, it's fine."

"It's the least I can do, Tessa," she said with a laugh. "You're letting me stay here. Keeping me warm with black tea. One of the best brands too."

Tessa tilted her head, her eyes lasering in on Caroline. "I thought you said you weren't from here."

"I'm not." She lifted her teacup and took another swallow. Tessa's imagination ran through several scenarios, and none of them were good.

"You must've visited before," she said.

"Many times," Caroline said. "My brother used to live here."

Tessa took an overly large sip of her tea. It was

more like a swallow. "Oh, that's lovely," she said. "Where did he live?"

Caroline's eyes flashed, and Tessa's hand shook as she put down her cup.

"Right next door," she said.

In a flash, Tessa was on her feet. "Who are you?" she asked, though she'd already questioned the woman for her name.

Caroline looked up at her, and her expression wasn't exactly full of malice. It definitely held an edge Tessa didn't like, and she had the very distinct feeling this woman had been on her way to see *her* when the storm had hit.

"Riggs only had one sister," she said. "She died when she was very young."

"From his step-mother and our father." Caroline took a calm sip of her tea. "I heard you were one of the women who helped find dear Louisa."

"I want you to leave." Tessa's fingers vibrated violently, and she curled them into fists.

"You'd put me back out into that storm?" Caroline asked.

Tessa put another step of distance between them. She wasn't going to let Caroline come up behind her the way Bobbie had. She stared at her sitting there, at her dining room table. Wearing her mother's clothes.

"I knew your mother," she said next.

Tessa opened her mouth to retort but found she had nothing to say. She missed her mother, and it seemed a wholly unfair and inappropriate time to have those feelings coursing through her. Grief could very much be like that. She'd be fine for a long time, and then reaching for the back of the chair in front of her to brace herself as it coursed through her and around her, making her weak.

"She was a lovely woman."

"How old are you?" Tessa asked.

Her smile this time held a hint of sadness. "Older than you think. Older than I'd like to admit." For a beat of time, she looked exhausted, but she wiped it away quickly with another of her near-manic smiles.

"Why did you come here?" Tessa asked. Caroline had to know Riggs wasn't here any longer. Louisa either.

"I came to see you." She nodded to the chair. "I'm not going to hurt you, Tessa. Please sit down."

She very much disliked being told to sit in her own house. She hated that this place didn't feel as safe as it once had. She remained on her feet just to spite Caroline, then pulled her chair toward her and all the way into the corner. That way, no one could sneak up on her.

She sat and folded her arms. "Why did you come here to see me?"

"I need your help to clear Riggs's name," she said simply. She took another sip of tea. "Then he'll be able to come home, and I can go tell our mother that all is well."

Tessa's pulse bobbed against her tongue in the back of her throat. "Riggs thinks your mother killed Louisa."

Caroline smiled. "Oh, I know. We've talked about it many times." She put her elbows on the table. "Now, here's what I need you to do."

Chapter 8

Julia hugged herself as she stood on Tessa's porch and waited for her friend to answer the door. The squall had come and gone. Annie was on her way from downtown—with their parents in tow. Julia had to do something.

The door finally opened, just as she raised her hand to knock again. Tessa didn't open the door very far, and she peered out from behind it, only showing about an eighth of her body. Julia frowned. "What's wrong?"

"Nothing," Tessa said, opening the door further. She looked past Julia and all around, then stepped back. "Did you get my text?"

Julia hadn't gotten any texts except from Annie. "No." She stepped forward to enter the cottage, because it wasn't exactly summertime on the porch.

Tessa closed and locked the door behind her, and a chill ran down Julia's spine. "Tessa," she said slowly. "Why are there broken pieces of a tea cup all over?"

She tore her eyes from the floor and looked at Tessa. Something was definitely wrong. Tessa's hair frizzed out on the side, and she reached to flatten it as Julia looked at it. The house smelled odd too. Wet. Tessa wrung her hands together, another huge tell of her nerves. Her eyes darted around the cottage, as if she couldn't settle on somewhere to look.

"What did you text me?" Julia asked. She reached out and touched Tessa's arm, and that seemed to center her.

"A woman took shelter here during the storm." Tessa closed her eyes and ran both hands down her face. "The noise of it, the sounds...I had a little panic attack before she arrived, and I dropped my teacup."

Julia didn't like the sound of "panic attack." She turned toward the house, looking for other oddities. She didn't see anything else out of place. "I'll help you clean it up." She went into the kitchen and got the broom and dustpan, noting the sink held two teacups, one of them nearly full of black tea. The chairs sat tucked under the table, though, and Julia glanced down the hall, remembering why she'd come over.

She swept up the broken pieces while Tessa stood there, mute and obviously out of it. "Tessa," she said, and the other woman jolted. "Come sit down and talk to me." She had no counseling training, but Tessa clearly needed someone with her. Before the storm, she'd agreed to help with the Thanksgiving dinner at the inn, and Julia and Maddy had expected to see her by now. Thus, Julia had volunteered to cross the sand and make sure she was okay.

She set the dustpan on the table and returned to the couch with Tessa. She sat right next to her, their knees touching. "What has you all spooked?"

Tessa swallowed, and Julia noticed how white her face had gone. "The woman who came. She said she was Riggs' Friedman's sister. His biological sister."

Julia's back went stiff and straight. "Really?" Her eyes widened, and she took Tessa's hands in both of hers. "What did she want?"

"She said we need to clear his name." Tessa's eyes closed again, and she took a long, deep breath in, then blew it all out. Her eyes opened, and she seemed more like herself with just that simple action. Oxygen could do a lot to help the mind line up its thoughts right, Julia knew.

"How are we supposed to do that?" Julia asked.

Tessa shook her head. "I don't know. She said she thought her mom had killed Louisa too, but I needed to clear Riggs's name so he could come back here and live." She shivered, and while Julia hadn't been on the island when Tessa had been kidnapped, she couldn't even imagine living next door to the man who had once done that to her.

"That's ridiculous," Julia said. "One doesn't just get cleared and get to go back to their regular life." She knew, because she'd seen plenty of people fall from grace. They always left the neighborhood, because they couldn't have a fresh start in a non-fresh place.

She herself was an example of that. Maddy too. Even Tessa herself, as she'd left Pennsylvania and moved here after her mother's death and her subsequent divorce. They were all starting over, and Julia was so glad she didn't have to do so alone.

"Her name was Caroline, and Julia." Tessa's eyes widened as if she'd just realized Julia was there. "She said terrible things. She said she suspected her mother in the death of Louisa, but if someone else took the blame…" She squeezed Julia's hands. "She said your dad was on the island in July in 1974. So was my mom. She said it could be either of them. She didn't care. She mentioned Helen and Viola too. Someone named Augustus…something. I can't remember."

Julia searched Tessa's face, sure she'd fallen down some rabbit hole into another world. "I don't know what you're saying."

Tessa pulled one hand back and touched her head. "I'm not even sure it was real."

Julia glanced into the kitchen. "There are two teacups in the sink."

Their eyes met again, and Julia didn't know what else to say. Her chest felt so tight, and she had to remind herself to breathe. "What should we do?"

Tessa gave herself a little shake. "It's Thanksgiving Day. We should celebrate the things we're thankful for."

Julia nodded, because that sounded wonderful. She thought of families who could do that today, stress-free. She wondered what that would be like, as her last few Thanksgivings had been filled with tension and apprehension, this one included.

She could see them in their cheery, soft yellow light, the table set in crimsons, golds, and pumpkins. The turkey wouldn't be dry, and the mashed potatoes would be bottomless and piping hot, with a lot of butter. All the seasonal spices, cranberries, and décor was perfect, and the house was warm against the chill of late November.

As it was, she sat in a small cottage, almost in the dark, the air heavy with fear between her and Tessa.

Tessa got to her feet, and Janey watched her as she went into the kitchen. "Give me a moment to change, and I'll come over to the inn." She paused in front of the fridge and turned back. "I'm late, Julia. I'm sorry."

"You had a major event," Julia said, getting to her feet. "It's fine. I came to check on you, but I also have a favor to ask." She clasped her hands together, trying to decide if now was the time to mention her parents had nowhere to stay that evening. "You'll have to tell everyone about this Caroline woman."

"We should ask your dad if he knew her," Tessa said, her eyes widening. "Do you think we could?"

Julia nodded and decided to go all-in on the favor. "Yes," she said. "I think you'll have some time to talk to him tonight. See...he and my mom were going to stay in that room at Harbor House, but the hotel got damaged in the squall. They have nowhere to stay tonight, and I thought..."

Tessa's shoulders went down. "They can stay here."

Julia's hopes soared, and she loved Tessa dearly in that moment. "Can they?"

"Of course," Tessa said. "I have lots of room."

"It's the man who cheated on my mom...with your mom," she said, because she didn't think Tessa truly understood what was going on right now.

"Janey won't be here," Tessa said. "I'll be fine. I have nothing to do with it, right?"

"Right," Julia said, though she actually didn't think so. And if Tessa was going to question her dad about a girl who went missing forty-five years ago and was then found in the balcony of the inn where Julia worked, she wanted to be there. "I'll come over with them, and we can all talk."

"I'll try to get Janey to come," Tessa said. "You should bring Annie too. This involves her too."

"How?"

"Ryan Harper is her dad too." She cocked her head and seemed to be lost inside her own thoughts for a moment. Then she added, "In fact, he seems to be the key to all of this." With that, she turned and went down the hall to change for Thanksgiving dinner.

Julia stared after her, quite sure the world had just turned onto a different ninety-degree angle. She was left holding on with two hands, trying to get her bearings, as usual.

"What could my father have had to do with Louisa Fry?" she asked herself, but the cottage only sat in silence, refusing to answer her. She looked around at the remodeled walls and floors, wondering what this cottage had seen in its lifetime.

She did what she was very good at doing. What she'd done to get through each day with Maddy at The Lighthouse Inn when they'd first started. What she'd done in the first few days and weeks following her separation and then divorce from her husband.

She took a deep breath; she compartmentalized the tasks that needed to be done; she focused on the most pressing need. Right now, that was feeding her friends, family, and the guests at the inn the best turkey dinner of their lives.

Once that was over... "Well, then we'll see what hits the fan," she said.

TEN MINUTES LATER, she and Tessa walked into The Lighthouse Inn, the scent of cinnamon and pine hanging in the air. The smell actually made Julia's stomach sick, but she'd never told Maddy. She thought it made the inn smell festive, and none of the guests had complained about it. Julia certainly wasn't going to.

Tessa went up the few steps to the hall that led into the dining room and kitchen, but Julia turned back to the glass entrance door. Annie, her kids, and their parents hadn't arrived yet, and they should be here at any moment. Julia didn't know what the roads were like out there, and downtown Nantucket was a twenty-minute drive under normal conditions.

She pressed her nose to the glass and looked left toward the parking lot, but she didn't see her sister's car. She sighed, her breath fogging the glass. "Help me pull this off," she prayed, her eyes adjusting to focus on her partial reflection only an inch or two in front of her face instead of the parking lot beyond.

She should've told her mother no. She could've ordered a Thanksgiving dinner from Gremlin's, and she and Dad could've lit candles and had a romantic meal together.

Movement caught her eye, and Julia immediately pushed outside. Annie led the way down the sidewalk, her girls trailing her, and Julia's parents bringing up the rear. Her sister had a fierce look on her face, and it only softened slightly when she saw Julia.

"What happened?" Julia asked.

"We should've told her no," Annie said, not bothering to slow down or break stride. She went right past Julia, and her girls looked like they'd just seen a whole army of ghosts. Julia put a smile on her face for them, her eyes trained on her parents.

She knew in that moment that there would've been no candles and no romance over turkey and stuffing had they stayed in Southampton and ordered their meal from the local gourmet deli. Her mother walked two steps in front of her father, her head held high. Julia wondered when she'd spoken to him last.

To him, not *at* him.

Her mother was extraordinarily gifted at speaking *at* people, Julia included.

"Hello, dear," she said, breezing into Julia's arms. "You look lovely."

"Mom." She squeezed her bony shoulders. "Are you okay? Annie said you had to shelter in the market for an hour."

"I'm fine," she said, and Julia noted the use of *I* and not *we*. In the past, she'd spoken for her and Dad, but Julia supposed it was the past that had shattered the present. Perhaps her mother was still grieving or still trying to figure out what to do next.

She indicated her bag. "Where should I put this?"

"The inn is full," Julia said, something she'd told her mom when she'd called on Tuesday. "But I found you a room at my friend's house." She twisted and pointed toward the blue cottage, the second floor of which could be seen past the sand swells. "It's in that blue cottage right there. Close. Easy. She has extra bedrooms. You'll be comfortable there."

Her mother looked toward the cottage, her nose wrinkled like she'd smelled something terrible. She didn't agree, but she didn't argue either. Instead, she simply walked toward the entrance of the inn, her wide-leg pants flowing easily around her calves and ankles. She wore a dark purple shawl for a coat, with a hint of an ivory blouse peeking through at the elbow and throat.

With her departure, Julia was left to face her dad. "Hello, Daddy." She hugged him, glad he still knew to hold her tight and chuckle as he did.

"Hey, Julia-Boulia."

She grinned as she pulled away. "Mom's not talking to you?"

His smile slipped, but the life in his eyes stayed bright. "Not really. I tried to get her to stay home. Everything I suggest is the wrong thing right now, so I'm afraid it's my fault we're here at all."

"It's fine," Julia said, because she knew her mother. How Dad had managed her all these years, Julia wasn't sure. She pushed the judgment out of her head, because people probably said the same thing about her and Alan, speculating how he'd put up with Julia for so long before finally leaving.

"I don't think staying in that blue cottage is a good idea," Dad said, drawing Julia's attention back to him. "Do you know who used to live there?"

Julia swallowed. She couldn't believe she hadn't thought about Tessa and Janey's mother. "Yes," she whispered. "Lydia's daughter Tessa owns the cottage now, and she lives there."

Dad nodded, his jaw tight and set. "I don't know, Jules."

"I'm not sure there's another option, Dad," she said. "Besides, Tessa said a woman had to shelter with her during the storm, and she said…" She trailed off, not sure now was the best time to be talking about this.

"Julia," Maddy called behind her.

Julia turned, suddenly realizing how chilled her skin was. She rubbed her hands up and down her arms as Maddy waved her forward. "Sorry," she said as she arrived at the entrance to the inn. "My parents just got here."

"Yes, I know," Maddy said, her voice dry yet professional. "Your mother is in the kitchen, and I need your help."

Julia's stomach sank all the way to her toes, and she sighed. "What else is going to go wrong today?" she asked, because that squall had really ruined her plans to keep her parents occupied until nearly mealtime. Now, they had hours to go, and her mother had nothing to do but be in the way.

"Dad," she whined.

"I'll suggest she make her apple pie," he said, grinning at Julia. She giggled, the sound morphing into a full laugh when she saw the horror on Maddy's face.

"I already made an apple pie," Maddy said.

"Come on," she said, squeezing past Maddy. "Let's go make sure she doesn't burn down the inn or hijack the menu."

Chapter 9

The heat in the kitchen itched under Maddy's skin, but she refused to look over to the long counter where Julia's mother stood. Annie had gone upstairs to her room, both of her daughters trailing in her angry wake. Maddy had called to her, but none of them had answered.

Sandy Harper had blown through the door next, and she definitely wore blinders over her eyes. Sure, she'd greeted Maddy, embraced her the way high-society people do, with kisses on both cheeks and the word "darling," and then she'd gone straight into the kitchen.

Panic crept into Maddy's heartbeat, but she kept it at bay by opening the top oven and taking out the first pan of stuffing. She'd put that in first, as the bread could easily be re-warmed right before the meal. The turkey roasted in the bottom oven, and Maddy had spent the time during the squall setting the dining room table for their initial round of dinner guests. They were serving in two sessions this afternoon, with all of the guests getting dinner first, and then Maddy and Julia's personal friends and family gathering at four for the second and last wave of turkey, yams, and mashed potatoes and gravy.

The second turkey had been in the oven for only an hour, as Maddy refused to reheat poultry. The mashed potatoes couldn't be reheated or kept hot either. But yams, stuffing, and rolls could. Maddy had been meticulously planning this day for weeks. Since before the inn had reopened, and she wasn't going to let Julia's mother ruin it.

Determination streamed through her, and then Julia said, "Mom, you don't need to cook today. Come on out of the kitchen."

Maddy looked over to them as she went back to the oven and got the second pan of stuffing out. She put it in the cooling rack too, simply because they took up room and she could store the pans there easily. The rolls needed to go in next, as she could only bake one sheet pan of them at a time, and she had four ready to go in. Everyone loved homemade bread on Thanksgiving, and Maddy really wanted this meal to be talked about online in guest reviews as one of the best holiday spots on the island.

"I can help," Sandy said.

Julia met Maddy's eyes, and volumes were spoken. "We need to get your bags over to the cottage," she said.

"Your dad can do that," Sandy said, not budging. Maddy's heart beat faster and faster.

"Mom, we have plenty of help in the kitchen," Julia said, and Maddy turned away as the smile blipped onto her face.

Good for you, she thought about her friend. Julia rarely stood up to her mother, but the tone she'd just used left no wiggle room.

"We don't need or want you in here," she continued. "Tessa is coming over, and you and Dad can go to her house and get settled. Wander the beach. Whatever you want to do until dinnertime."

Sandy didn't say anything, and Maddy picked up another potato and got peeling. She'd been peeling them in between all the other tasks, and she very nearly had enough for their first wave of guests. She kept her head down and her shoulders bent so as to not invite conversation, but Julia said, "Maddy, tell her what we're having for dessert—and who's making it."

She turned away from the huge industrial sink against the far wall. "What? Sorry, I wasn't listening."

"We don't need another apple pie, Mom," Julia said. "We don't even have all the ingredients for it, and the stores on this side of the island are closed."

"Helen Ivy is making most of our desserts," Maddy said. "She's bringing several pies with her to complement what I've made, and she's going to make her famous cranberry sheet cake when she gets here." She glanced up to the clock above the door that opened in both directions and went into the dining room. Tessa should've been here by now too, and Maddy hadn't heard why she wasn't. "She'll be here any minute."

She hoped.

She looked at Julia again. "Is Tessa waiting for your folks to arrive before she comes over?"

"No," Julia said. "She's on her way." She turned back to her mother. "She said you and Dad could have any room you wanted in the cottage," she said. "There's one on the ground floor and a few upstairs. I want you to take your things over there and find something to do until dinnertime."

Sandy Harper raised her chin, and Maddy could see the defiance in her expression. It radiated from her shoulders, and it was only matched by that of her daughter.

"Mom," Annie said as she came into the kitchen. "You shouldn't be in here."

"That's what Julia just told me," she said. "You two don't want me here."

"Mom, it's not that," Julia said with a sigh.

Annie, however, said, "You're right, Mom. We don't. You've made things very difficult for us today, and we're all trying to do the best we can with it. You could at least give us that same courtesy."

"Annie," Julia said in a shocked voice. "Mom, it's fine that you're here."

Annie cocked her hip, and Maddy couldn't look away from the sporting event in front of her. She volleyed her gaze from one woman to the other, trying to find the weak link.

"None of this is our fault," Annie said.

Julia followed that with, "You're being very selfish."

"It was forty-five years ago," Annie said. "You're going to have to meet Janey. If you can't handle it, then *you* should go."

"Girls." Ryan Harper entered the fray, and Maddy wanted to slide behind one of the cooling racks so they'd continue to talk in front of her. She truly understood what a fly on the wall must feel like as she stood behind all of them as they prepared for this family feud.

She didn't need this today. She pushed away from the sink and strode toward them. "All right," she said just as Ryan started to speak. "I know you guys have a lot of family drama and all that. But we can't have it here today. Julia and I run this inn. We have to be professional. No one is authorized to work in this kitchen except for me, and I'm responsible for the food that goes out."

She hoped Sandy wouldn't bring up how she'd

invited two of her other friends to cook with her that day.

"We're serving not just one Thanksgiving dinner here today. Sandy, if you'd like, you can dine with the guests. Their meal is at two-thirty, which is getting dangerously close. If you think you can be polite and kind to everyone we've invited to our Thanksgiving Day table for the family and friends meal at four, you're welcome to that. But you're not welcome in the kitchen." She nodded like that was that, and Sandy's dark eyes bored into Maddy.

"Come on, Sandy," Ryan said, reaching for her. She pulled her arm away before he could touch her. He didn't react at all. "I've got our bags, and you can pick which room you want at Tessa's." He spoke in a tired, quiet voice, and Maddy had never known him to act that way. True, she hadn't interacted with Julia's parents for a long time now, but whenever she'd spoken with them in the past, her father had been vibrant and full of life.

He almost seemed like a shell of himself, and she couldn't help wondering if her ex-husband felt and acted like that sometimes. Chris had acted like Maddy had done nothing but hold him back, but she'd learned since coming to Nantucket that he'd done and said what he'd had to in order to drive her away. Hardly any of it was true.

"Fine," Sandy said. "I need a nap after that squall.

I have quite the headache."

In that moment, Tessa entered the kitchen, and Maddy had once thought that this room was absolutely cavernous. It could never be full of people or activity, but with the six of them there now, it felt stuffed to the gills.

She could barely get a full breath as Sandy looked at Tessa, and she wasn't even Janey. Maddy's pulse vibrated in the back of her throat, but she managed to say, "We have some painkiller out in the lobby." She cleared her throat. "In the office. Julia?"

Her friend startled and blinked. "Yes," she said. "Come on, Mom." She smiled at Tessa as she led the way out of the kitchen, and thankfully, Sandy followed her. Annie went too, after casting a glance at Maddy.

Ryan looked at Tessa, and she stared back at him. He took a few steps toward her and gave her a smile. For some reason, Maddy wanted to jump between them, but she wasn't sure why.

"Hello, Tessa," he said. "It's great to meet Janey's sister. She speaks of you often." He extended his hand, and Tessa shook it firmly.

"Thank you," she said. "It's...lovely to meet you too." She swallowed, and Maddy's heart tore and bled a little bit for the other woman. She'd been through so much in such a short time. She'd been on Nantucket for less than a year, and absolutely everything in her life had been turned upside down.

"Thank you for letting us stay in the cottage," he said, and he swallowed too. "I'll admit, I'm nervous about it."

Tessa released his hand. "We have some things to talk about anyway. It'll make it convenient. And private." She drew a deep breath and looked at Maddy. "I'm sorry I'm late. The squall shook me." She wore a haunted look in her eyes. "You wanted me on potatoes, I think."

"Yams," Maddy whispered, and Tessa nodded as she stepped past Ryan. If only Maddy could handle everything with as much grace as Tessa Simmons did.

Her gaze switched back to Ryan's after Tessa had moved beyond her, and he gave her a smile too. It again looked sad and exhausted. "Maddy, I'm sorry," he said, and then he turned and left the kitchen too.

The tension and awkwardness went with him, and Maddy sagged against the counter behind her. Silence reigned in the room now, and every sweep of the peeler along a yam grated against Maddy's nerves.

With a slight tremble in her fingers, she pulled out her phone and sent Ben a quick text. *Next year, for Thanksgiving, we're boarding a plane and flying far away. Just the two of us.*

It took less than a second from when she sent her text for his response to come in.

Done.

Maddy smiled, feeling more settled, and she shoved

her phone in her back pocket and went to help Tessa with all the peeling they had to do. As they stood shoulder-to-shoulder at the sink, Maddy simply let her presence say all that needed to be said.

It wouldn't take long for Tessa to start talking, should she want to. So Maddy wasn't surprised when she said, "What else is in the Seashell Promise besides sharing a secret?"

She didn't want to talk about the squall, though something had happened there. Tessa was never late without texting, and Julia had gone next door to check on her when they hadn't heard from her or seen her when they expected to.

She didn't want to talk about Abe, the man she'd been talking to on a dating app.

She didn't want to talk about Ryan Harper staying in her house. Maddy couldn't blame her for wanting to avoid all of it.

Tessa looked over to her, and Maddy smiled. "Well, Julia wrote it, but I seem to remember having to write down my biggest fear. We then went up onto the roof of her building and lit them on fire and let the wind scatter the ashes across the city." She giggled at the memory of her and Julia, as college students, thinking they could get rid of fears simply by striking a match.

Tessa grinned too. "I like that. Did it work?"

"Heavens, no," Maddy said, nudging the other woman with her hip. "Don't you know the only things that help with big, huge fears are therapists and alcohol?" They laughed then, but Tessa sobered quickly.

"Maddy," she said, and Maddy hummed. "I thought...I have another secret, but I don't want to tell anyone else yet."

Maddy slowed the peeling as Tessa did. "You can trust me. I won't say anything."

"Nantucket used to feel...different," she said. "I loved coming here as a girl, and I thought I wanted to live here, in that cottage of my mother's." Fear edged her eyes, and Maddy wanted to wrap her in a hug the way she did her daughter when everything went wrong. When she'd fallen and scraped up her hands and knees and everything hurt and stung.

"But you don't," Maddy supplied for her when Tessa remained silent.

Tessa shook her head and went back to peeling potatoes. "I just don't have anywhere else to go," she whispered, and it was the saddest statement Maddy had ever heard. She understood on the deepest level possible, and tears sprang to her eyes.

She wouldn't wish this drifting, untethered, unwanted feeling on anyone. She sliced off the brown peel, one stripe after the other. "I know how you feel," she said, her voice barely louder than the peelers doing their job. "After my divorce, I had nowhere to go. No one was talking to me. No family I could lean on or trust. Just…" She waved her peeler, the potato in her hand a cold lump.

She stared at the wall in front of her, not seeing it. She saw the city at night, as she'd walked the street that first night after moving out of her beloved home. "It's so lonely," she said. "So cold. Dark. It's terrible."

"Where did you go?"

"I stayed in a hotel," she said. "Once the holidays pass, Tess, you can stay here. Or get a hotel in town. Get out there. Look beyond the walls you think you have in your life."

"Is that how you ended up here?"

Maddy nodded. "I needed a job, and this one came up. I applied and got it. It's been a good start for me."

"Will you stay for very long?"

"I don't know," Maddy said thoughtfully. She'd always be on the East Coast, she knew that. Her children were here. "Ben's job is turbulent."

"So you're serious with him?"

"Serious enough for now," Maddy said, keeping things vague at best. The relationship was new, and while Maddy was enjoying herself, she didn't know how serious it would become.

"They're gone," Julia announced as she returned to the kitchen, a loud sigh following. "Maddy, I am so sorry. But they're gone until dinnertime."

Maddy put a bright smile on her face, hoping it would erase the melancholy memories and low conversation she and Tessa had been having. "Great," she said. "And Jules, you did great handling your mother."

"I did, didn't I?" Julia wore a flush in her cheeks as she tied an apron around her waist. She seemed flustered and jittery, but Maddy knew she'd calm down soon enough. "All right. Where am I?"

"Earth," Tessa said in a dry tone, and the three of them burst out laughing. Whoever had said that laughter was the best medicine had been a genius, because it chased away everything that had been said and done in the kitchen in the past half-hour, and by the time Helen arrived with her Grumpy-Grandmother face firmly in place, Maddy had gotten out a bottle of rosé and they all had a glass they were sipping slowly.

"What is going on in here?" Helen demanded as she slid a tray laden with ingredients onto a spare space of stainless steel counter. She looked around at Maddy, Julia, and Tessa. "Why don't I have a wine glass in my hand?"

Maddy giggled as she hurried to pour the older woman a drink. Helen took a delicate sip and said, "All right. I'm ready to bake," to which they all cheered and laughed again.

Now, if she could just survive preparing and serving two Thanksgiving dinners back-to-back, Maddy could wear a cape for the rest of the year—until the holidays next year.

Chapter 10

Janey pulled the big van she'd rented up to The
Lighthouse Inn and into an available parking space. In
the back, Rachel wasted no time pulling open the door
and spilling out of the vehicle. Travis followed her, still
chattering with Cole about something Janey didn't
understand. Video games or golf or something.

She looked in the rear-view mirror at Sean, who
rode directly behind her, and then over to Viola, who
occupied the passenger seat. She smiled warmly at the
older woman whom she lived with. "Sean will come
help you, okay?"

Viola frowned, but she nodded. Sean got out of the
van and turned back to first help Bradley Denney,
Maddy's father. Janey couldn't procrastinate any
longer, and she got out of the driver's seat too.

"Daddy," Maddy called, and Janey turned toward

the inn. The blonde woman came striding toward them, and she wore radiance on her face. "I'll take him. Thank you so much for picking him up."

"It was no trouble at all," Janey said. She met Maddy's eyes, and she saw entire wars being fought inside the woman's soul. "The Harpers are here, aren't they?"

She nodded, and Janey's stomach turned for the twentieth time that day. She reminded herself of something her counselor had told her. *You aren't a mistake. You're not the one at fault here either. There is no fault here. It happened a long time ago, and you honestly didn't have anything to do with it.*

She didn't. She hadn't known about her mother's affair or that Ryan Harper was her biological father until a few months ago. She certainly couldn't be blamed, and yet, she felt certain Ryan's wife blamed her.

McKenna exited the van too, and Sean went to help Viola, and that left Janey to walk with the two of them toward the inn. She had a large contingent of people with her. She'd been up half the night telling herself and devising ways she could hide behind the six people she'd brought with her.

Sean reached for her hand as they neared the entrance of the inn, and he squeezed. She looked at him, relieved to have such a steady anchor in her life. "We can walk the beach after we eat," she said.

"It's already getting dark," he said with a smile. "So I don't think so."

"You should wait for the island cleanup before you go out on the beach after a squall," Viola said. "It can sometimes wash up dangerous things. Once, we found this long piece of barbed wire, and it was wrapped around the neck of a statue."

"Oh, that's not true," Janey said, teasing Viola.

"It most certainly is," she said in a haughty voice. "There's a company that takes you out to see all these gold statues. Someone threw them all into the ocean when he found Christianity hundreds of years ago."

Janey looked at Sean, and they shook their heads together, and Janey took a deep breath of the spiced air inside the inn. The interior had been painted in beautiful shades of beige and gray, which she found cooling and calming. The furnace pumped this afternoon to keep everyone warm, and the scent of the incense or potpourri or whatever Maddy and Julia used to fragrant the air mixed with the more savory scents of brown gravy and baked bread.

Janey hadn't eaten since breakfast, and her stomach did another roll. Her mouth watered this time too, and her head felt a little bit light.

"Janey," a man said behind her, and she knew the voice.

She turned toward Ryan Harper—her father—and found him entering the inn with a dark-haired woman.

His wife, Sandy. He wore a huge smile and a pair of dark gray slacks, a pale blue dress shirt open at the throat, and a pair of dress shoes that probably cost as much as she'd paid to rent the van for this weekend.

She didn't care that he screamed wealth and she didn't have much—at least before Mom had passed.

He'd welcomed her into his life, even when it was very difficult for him to do so personally. He sacrificed for her, and Janey felt it keenly as he came nearer and opened his arms.

They met in an embrace, and her soul lit up with a smile. She'd felt so alone after her mother had passed away earlier this year. Orphaned. Solo. So very isolated. Finding out she wasn't completely alone in the world yet had been a balm to her weary soul, and she only had Ryan Harper to thank for that.

"You look great," he said as they separated. "Everyone got in okay? Before the storm?"

"Oh, it's been raining here for days," Janey said with a wave of her hand. "My kids got in during this torrential rainstorm, but at least it wasn't a squall." She smiled at him, refusing to let her eyes drift to Sandy yet. They would soon enough. "Annie said you guys barely made it off the ferry. Can you imagine if you'd been on it?" She shuddered. "I had the news on the moment the power returned. Apparently, they held the ferry at the dock because they'd seen the squall on the radar, so no one was out there."

"A miracle," he said.

"Truly." Janey's grin started to slip. "I can't wait for you to meet Sean." She indicated the way he'd gone with Viola. "You've heard so much about him."

"That I have," Ryan said, his smile not dimming even a little bit. "Janey, this is my wife, Sandy." He brought her right to his side, though it was clear she didn't want to be there. He smiled at the side of her face and then back at Janey. "Sandy, this is my daughter, Janey."

The way he said things just so matter-of-factly made Janey want to do the same. Her father—the man who'd raised her thinking he was her father—had told her that a situation was only awkward if she let it be that way.

So she shoved against all of the trepidation and awkwardness she felt coursing through her, pasted her own smile back onto her face, and reached for Sandy's hand. "It's so great to meet you," she said, taking one of Sandy's hands in between both of hers. "Ryan talks about you constantly."

Sandy looked like she'd been whiplashed from one side of the continent to the other. "He does?"

"Yes." Janey told herself to stop shaking this woman's hand so violently, and she dropped it abruptly. "Sorry." She gave a light giggle, wishing the ground would open up underneath her and draw her down,

down, down into the depths of the earth. Away from here.

No, she told herself. *Be present. This is the situation. Make the best of it.*

"What have you two been doing this afternoon?" she asked.

"Oh, Sandy napped," Ryan said casually. "I went and visited the bakery. Got a few goodies to try in the morning before we head back to the Hamptons." They started toward the dining room in slow steps. "What about your family?"

Janey's smile became more relaxed, more sincere. "We played games," she said. "My children used to love playing games on holidays. My husband and I would get a new family game every Christmas Eve, and another one on Christmas Day." She looked over to Sandy and Ryan. "It was nice."

"Sounds wonderful," Ryan said.

Sandy walked like her legs wouldn't bend at the knee, and she said nothing. Janey supposed she couldn't ask for more than that. She had no idea how she'd react if she came face-to-face with someone who said they were the offspring of her husband. The evidence of his affair.

Her face started to heat, and thankfully, the door to the kitchen opened and Tessa spilled out. "There you are," she said, her eyes scanning over to the Harpers. "I saw your kids, but not you."

"Here I am," Janey said in a falsely bright voice. Something with Tessa was very, very wrong, but she couldn't put her finger on what it was in only a moment. "What's going on?"

"Nothing," Tessa said far too quickly. She drew Janey into a hug as the Harpers continued down the hall toward the dining room. "Are you okay?" she whispered.

"I survived," Janey whispered back. "Surely I won't have to sit by her at dinner."

"Opposite corners," Tessa said. "Maddy and Julia made sure of that."

Of course they would. Maddy and Julia were two of the kindest women Janey had ever met. She hadn't treated them as well as Tessa had, and thus, she wasn't as close with them as Tessa was.

Her sister had gone through a lot in recent months too, and she really was all alone in the world. No mother. No father. No full-blooded siblings. Janey only had Ryan to her credit, and she couldn't understand why she needed someone on the planet with her. Maybe Tessa didn't need that same reassurance, but the grayness in her skin suggested maybe she did.

"Something's not right," Janey said as she looked into her sister's eyes. "What happened?"

"I'll tell you tonight," she said. "I need you to come to the cottage after this. If I need to give you a ride home, I will."

Janey continued to search for answers in Tessa's expression. "What are you talking about?" She didn't want to stay at the inn or go to the cottage for longer than she had to. She'd brought her family for dinner, and they had plans to return to Viola's, make caramel popcorn, and put on the first Christmas movie of the season.

They'd stay here for as long as socially acceptable, of course. She wasn't going to dine and dash. But she didn't want to stay for longer than necessary. She hadn't had her children with her for the holidays for a while, and perhaps she was feeling a bit selfish this year.

Her therapist said it was allowed, and Janey had worked past feeling guilty about it.

"I had someone come to my door during the squall," Tessa said in a quiet voice. "I need everyone to gather at my cottage after dinner. Please, Janey. Just for a few minutes."

Fear streaked through Janey, and she wondered if she'd ever be free from the phantoms out there. She didn't even know what these ghosts were, but they were big and scary if they'd turned Tessa this sickly shade of gray.

"Okay," Janey said, because she didn't know how to deny her sister in this instance.

"Come eat," Maddy chirped, and Janey turned toward the dining room. She and Tessa linked arms, and they walked toward Maddy. She gave Janey a hug and a smile, and Janey stepped inside.

The table bore trays and bowls of food that made Janey's mouth water. Everywhere she looked, she saw something delicious and delectable, from the enormous, golden turkey in the middle of the table to deep, dark cranberry sauce, boats of gravy, plates of butter, and toasty marshmallows over candied sweet potatoes.

People stood about, laughing and chattering, but Janey didn't go to the bar on her left and pour herself a drink. She wanted to be clear and level-headed tonight. She migrated with Tessa to Sean's side, the three of them standing together as they surveyed the room.

Julia, Annie, and their parents did the same thing in the opposite corner, Julia desperately trying to engage everyone in conversation. Helen eyed Viola with some level of distaste, and Janey had forgotten about their old animosity. Oops.

Rachel, Cole, McKenn, and Travis seemed oblivious to the tension in the room, and they stood talking to Annie's girls, thankfully. Otherwise, they'd have been completely out of place and probably absolutely petrified to be at this dinner.

Maddy raised her hands above her head and yelled into the fray. "All right. Everyone's here. Please find your place and sit down. Then we'll start our festivities."

Janey groaned inwardly, but she made no noise on the outside. She wouldn't ruin anything for Maddy, who'd clearly been working on this afternoon's meal for days and days. Not only that, but this was the second meal she'd served in as many hours, and Janey didn't even want to see what the kitchen looked like.

She sat in her assigned spot, Sean on her right, and Tessa just around the corner at the head of the table. Her children sat in pairs on either side of her as well, Rachel and Travis beside Tessa, and Cole and McKenna by Sean. From there, Viola sat beside Travis, then Annie and her children took up three spots, then Julia and her parents, and then Maddy and her father down at the other end of the table on Janey's side. Helen sat between Brad and McKenna, and Janey noted that Julia and Maddy had done a good job keeping the two older women apart too.

Part of her wanted to stand up and blow up the seating chart. She wanted to sit right next to Sandy and force her to talk to her. To accept her. She wanted to plant Helen next to Viola and demand they talk until they worked out all the misunderstandings of the past.

She said nothing, and she bowed her head as Annie said grace. She hated the walls and distance between people, and she ached to erase it. She simply didn't know how, and as Maddy said, "Be thinking of something you can share with us about what you're grateful for," Janey added her own silent prayer to that which had already been offered.

She reached for Tessa's hand and leaned toward her. "I'm grateful for you," she whispered.

Tessa grinned at her, squeezed her hand, and said, "I'm grateful for you too."

Janey allowed herself to believe it. Not that long ago, Tessa had been horribly upset with Janey. She had every right to be, and Janey still had a very long way to go before she could truly be forgiven for firing a gun near her sister, with her eyes closed.

She knew that. She knew she needed forgiveness and grace more than anyone else at this table. It also allowed her to feel absolute love for every person seated there—including Sandy Harper. In truth, Janey had no issue with the woman. It wasn't her fault her husband had cheated on her so long ago.

After taking a roll, she looked down and across the table to Sandy and found the woman watching her too. She smiled, and she could've sworn Sandy returned the gesture. Just for a moment. A blip of time. There, then gone, her eyes falling to the bowl of creamed corn her husband had passed her.

But she'd smiled for that brief moment in time, and Janey had seen it.

A COUPLE OF HOURS LATER, Janey walked with Helen, both of them carrying desserts across the sand to the blue cottage at the end of the lane. Her heart grew heavier and heavier with every step, but she said nothing.

Helen didn't either, and the darkness around them seemed all-encompassing. Janey had sent her children back to Viola's with the older woman, Sean, and Brad. Helen had said she could take Janey back to Wainscott. Or Tessa could. No matter what, she wouldn't be staying in the blue cottage, because Ryan and Sandy were.

"Here we go," Helen said as they reached the steps and started climbing. "Into the belly of the beast." She flashed a smile at Janey, who did her best to return it. The porch light cast strange shadows across Helen's face, and monsters swam behind Janey's closed eyes in the time it took for her to blink.

She didn't knock but went right inside, the interior of the cottage brightly lit. Tessa had every light burning, and Janey and Helen were the last to arrive. Julia, Annie, and Maddy all sat on the couch. Tessa handed a mug to Ryan, then looked over to Janey and Helen. "Okay," she said. "Everyone's here."

Sandy wasn't in the room, and Janey's anxiety dropped a notch. She led Helen over to the recliner and helped her sit down. She couldn't sit. She'd stand, because then she could get some of the nervous energy bolting through her out and into the ground.

Tessa took a seat on the loveseat with Ryan, and the pair of them there together made Janey wince. They shouldn't be friends. They didn't go together, and yet somehow, they...did. She couldn't make sense of any of it, because Tessa then said, "A woman came to visit me this morning. Her name is Caroline Fyfe, and she's looking for her brother, Riggs. She wants him to be able to come back to Nantucket, his name cleared."

She looked around at everyone, taking a moment to meet their eyes singly. She looked right into Janey's. "She wants us to clear his name, and she made it sound like she'd do anything she could—even pin Louisa's disappearance on one of us or someone close to us—if we didn't help her."

Her hand shook as she lifted her mug to her lips and took a sip of her tea. Janey knew it was tea, because her sister didn't drink coffee this late at night. Or at all. Janey needed some tea too, or something hot, because her insides had iced over.

"One of us?" Maddy asked.

Tessa instantly looked at Ryan. "You were here that summer. My mother was too."

"No," Janey said instantly. She rocked back and forth, her weight shifting from one foot to the other. "Neither of them had anything to do with Louisa's disappearance." She couldn't believe they were even *talking* about this.

Anger rose through her, and Tessa's eyebrows went up. "We don't know that," Tessa said evenly. "We weren't there."

"Exactly," Janey shot back. "Why is this our problem? Why can't we just say Riggs did it and move on?"

"You know he didn't do it," Tessa said quietly.

"No," Janey said, all rational thought flying from her mind. "I don't know that. You don't know that. None of us know that!"

She looked over to Julia, Annie, and Maddy. They hadn't even been here over the summer, when Bobbie and Riggs had taken the sunny, happy Nantucket from Janey and twisted it. Made it into something ugly to be feared. Why were they here? How did this involve them?

She didn't even know how it concerned her.

"She mentioned Helen," Tessa said next. "Viola. She knows all the players." She twisted and set her mug on the side table. When she faced everyone again, she wore absolute fierceness on her face. "I don't want to see any of us, or anyone we love, go down for something they didn't do." She took a breath and folded her hands. "So. We need a plan. We need people to start talking about what they know about the summer of seventy-four, Riggs, Rick Fry, Louisa, everyone." She looked at Helen and then Ryan. "Then we'll go from there."

Janey wanted to ask her where they'd go from, and what they were driving to, but she didn't. Instead, she sank onto the arm of the couch beside Julia as their father opened his mouth and said, "I knew Rick Fry. He was a nice guy…"

Chapter 11

Tessa listened to what Ryan Harper said. It wasn't anything different than what she'd researched only a few months ago.

Rick Fry had come to Nantucket Point with his family. Caroline, who was older than Rick, hadn't come. She'd been engaged, and she'd spent that year— 1974—in New Jersey with her soon-to-be husband.

Tessa had never heard Riggs speak of a sister, but that didn't mean she didn't exist. Ryan and Helen both said they'd met Caroline on previous occasions, she simply hadn't been present on the island that fateful summer.

Ryan said, "We all had a relationship with Lydia." He shifted in his seat, his eyes suddenly trained on the floor. "She was a beautiful woman, full of...spirit." He smiled seemingly to himself, but Tessa had to agree.

She missed her mother so very much sometimes, because Mom did everything with spirit. She'd taught Tessa to do the same, and somewhere along the way, in her boring library job that she'd actually enjoyed, or living alone for weeks at a time as she enjoyed her garden more than her husband, she'd forgotten to live with spirit. With spunk. With laughter and purpose.

"I knew she loved Greg, and." He cleared his throat. "I went home to my wife. I didn't see Lydia again after that, not for a long time. She and Greg got married, but Sandy and I didn't come. I made sure I was too busy at work to make the trip, though it was easy to do so from the city to Nantucket."

Tessa appreciated the distance Ryan had put between himself and her mother, and Janey had told her he hadn't known about her until that summer. Listening to him talk, the truth of his words sunk into Tessa's soul. A sense of invigoration filled her, and she suddenly didn't feel so heavy and so…slow.

"We still came to Nantucket, of course." He glanced over to Helen and smiled. "We always came to the bakery, though I usually booked a house some-where besides the Point. I knew Lydia had the house here, and I knew it was important to her."

"Thank you," Janey murmured.

Ryan looked at her, and then Tessa, and while Tessa didn't speak, she nodded in silent acknowledge-ment of what Ryan had done all those years ago.

"Rick…I don't know what happened to Rick. I had a new baby. I had a busy job, and I was trying to climb that ladder fast, you know? I didn't know Riggs Friedman very well, because as I said, I tended to avoid the Point."

"Riggs came to the bakery all the time," Helen said. "I didn't recognize him as Rick Fry. He wasn't an inhabitant of the island under that name. Only a tourist, and I never made it a point to get to know the tourists."

"You knew me," Ryan said with a smile.

Helen folded her arms. "I make a few exceptions for the good ones." Her crabby façade didn't crack despite the obvious compliment she'd just paid Ryan.

"Surely you must've known about his sister going missing," Tessa prompted. "Both of you."

"Of course," Ryan and Helen said together. "It was huge news," Ryan said. "Huge." He paused and waited for Helen to say something, but she didn't. "Since I knew Rick, I followed it closely, but I wasn't here on the island at the time."

"At all?" Tessa asked, leaning forward.

"I'd gone home a couple of weeks before," Ryan said. "Sandy and I didn't come again that summer. Lydia and Greg were married that fall."

The timeline fit, but Tessa was sure Caroline could spin something to make it seem like Ryan had been here in July of 1974. Two weeks was nothing, and as he'd said, it was an easy trip from New York City to Nantucket. Then, and now.

"I followed what I could from the city, and communication then wasn't what it is now. I couldn't just call Rick and ask him what was going on. The newspapers said he was on the run, and he didn't have a mobile phone."

"The island was in an uproar," Helen said, which Tessa had heard before as well. "Everyone was scared, but then…then it sort of died down."

Until this past fall, when poor Louisa Fry had been found in the balcony of The Lighthouse Inn. Society at large believed Rick Fry aka Riggs Friedman had killed his sister, hid her body, and then disappeared.

He'd returned to Nantucket a few years later, married Bobbie Friedman, and they'd lived next door to Tessa's mother for decades. There was no other evidence to indicate anyone else, except Rick and Louisa's mother, of the crime.

Tessa once again thought she needed to get up to New Jersey to visit with the woman, but at the same time, the very idea of coming face-to-face with her sent a tremble through Tessa's stomach that spoke of terror.

Helen and Ryan continued to reminisce about days gone by, but nothing new was shared. Julia, Annie, and Maddy left for the inn. Ryan retired up the steps while his wife had chosen the room on the main level where Janey had stayed over the summer.

Tessa put away the coffee mugs and teacups while her sister helped tidy up the living room and put the kitchen chairs back at the table. She finally faced her sister, and the two of them held a conversation without saying a word.

They'd kept plenty of secrets from one another when they'd come to the island to go through their mother's cottage after her death. They'd been through so much since then, and Tessa saw no need to hold anything back from Janey.

"What do you think?"

"I think this isn't our problem."

"You weren't in this house with Caroline Fyfe." Tessa frowned at her sister, the words she wanted to say building beneath her tongue. How wonderful it must be for her to have her children here with her. A new boyfriend. All the love in the world surrounding her. No matter how hard and far Janey fell, she always had so many people lifting her back up.

Tessa had do all of that herself. She'd had no man there to help her when she'd been kidnapped. Her son barely responded to her texts, and he hadn't answered a call in weeks. Janey herself had been there, and they had grown closer over the past handful of months, but Tessa never felt like *she* was enough for Janey.

Janey always needed more than Tessa could give, and somewhere deep inside, that continued to stab at a wound that wept continually and never truly healed.

"She's dangerous," Tessa said, a chill sliding over her skin. She didn't hide the tremble. "I just don't know what to do."

"I just want to enjoy the weekend," Janey said.

"Me too." Tessa didn't have to work until Tuesday, and she imagined the thousands of families enjoying after-dinner pie right now, and tomorrow they'd wake up to breakfast casseroles, huge Black Friday sales, and leftover turkey sandwiches for lunch.

They'd spend time with their families the way Janey had all day today, and when Tessa had enjoyed that life, she'd never given much thought to people who didn't have loved ones to celebrate with or to simply be with.

She knew now how lonely, dark, and long holidays could be.

"Maybe we don't need to do anything," Janey said.

Tessa wanted to argue, but she said, "Maybe."

"What could she possibly do?"

"Janey," Tessa said. She worked to keep the frustration out of her voice, and she succeeded well enough. "I think she'd do something like frame Ryan Harper." *Your father*, she thought but didn't say. The words echoed in the quiet kitchen anyway. "It wouldn't be that hard, honestly."

Janey's fingers curled into fists. "He's got money," she said. "He'd fight it and there's no way it would stick. Riggs still wouldn't just be able to waltz back onto the island and start living next door again."

"They haven't sold the house," Tessa said.

"Does anyone ever come?"

Tessa sighed as she pulled the chair away from the table and sat down. "No."

"Bobbie will be sentenced in January," Janey said. "It'll be over then."

Tessa had thought so too. She closed her eyes, and a chill wafted across the back of her neck. She startled and yanked open her eyes again. She looked over her shoulder, her pulse pounding in the back of her throat.

"You weren't here," she said. "Caroline doesn't just want this thing with Bobbie done and over with. She wants the case from forty-five years ago to be final and closed."

"To what end?" Janey sat down too, pure exhaustion in her expression.

"To clear her brother's name." Tessa shrugged. "She really wants her mother to admit to something, and she won't. She thinks if Riggs—Rick, whoever—is cleared, her mother won't have any reason to keep lying."

Janey shook her head. "That makes no sense. Whether it's Riggs taking the blame or Ryan, she's still not going to admit to anything."

"She thinks she will," Tessa said. "And Caroline has things in her head that won't budge." Tessa had inter-

145

acted with people like her before, and they were dangerous. "She said she wanted me to get everyone together and tell them about her. That all together, we could come up with something that could clear Riggs's name. I honestly don't know what."

"She didn't give you anything?"

"Just the creeps," Tessa said. "Nothing tangible or physical. She wanted everyone to know she'd been here." She put her head in her hands, trying to remember what Caroline had said.

Now, here's what I need you to do.

Get everyone together and tell them I want Rick's name cleared.

Tell them about me.

Find a way to clear Rick's name so we can get my mother to admit to Louisa's murder.

If you can't, well, I'm going to have to do something to get my brother's life back, and there are other potential suspects for the murder.

She opened her eyes. "She really wanted everyone know she existed." She searched Janey's face. "What if she's not really Rick's sister?" She thought of the gray hair and how Caroline had said she was older than Tessa might think.

"Who would she be?" Janey asked. "Who would run through a squall to this house, to tell you all these crazy things, if she wasn't his sister?"

"I don't know," Tessa said. Caroline had left her

teacup on the table, and she'd left the moment the sky had started to lighten again. She hadn't given Tessa her phone number, nor had she said where she was staying.

Tessa had no doubt she was close by, and while it was a bit off-putting to have Janey's father and Sandy staying with her, at least Tessa didn't have to be alone tonight.

She got to her feet and said, "I'm beat. Let's talk more tomorrow."

Janey stood too and drew Tessa into a hug. It felt so nice to be held, and in moments like these, Tessa felt as close to her sister as she always had. "I love you," Janey whispered.

"Love you too," Tessa said as she pulled away. She put on the best smile she could muster and walked Janey to the door. She watched as she got in the car with Sean, who'd come to get her and Helen, then retreated into the house and locked the door behind her.

Safe in her bedroom, with that door locked too, Tessa pulled out the folder of papers, interviews, pictures, and everything else she'd collected on the Louisa Fry case. She laid it all out again, read a few things, and then stopped.

Caroline Fyfe... She needed to do more research on this woman and find out if she existed or not. She picked up her phone and saw a few messages from

Abe. Her heart grew wings, but she had one thing to do before she could flirt with him and tell him all about her Thanksgiving Day.

She hadn't seen Riggs since the day he'd shown up at the house next door, Janey had fired a gun, and he'd run again. But he'd managed to leave her a note in the garage behind the house, and that had been a single slip of paper with a phone number on it and the words *for emergencies.*

She didn't know for certain if it was from him, but she'd made a very good assumption based on the handwriting.

And his supposed sister showing up during a squall was an emergency if Tessa had ever had one.

She opened the top drawer of her dresser, which was slim and barely deep enough to hold a pair of balled socks. The note sat there, and Tessa tapped in the numbers. Then she wrote a quick text, something Riggs could answer with a single word, as she didn't know what access to this phone he'd have, and for how long.

Your sister came by this morning. I hope you had a good Thanksgiving with her. Did you?

She hoped he could decipher what she was really asking. *Do you even have a sister? If so, did you know she's here on the island?*

She stacked all the pages and put them back in the folder, then plugged in her phone, changed into her pajamas, and climbed into bed. She didn't know what to do about Caroline or Riggs, and she wouldn't tell Abe about any of it just yet.

But a long breath of relief moved through her at his first message, which was a picture of him and his loved ones, all of them standing around their Thanksgiving feast table—with its near-complete meat dominance. She grinned at it, her thumbs already flying across the screen.

Did you eat any veggies today?

There were some olives in the olive loaf, he said, and she giggled to herself. She marveled at the resiliency of human beings—of herself—and how she could switch from something troubling and terrifying to something flirtatious and fun.

Caroline never truly left her mind, but she could set her on a shelf for a few minutes before those dark eyes and foreboding presence crept back in. When Abe went silent, Tessa tapped back out to her main texting list.

The number she'd texted earlier hadn't responded.

Chapter 12

Annie pushed aside the hangers with the ugly black dresses, looking for something she thought Paige would like. It would be suicide to purchase something for her teenager without at least snapping a pic and sending it to the girl. Paige would be asleep for a few hours yet, and Annie did like having a surprise for her daughter's birthday.

The older Paige got, though, the harder it was to surprise her with anything but cash. Even then, Annie often felt like the amount wasn't significant enough. Her mind wandered as she turned away from the dresses and started looking at the sweaters. Bri loved those, and with winter descending upon the Atlantic Northeast, everyone in the family could use another sweater.

Annie saw one she liked, and she rifled through the

stack for the right size. If she liked things from this store, it was a given neither of her girls would, and she gave up the search to find something for them.

The store was extraordinarily busy, but she supposed she should've expected that for Black Friday. She waited in line for a dressing room, just to make sure the sweater hung right across her chest, and when it was her turn, the woman there managing the crowd of ladies gave her a smile. Annie wondered what time she'd come in to work today.

"Just the one item?" she asked, eyeing the sweater.

"Yes, please."

"You need help finding anything else?"

Annie shook her head. She hadn't gone far; a row of shops and restaurants sat just down the road from The Lighthouse Inn. She hadn't wanted to brave downtown Nantucket by herself, and neither Julia nor Maddy could take the morning off work. Bri and Paige preferred sleep, but Annie found herself restless.

She wasn't sure why. She had a couple more days here on Nantucket, and then she'd return to Chatham, and everything would settle down again. Except, somewhere in the back of her mind, she didn't think it would.

In the dressing room, she shrugged out of her coat and thin T-shirt and into the sweater. The bright green made her smile, and the pink and brown and white geometric patterns helped her to feel younger and hipper than she currently was. Than she'd probably ever been.

For maybe the first time in her life, Annie didn't take off the garment and check the price tag. She wanted the sweater. She was going to purchase the sweater. With her own clothes back on, and the sweater draped over her arm, she left the dressing room and headed for the check stand.

Another long line. Another woman with raised eyebrows that Annie had managed to make it through the store and had only found one item to buy. She left the women's wear store a hundred dollars lighter than before, her panic stuck deeply in the back of her throat.

The sun hadn't burned off the gray mist yet, but Annie held high hopes for the day as she walked from one shop to the next. The Holiday House boasted lights with yellow and white lights along the sign, and they made Annie warm from the inside out.

A woman stood at the door, greeting people as they walked in, but this definitely wasn't the most popular shop. "Welcome," she said. "We have all of our fall décor on sale today, and some select Christmas items."

Annie took the pamphlet, not really sure what she was looking for. She barely had time to water her plants, let alone decorate for Halloween or Thanksgiving. She and the girls would drag the Christmas tree out of the storage closet, hang stockings, and bake cookies on Christmas Eve—if Annie didn't have to work.

She normally didn't mind picking up the holiday shifts, because Paige and Bri could go to their father's. This year, though... She banished the thought. She and Donovan would work out how to get the girls where they needed to be.

She'd been able to calm herself with thoughts like these before, but they didn't do much today. The scent of Christmas hung in the air, and Annie took a deep breath of it as she became aware of someone coming into the store behind her. She half-turned and saw a couple of women taking the pamphlet.

One with almost golden hair and one with hair a shade or two or three darker than that. They looked at the papers and then each other, and Annie liked the joy she saw there. She wasn't what it was about them, but they felt like women she'd like to know. Like the other nurses she worked with at the hospital.

She told herself she had friends back home, but the truth was, she felt like a drifter. Like this island wasn't tethered to anything solid, and if she stayed too long, she'd float further and further from anyone she knew.

The two women approached, and Annie noticed the baby bump on the one with the darker of the blonde hair. She gave her a smile, and she got the same gesture in return. "When are you due?"

"Oh, not for months yet," she said, looking down

at her midsection. "How did you know I was pregnant?" She looked at her friend. "You said I wasn't showing."

"You aren't," the woman said, her bright blue eyes blazing. She looked back at Annie with interest.

"I'm a nurse in a radiology unit," Annie said. "I can almost sense a pregnant woman. It's not you. It's me."

The other woman nodded in acceptance, and the moment turned awkward. Annie ducked her head and turned away, ready to find some amazing deals on holiday accessories. She'd driven onto the ferry, so she didn't have to limit herself to what she could stuff into her suitcase. Anything she could get into her car, she could get home.

She wandered around, looking and wasting time. She'd picked up and smelled every scented candle in the place, finding most of them to be too strong for her taste. Too much cinnamon. Too soapy. Far too much lavender, a scent she'd never understood. With a whole cupboard of scented candles at home, Annie certainly didn't need another one.

She'd just arrived in the nutcracker section when she heard someone yell, "Hey," behind her. Annie turned and found the blonde jogging toward her. She looked like she did a lot of running, her stride even though her expression held only anxiety.

"You're a nurse, right?" she asked.

"Yes." Annie turned toward her. "What's wrong?" She looked past her to find her friend, but she wasn't there.

"Heidi's having some pain." The woman wore wildness in her eyes, and she pulled in a breath. "It's her first baby. She'd nervous. Can you…?" She glanced over her shoulder. "Can you just come talk to her? I've had children, but it was a while ago, and she needs some reassurance from someone younger than me."

"Sure," Annie said, because she saw no reason not to go help. She wasn't going to buy anything at The Holiday House, and she followed the woman back down the wide aisle toward the front of the store.

"My name is Robin," the woman said. "Robin Grover. My friend's name is Heidi Baker. She's married to a cop, and she said she was going to call him. He'll be on the next ferry here from the Cove."

"The Cove?" Annie asked, glad Robin was short enough to keep up with. Annie couldn't run should Robin try to do that, but Heidi came into view. She sat on a bright blue couch in the spring section, and Annie found she did want to explore more of this store. Perhaps there was more to The Holiday House than decorations.

"Five Island Cove," Robin said. "It's a thirty-minute ferry ride southeast of here."

"Are there really five islands?"

"Yes." Robin smiled. "I've lived there my whole life. It's great."

"Is it like Nantucket?"

"Do you live here?"

"No," Annie said. "Chatham."

Robin nodded like that answer gave her the confirmation she needed. "Nantucket is a bit...stuffy. Five Island Cove is more casual. It's beachy and fun. Bright blue skies and festivals and great little restaurants. A fabulous ferry system." Robin smiled with plenty of joy in her expression. "I love it there, obviously."

"I can feel that," Annie said. To be honest, the way Robin talked about Five Island Cove made Annie want to go there and see the place for herself. "Maybe I should come visit."

"Come in the summer," Robin said with a smile. "I'll take you to the best beaches and we'll get the most delicious ice cream from this new shop that just opened last July."

That sounded absolutely wonderful, but Annie would never do it. Even so, she said, "I'm in." They arrived in front of Heidi, who looked up at them sheepishly.

"I'm fine," she said. "The pain is all gone. Maybe I just got a little over-excited about the bird feeders." She gave a light laugh.

Robin sat down beside her, and as the couch only

held two, Annie stood awkwardly above them. "This wasn't brought on by bird feeders."

"The Internet says the uterus can cramp during pregnancy, and it's normal." Heidi's fingers twined around one another.

"It can," Annie said. "Are you bleeding?"

Heidi and Robin both looked up, and Heidi shook her head. "I don't know."

"I'd go check," Annie said. "Sometimes the baby is twisting or turning. How far along are you?" She crouched down in front of Heidi and put her hand on her knee.

"Four months," Heidi said. She looked up as a third woman arrived, this one carrying a baby who couldn't be older than a couple of months. Annie loved babies, and she straightened with a smile on her face.

"What's going on?" the woman asked, her keen eyes taking in everything. They landed on Annie the longest and then switched to Robin.

"Heidi got lightheaded and had some cramping," Robin said. "Annie's a nurse, so she's helping her." She indicated Annie, and then the other woman. "This is Laurel Lehye. Don't let her stern look fool you. She's sweet as pie when she's not in cop mode."

Laurel's attitude dissolved right in front of Annie. Her face relaxed into a smile, and she bounced her baby on her hip. "Did you call Royce?"

"No," Heidi said. "He didn't want me to come to Nantucket this early anyway."

"You have to tell him," Annie said, turning back to the pregnant woman. "If it happens again, then you'll have a record of it." She extended her hand toward Heidi. She was probably a decade younger than Robin, maybe more. Which meant she was younger than Annie as well.

"Go check yourself in the bathroom, and then make sure you're drinking enough. If you feel tired or weak, tell your friends. Sit down. Keep track of what your body is telling you."

Heidi put her hand in Annie's and got to her feet. "Okay." She glanced at Robin, who jumped to her feet too.

"I'll go with you." They bustled off together, and Annie looked at Laurel. She offered her a smile, but Laurel seemed to have her policewoman mask back in place.

They took a breath at the same time, and Laurel blew hers out first. "I can't wait until they bring The Holiday House to the Cove."

"Oh, are they moving?" Annie asked, though she really didn't have local interest in the happenings of Nantucket, or this little section called Nantucket Point.

"Opening a second store," Laurel said. "My parents live here, and this is one of my favorite stores." She smiled in a more genuine way now. "So I'm excited to have it closer to me. It'll make shopping for my mother much easier." Her baby squealed, and both women gave the little girl their attention.

"I understand that," Annie said, though she didn't. Not really. She sent her mother flowers on her birthday and she went in on an edible fruit arrangement for Mother's Day. Julia always organized it, ordered it, and ensured it got delivered on time. Annie and her brother paid Julia what she said their share was.

She swallowed. "I walked by The Glass Dolphin earlier," she said. "It's right next to The Lighthouse Inn, and I'm staying there."

Laurel tugged her baby's hat lower onto her head so it wouldn't slip off. "Have you eaten there? The Glass Dolphin?"

"No," Annie said.

"It's fabulous." Laurel ignored her phone as it rang.

"They said they were opening a café somewhere called Sanctuary Island. I'm not sure where that is. It feels like everything about here has some strange combination of Cs and Ks and 'tucks.'" She laughed, because Nantucket fit that bill, as did Tuckermuck Island, and nearby Chappaquiddick Island.

"Sanctuary Island is one of the five that make up Five Island Cove," Laurel said. "We all live there. Me, Robin, and Heidi."

Annie nodded. "So it seems like quite a few places are expanding to the Cove."

"It's been growing a lot lately," Laurel said.

"What has?" Robin asked as she approached.

"Five Island Cove."

"That it has." Robin emitted a long sigh. "She's not bleeding."

Heid wore equal relief on her face, and Annie felt a connection to her she didn't understand. All three of them, actually. "That's good news," she said. "Did you skip breakfast this morning?"

"I wasn't feeling well," Heidi said. "We left early."

It was still early, and Annie nodded. "Eat and drink. Slow down when you feel like you need to." She tugged her phone free from the pocket of her purse. "If you'd like, I can give you my number, and you can call or text if you need anything else while you're here on the island."

Nantucket had a hospital, and Heidi could easily go there too.

"That would be great," Robin said, and she looked at Heidi with encouragement.

Annie tapped in her name and number and sent a quick text to Heidi. "All right." She looked up, feeling some measure of light fill her up. She hadn't even realized how dark she'd been inside until that moment. She blinked, the moment breaking.

"It was great meeting you three." She stepped

awkwardly into Robin, who smoothed over the motion by hugging her tightly.

"Thank you, Annie." Robin gave all the light back to Annie, whose soul couldn't seem to absorb enough of it. She patted the baby's head, and hugged Heidi, then turned and examined the spring collection here in this section. "I think I'm going to get a bird feeder too."

They all laughed then, and Annie stayed with all the florals and brighter colors while the three women from Five Island Cove moved on. She didn't feel left out, but the morning's high had definitely been reached.

She wandered through the store, then went to the last one in the row—a shop Janey had recommended for "amazing beachwear." Sandy Waves did have some great items for sunbathing and lounging on the deck of a large yacht. Annie didn't spend much time doing anything outside, because people needed emergency care every day of the year, and Annie had to be there when they did.

She left that shop empty-handed too, and she faced west and looked down the sidewalk. Shops on the right. Thin parking lots on the left. Down at the end of the row—probably three-quarters of a mile away—she could make out the upper level of what used to be a functioning lighthouse.

The inn.

Annie didn't want to go back, but she couldn't stay away forever. She hadn't been able to make much sense of the tales her father had told last night, though they'd meant more to Julia and Maddy, Tessa and Janey. Julia had tried to explain more about the happenings of the fall while she and Maddy had been renovating and preparing the inn to reopen.

In Annie's opinion, it was a beautiful building. Her sister and Maddy had done an amazing job on the inn, the rooms there, and all of the activities they ran. But The Lighthouse Inn almost seemed to be a place that collected bad energy and hung onto it, and Annie thought the best thing that could happen would be to shut it down.

Julia would need to find another job, and Annie knew the price her sister had paid to come to Nantucket Point and start fresh. Annie knew a little something about having a very stable life blown up and about trying to catch all the tiny little pieces as they came raining back to Earth.

It was an impossible feat, and Annie looked up into the sky, the grayness gone. Blue shone through all the puffy clouds, and she wished she could gather the fluffiness into her hands and make cloud-castles with it the way children did with sand.

A smile touched her face as she rearranged the clouds into great structures in the sky, and the daydream was enough to get her back to the inn. Julia waved to her from the back patio, that bright pink book in her hand. "Annie!"

He lifted her hand in a wave and changed directions when she saw Paige sitting with her sister and Maddy.

"Come on," Julia said. "We're doing some Seashell Promise stuff."

Annie very nearly turned around and went to put her single bag containing the green sweater in her car. She didn't want to do all of the things in her sister's fanciful college book, but she also didn't have the heart to cause any more heartache for Julia. So onward she went, down the sidewalk that ran alongside the lighthouse and to a set of stairs that led up to the back deck, confining herself to whatever happened next.

Chapter 13

Julia grinned at her sister and eyed the bag. "What did you get? Anything good?"

"A sweater," Annie said, handing her the bag. "Mom and Dad must be gone."

"Their car left twenty minutes ago." Julia's smile only got wider, and Annie couldn't blame her for that. Yesterday had been a very long day filled with tension and eggshells, and Annie had never taken more painkillers in one day than she had yesterday.

"I know you don't want to do the Promise stuff," Julia said. "Which is fine. But come hang out." She nodded to the table filled with all manner of delicious things. "Helen's obviously here; she'll be out in a few minutes. She ran into a guest she knows inside." Julia sank into a padded wicker chair with a sigh. Annie sat beside her and nodded to Maddy, who lifted a steaming cup of coffee to her lips.

"There's coffee and tea," Maddy said. "On the table beside the slider."

Annie got up to fix herself a cup of coffee and collect a couple of pastries. "No activities today?"

"No," Julia said. "Not until this afternoon. We figured this morning would be dedicated to sleeping or shopping." She waved the bright pink book as if she needed it to ward off heat exhaustion or a multitude of flies. She really just didn't want anyone's attention to get too far from the Seashell Promise.

Tessa turned from the back railing, and Julia glanced over to the sliding glass door, almost willing Helen to walk through it. If she didn't get started soon, she'd lose more than Annie's attention.

Maddy kept looking out over the water toward the Coast Guard base, the morning stillness making everything seem louder and more enunciated. She sipped her coffee without making a sound, which meant she was working very hard to be silent.

Julia flipped open the book and said, "All right. Helen can get caught up."

"I'm here," the older woman said. She slid the door closed and limped over to an available chair. "You didn't need to wait for me."

"Of course we did," Julia said. "You told us all your deepest secrets last time."

Helen scoffed, as she had the grumpy older woman down to a science. Not only that, but her secret had been that she read romance novels…so not really a secret activity.

She picked up a chocolate croissant without a care in the world for calories and took a bite of it. Maddy scoffed and then giggled. "You don't have to do it like a neanderthal," she said.

Helen very nearly chewed with her mouth open too, obviously a challenge to everyone. Julia rolled her eyes and said, "Okay, now that everyone is finally here."

"I said you didn't have to wait for me," Helen said past all that croissant.

"You're part of us," Julia said, and all eyes moved to her. A sense of discomfort stole through her, but she held her head high. "We are all we have." She didn't mean for her voice to come out super-charged or choked, but it did both. "My sons weren't here for Thanksgiving. Maddy's children didn't come. Her boyfriend was off with his parents."

A sense of wildness she couldn't have predicted crept through her. "Tessa didn't have her son here. Janey had all of her kids, but she was the only one, and we all had to put up with my very awkward parents."

"It was okay," Tessa said gently.

Julia's gaze flew to her. "I know it was, and that's because I'm your friend and you care about me." Her eyes darted to Annie, who stared steadily back at her. "You're not all alone, Annie. I know you feel like you are, but you're not. None of us are, because we have *each other*."

She slapped the book onto the table in front of her. "I don't care if we do this."

"Yes, you do," Maddy said with plenty of force in her voice too. "Don't get all bent out of shape just because we're not all as excited about it as you are."

Julia glared at her, because when they'd found the book, they'd *shared* the enthusiasm over it. "We need something good in our lives right now," she said, her voice much quieter than it had been a moment ago. "There's this...this dark cloud above us with everything surrounding Riggs and Louisa. I thought it would finally be over, and we could do this fun, pink, sparkly thing and move on. Finally move on."

Foolishness flooded her. "I was stupid." She shook her head in quick little bursts. "Sorry to make you bring so many things from the bakery, Helen."

"Please," she said. "No one stops by on the day after Thanksgiving. They all have pies and leftovers for days." She indicated the platter. "In fact, I think some of these might be from a day or two ago."

"Great," Maddy teased. "You brought us stale pastries." She laughed, and Helen's craggly exterior cracked as she smiled too.

Paige leaned forward and picked up the book. Julia

watched as she flipped it open and asked, "You wrote this, Aunt Julia?"

She swallowed, met Annie's eyes, and then nodded at her niece. "Yes. It was a silly little thing from college."

"The Seashell Promise," Paige read. "Is a friendship pact between women." She looked up, clear interest in her eyes. Julia's heart thumped, because she'd spoken true. She didn't have anyone else but the women on this deck. Yes, she could text her brother or his wife. She could do the same to her parents. But day-to-day? Someone who knew her inside and out? Someone who could walk into a room, take one look at her, and *know* without either of them having to say a word?

That was Maddy. Or Tessa. Or Helen. Or Annie.

Annie reached over and took Julia's hand in hers. "Go on, Paige," she said quietly.

"In order to bond as true, lifelong friends, hardships must be faced. But when women face them together, they come out stronger and more capable than when they must navigate life's storms alone." Paige turned the book around as if it were kindergarten storytelling time and showed the boat Julia had drawn.

It was a real piece of art too, not a child's rendition done in crayon. Julia loved to draw with ink and paper, making everything in shades of black, gray, and white. She'd done a big yacht, which usually felt safe and didn't capsize. As a twenty-two-year-old, she'd believed the tales of boats and ships overcoming storms.

Now, twenty-five years later, she knew there were some things that could capsize a woman, leave her gasping for air, and utterly stranded in an ocean that went on for miles and miles and miles.

"That's beautiful," Helen said. "The words and the art." She smiled at Julia and finished her croissant without fanfare.

"Step one," Paige read after she'd faced the book in her direction again. "Tell each other a secret. Secrets should be kept within the group, even if there's only two people. Trust must be established between friends in order to build a strong foundation."

"We did that part already," Maddy said.

"Almost," Annie said. She looked from Maddy to Julia to her daughter. "I didn't tell anyone a secret."

"You don't have to," Julia said, her chest constricting with the texts her sister had sent after their first Seashell Promise session.

"I want to," she said, but she swallowed hard. Julia waited, because she'd known Annie for her whole life, and her sister had been carrying a burden all alone for a while. What it was, Julia hadn't been able to get her to say. Yet.

"My ex-husband, Donovan." She licked her lips

and looked right at her daughter. "He left Mass-achusetts."

"What?" Paige asked. The book fell to her lap. "When?"

"Last week," she said, and Julia felt the bravery pouring from her sister in waves. "He and Mitch went to Vermont. They had an opportunity there."

"But," Paige said, and it was more like a sputter. "I can't—we can't go see him every weekend or whatever if he's in *Vermont*."

"No," Annie said. "You can't." She lifted her arm and put it around Paige, who leaned into her. "That's my secret. I didn't know what to do. I still don't know what to do. I suppose there's nothing to do." She met Julia's eye. "But Julia's right. I don't have him to rely on anymore. I feel...alone, and I don't want to feel that way, so if I can rely on you ladies here, maybe I won't feel one breath away from drifting up into the sky and never coming back."

Her voice broke on the last word, and Julia's heart pumped out strong beats that ached as they echoed through her body. "Annie," she whispered, squeezing her sister's hand. "You are not alone."

"No," Maddy said. "You are not. Julia and I are right here with you. We know *exactly* how you feel."

"So do I," Tessa said. Julia looked at her. "I lost my mother this year, and then I found out my sister is only my half-sister. I feel exactly the same: If I breathe too deeply, I'll just float away, and you know what? No one will even notice."

"I would notice, dear," Helen said, patting her hand.

Julia loved Tessa with her whole heart. "Who came over only ten minutes after you didn't show up to help with Thanksgiving dinner?"

Tessa didn't need to say Julia had, because everyone already knew it. She looked around at the small group of them again, folding Paige right into their sisterhood though she was so young. "None of us is alone. We don't have to do anything by ourselves." She nodded to Paige, who looked at the book again.

"Respect each other's privacy and honor their confidence," she said. She looked up. "Does that mean like, keep their secret?"

"Yes," Julia said. "It doesn't mean how good you think you are at something. It means, I tell you something in confidence. And you'll keep it safe for me. We have to be safe with each other, because sometimes..." She looked beyond the railing to the Sound beyond. "Sometimes it doesn't feel safe out there."

Paige flipped the page, the only sound among them now. "Step two is to share your biggest fear. Fears come and go. We conquer them and new ones rise up. Women should champion each other and help them face fears, rationalize through them, and overcome them. Never mock someone for their fears, as they all have a very real basis inside us." Paige turned the book around, and though Julia had drawn the images and had looked through this book more than anyone else, she was still surprised by the level of emotion in the woman's face on the page.

She sat behind a windowpane, drips of water running down it, distorting some of her features. She looked absolutely terrified of something, and Julia's own pulse picked up speed.

"You're supposed to share something you're afraid of," Paige said when no one said anything.

"I'm afraid of living an unimportant life," Annie said, and surprise filtered through Julia that she'd shared first. "I'm afraid I'm clinging to Chatham, because I've lived there for so long. I'm afraid there might be something else for me, and I'll miss it, because I've got both hands gripping the life I have now, afraid that a better one isn't out there." Her hands shook as she tightened them into fists, her knuckles turning whiter and whiter as she gripped the phantom life she'd spoken of.

Paige stared at her mother. Everyone did, even Julia. She normally didn't hear Annie speak this way.

Julia didn't know what to say. She had fears. Of course she did.

"I'm afraid of being forgotten," Tessa said, and all eyes moved to her. No one tried to reassure Annie or

Tessa that they were wrong about their fears, and Julia allowed herself to start to open up.

"I'm afraid I've already done what Annie said," Helen said. "I've been holding so tightly to the bakery here on Nantucket, and I'm terrified to let it go."

Tessa nudged the platter of baked goods closer to her, and most of them smiled. Helen's was the widest, but she did pick up a raspberry fritter.

"Mine kind of goes with what my secret was," Maddy said. "That I'm still hurting from losing my family?" Her eyes grew distant. "I'm afraid that if I allow myself to move on, that I'll be giving them permission to cut me loose, when I don't want to be cut loose."

Julia swallowed, because she was the only person who hadn't told her greatest fear. Besides Paige, who she didn't think would participate. One by one, each woman looked at her.

She tried to organize the words. She couldn't, and then she realized she didn't owe anyone an explanation. Helen hadn't expounded on why she felt like she needed to hold so tightly to the bakery. Tessa hadn't explained why she felt forgotten, though it wasn't hard to see.

"I'm afraid I'm invisible," she finally said. That summed it up nicely, and she looked at Paige. "We only do one—"

"I'm afraid of making the wrong move," Paige

said. Julia clamped her mouth shut, her shock echoing Annie's. "I only have a year of high school left, and then there's this big, scary world out there. What if I choose the wrong college?" She looked wildly over to Helen. "Or the wrong man?" She looked at Maddy. "I can't even order at Wendy's without a major crisis."

She met Julia's eyes. "And you're not invisible, Aunt Julia. I see you. I see you everywhere in this inn, and it's amazing. And Maddy, your family won't cut you loose if you move on. They're watching you with admiration for not letting a really crappy situation beat you into the ground. They just don't know how to say it."

Tears filled her eyes, and Julia's own burned as well. "I know, because I've seen my mom do exactly that. Life handed her a huge stinking platter of crap, and she took it, turned it into cake, and keeps moving forward."

Annie wiped her eyes, and Paige sniffled. "You're not going to make the wrong choice for us, Mom. You never have."

"What if it's not in Chatham?"

"Then we move," Paige said. "It's fine. People do it all the time. We're not special. Isn't that what you're always telling us?"

"You tell your kids they're not special?" Tessa asked, her voice full of teasing. "Annie, I'm shocked." That broke the tension, and Julia's right eye leaked tears down her cheek. She swiped at it quickly, glad she wasn't the only one.

"You aren't forgotten," Julia said to Tessa. "And Helen, if you want to sell the bakery and retire, do it."

"I just might," she said.

Julia looked around at everyone, and they all gazed at each other too. She took a deep breath and took the book from Paige. "All right," she said. "We only do one per day, because wow." She gave a laugh that didn't truly hold any humor. "That was some heavy stuff."

"I want to know how things are going with Abe," Helen said, focusing on Tessa. "Can we talk about *that*?"

"No," Tessa said. "Unless you're going to start talking about who that gentleman was inside that kept you for so long." She batted her long eyelashes at Helen, who suddenly turned a shade of red Julia had never seen someone over sixty turn.

"Helen," Maddy said, her voice mostly air. "Do you have a gentleman caller?"

"No," Helen barked. She pinched off a piece of her doughnut and tossed it at Tessa. She laughed, the sound full of joy. Julia wanted to bottle the sound and let only a beat or two out when she needed to infuse her soul with happiness.

Sitting right there on the back deck at the inn, she captured the moment and pocketed it in her memory. She knew she'd need it later, but for right now, she could bask in the sisterhood flowing around her and binding them together exactly the way she intended the Seashell Promise to do.

"Okay," Tessa said as the laughter died, and the moment sobered. "Now, does anyone have any ideas about what we can do to pacify Caroline?"

Julia's mind blanked, because she honestly felt like the stories she'd learned and been told belonged on a true crime podcast. They weren't real. They were larger than life. Stranger than fiction.

"Because I don't think she'll stay away for long," Tessa said. "And I'd rather not allow her to cause problems for any of us."

"We need to get ahead of it for sure," Maddy said, but she didn't offer a way to do that. No one did, and Julia once again felt stuck between two impossible situations. Her father hadn't had anything to do with Louisa's disappearance or murder. But Caroline didn't care about that.

And this time, just like last time, Julia didn't have to tread this path alone.

Chapter 14

Maddy wiped the last counter in the kitchen, a sense of accomplishment coming over her. She poured so much of her heart and soul into this single room, all so she could turn out amazing feasts for the guests in the one next door.

The Lighthouse Inn had only been open for about a month, but they'd gathered nearly three hundred reviews online. All of them mentioned the quality of the food and how good it was. She needed that. It fed her pride and kept her from hitting snooze on her alarm—on her life—every single morning.

Someone needed her, in a world where she hadn't felt needed since her divorce. Her mind went down whatever path it wanted to as she cleaned, and she'd been going over the get-together from only an hour ago. The emotions out on the deck had been sky-high, and Maddy's had gone with them.

She felt like Tessa too. Forgotten.

And Julia. Invisible.

And Annie, like she'd been holding too tightly to the wrong life for too long. She'd been forced to release her fingers quite against her will, and the pain of such events still pulled through her despite the pristine condition of her kitchen.

She rinsed out the washrag and laid it on the counter to dry. She'd gotten Vivian to approve a higher budget for food for the holidays, and she didn't have to cook tonight. She'd have to make the drive to Wain-scott to pick up the catering order she'd put in—and her father.

Her mind moved away from the mystery still surrounding Riggs Friedman—or Rick Fry—and now his sister, Caroline and to her dad. His health had declined to a point where it now seemed to have stuck. He wasn't getting worse; he wasn't getting better.

He had good days and bad ones. Maddy was there for all of them, and she went into the quiet, still dining room to catch up with her family. She tried to keep Brittany and Tony up to date on their father's health, and she'd taken several pictures yesterday and sent them to her siblings.

As she hadn't seen her father yet today, she simply sent a quick message that she was glad the holidays here had concluded, and she was looking forward to a slower weekend before another week began.

I'll see Dad tonight, and I'll let you know if he got your gifts, she sent, as both Tony and Brittany had sent him a gift basket filled with all of his favorites—pears, flavored mustards, pretzel rods, summer sausage, and candied nuts. Dad spent a lot of his time on the porch, listening to news, podcasts, or audiobooks, as his eyesight wasn't what it had once been.

How was Thanksgiving? she sent next, and then she navigated away from her sibling text string and to her children. They'd spent the holidays with their significant others. Kyle, her son, with Bea's family. And Chelsea with her father.

Maddy had already invited everyone to Nantucket Point for Christmas, and her daughter had confirmed. Kyle hadn't yet, and while Maddy didn't want to pressure him, she did need an answer.

She only texted her children on the same group string with good things, so she sent a personal message to Kyle. *Hope your holiday in DC was amazing. Have you talked to Bea about Christmas here on the island?*

She hastened to add, *No pressure, but I'll need to arrange lodging as the inn is full. There are a few options now, but they'll diminish the closer to Christmas we get.*

She texted with Chelsea about the food at her father's, and her daughter could talk and talk and *talk* once she got going. Apparently, the turkey had been dry in some places and undercooked in others. The marshmallows on the sweet potatoes had burned, and Chris's new girlfriend certainly wasn't handy in the kitchen.

Maddy experienced a deep satisfaction at this, though she tried to push it away. She giggled with every story Chelsea told, and she cherished each moment for what it was. A moment with her daughter that was untarnished by Chris's influence. A life and experiences Maddy had once had with both of her children.

Kyle's name blipped down from the top of her screen, and she quickly tapped over to his texts. *We'll be there, Mom.*

Those four words made her happier than she knew she could be post-divorce, and she looked up at the sky and murmured, "Thank you, Lord." She'd experienced more miracles since Chris had said he wanted a divorce, and she'd been blind to them for long enough. "Thank you."

⸻

MADDY SCRUBBED the window of the yacht, the gentle back-and-forth movement of the vessel in the water soothing and comforting. They hadn't run any tours today, but tomorrow would be back to business as usual. The inn was full for the weekend, and she and

Julia had specifically designed Thanksgiving-themed meals, activities, and outings for their guests.

Since Maddy had a hard time being idle, she'd finished texting her family and moved onto the yacht to make sure it would be ready for its morning voyage the following day. She'd checked the weather, and everything should be smooth sailing for the next week. After that, she'd have to double-check everything.

She looked up, her tasks almost complete, when she heard Julia's voice. Had she lost track of time? Maddy looked down at her phone, but she hadn't been out here that long. Not even long enough for her stomach to grumble for lunch. She frowned and started to call for Julia.

Something in her friend's tone stopped her. Julia sounded...angry. Since they'd been working together at the inn, her mood had improved a lot. Julia rare got angry about things going on here in Nantucket. She'd get frustrated, sure. She'd go quiet when she needed time to think. But she didn't have the anger in her that Maddy once had. For Julia, her default was feeling hurt, not going into denial and getting furious.

Maddy edged closer to the doorway that led up to the deck, her ears straining as she tried not to make a sound. *You're eavesdropping*, she told herself, and yet, she couldn't make herself stop. The yacht was Maddy's territory. She was the one with the pilot's license and all the sea knowledge. Julia never came out here. Never.

Or maybe she did…

Maddy peered up the steps, but she couldn't see Julia. Her voice didn't waver or move, so she stood somewhere out of sight. Maddy would've only been able to see her feet anyway.

"No, Dad," she said. "You can't tell them that." A pause, barely a breath, and then Julia said, "Tessa will think you did it. Janey nearly *shot* Riggs a month or so ago. No."

Her feet moved then, the steps loud against the deck upstairs, and Maddy pulled back, her heartbeat pounding in her throat, her mouth, her head.

"I can't believe you were on the island that day," she said. "And that you didn't say so!"

Ryan Harper was on the island after he'd said he'd left. That much was clear. The reason why he'd come back wasn't hard for Maddy to guess. Julia wouldn't want to hear it though, and honestly, Maddy didn't blame her father for not telling them last night. He and Helen had been put on the spot, with four other women looking at them for answers from almost five decades ago.

Maddy drew in a slow, shallow breath. She just wanted this case with Louisa Fry to go away. A wall of emotion hit her, the same way it had when she'd first walked into the office here at The Lighthouse Inn and seen Julia Harper sitting there. Maddy had very nearly walked right back out, and the urge to do so once again intensified inside her.

She didn't need this job, not for the money. She needed something to keep her busy and occupied, and she did like being near her father. But she didn't have to work here. In that moment, she didn't want to be on this yacht or worried about anything happening at the inn—or what had happened so long ago. She'd barely been born, and she really didn't need all the drama. She had enough of her own real-life drama, thank you very much.

"Dad," Julia said next, the word clipping from her lips. Maddy could only imagine the irritation on her face, burning in her eyes. "Of course I'm not going to tell them. There's nothing for them to find, is there?"

She moved again, and Maddy backed up a step.

"You have *got* to be kidding me," Julia said, her voice getting dimmer and dimmer. Maddy took a couple of quick steps up, wanting to hear more. "Maddy keeps all of that in her room. I'll see what I can find."

Maddy continued to the top of the steps, her mouth open, ready to call to Julia. But her friend walked with purpose, her long, dark hair streaming behind her she moved so fast. The wind played a part too, but she looked fierce and frightening, and Maddy suddenly didn't want her to know she'd been lurking below, listening.

"Maddy keeps all of that in her room," she murmured to herself. She lived in what had once been called the Blue Room. She'd found the historical scrapbooks and journals of The Lighthouse Inn, as well as an ancient recipe box full of brotherly love notes from Riggs to his sister Louisa.

Some of the pictures now hung on the walls of the lobby. She and Julia had gone through them all and chosen select ones that illustrated the concepts they wanted to recreate for the inn. She and Tessa had made copies of everything in the recipe box, the journals, and the scrapbook before they'd turned everything over to the police.

She shook her head. Why did she think she'd know more than trained professionals? "You and your friends did find her in the balcony," Maddy told herself as she turned around to go finish cleaning down below. Now, she wished she hadn't. She wished the location of the little girl had remained a mystery.

A shiver ran down her arms. No, that wasn't right either. If they hadn't found her, she'd still be in the balcony, and that thought chilled Maddy right to the bone. So did the idea that the person who could've harmed her had sat at her Thanksgiving dinner table last night. And that his daughter was probably now entering Maddy's private room to find any evidence of his stay on the island the week Louisa Fry and her family were here.

Her phone caught her eye, and Maddy reached for it, her hand moving slowly as if someone had poured quicksand over her head. She and Tessa had made copies in the form of photos. They'd each taken a photo of every card, every piece of paper, every photo, every everything that had come out of the Blue Room.

She had it all right at her fingertips—if only she knew what she was looking for.

Julia does, her mind whispered, and Maddy turned back to the steps. Her mind spiraled as she thought about what she should do. Confront her best friend? Let it go? She shouldn't have heard the conversation anyway. Julia had obviously come to the yacht for privacy.

How strong was their bond? How far would Maddy go to protect Julia and Ryan Harper? So much of her life had been lived in shades of gray, and Maddy suddenly understood why. Friendships and relationships were complicated. The love of a mother knew no bounds, but she and Julia weren't a mother-daughter pair.

Her relationship with Julia felt just as important to Maddy, and yet...

Her loyalty wavered.

"Stop it," she told herself. She turned and threw the bottle of glass cleaner in the bucket. Off came her gloves, and Maddy put away the cleaning supplies. "You don't know anything. You heard a few sentences. If you want to make a judgment and know what to do, go get the facts."

She'd learned that from her politician ex-husband, and she marched up the steps and off the yacht, praying she could be brave for just a few minutes.

Be brave, she chanted at herself. *Get the truth. Be brave. Get the truth.*

Chapter 15

Summer, 1974:

Lydia Merrill could not believe what she was seeing. Or rather, who. She glanced left and right, trying to decide if she should head inside the cottage or go and meet Ryan Harper head-on. She couldn't see around the corner of the house, and she had no idea if Greg and Dale had left the front door open or not. She'd said she'd be right in, and she'd just wanted to watch the sun finish painting the sky in such marvelous golds, silvers, and bronzes.

Dale's kiss burned on the left side of her neck, and Greg's on the right. She didn't want Ryan here, not now that she knew he was married, at least. She reached the corner of the cottage and stole a peek down the lane. No movement. Cars wouldn't come this way, as there wasn't any parking or public beach access.

Her cottage sat right at the end of the lane, faced the Sound, and Lydia had given her whole heart to it the first time she'd come for a visit.

She dashed along the front of the house, nudging the door closed with one sandaled foot as she went by. She flew down the steps and to the left, her feet getting sluggish in the sand. "You can't be here," she hissed in Ryan's direction.

He came from The Lighthouse Inn, and she had no doubt he'd booked a room there. How, she didn't know. The inn only had five of them, and with it being the middle of July in peak summer tourist season, it should be hard for him to find a room on the island anywhere.

"I had to see you," he said.

"No, you didn't."

He caught her around the waist even as she denied him. When he lowered his head and kissed her, Lydia didn't fight back. She hadn't wanted to give him up, but she'd been so terribly angry with him when she'd seen him and another woman in downtown Nantucket a couple of weeks ago. She'd said nothing then, but she'd confronted the married man when he'd come by her cottage in the dead of night.

Their ritual. Sometimes Greg was still there, and neither of them seemed to mind making love to her simultaneously. Lydia's father would fillet her alive if he knew of her encounters here on the island, but she had a plan to make sure everything turned out okay.

Ryan kissed her deeply, their breath mingling as she fought him for control of the stroke. He wouldn't give it to her, and when *he finally pulled away, he panted, "You're not convincing me that I need to go."*

"You do," she said, glancing over her shoulder to the cottage behind her. It sat in darkness, which meant Greg and Dale were waiting for her. Would they be able to taste Ryan on her tongue? Perhaps she could invite him in for one last rendezvous.

No, *she told herself.*

"Where's your wife?" she asked.

That got Ryan to back up a step. The last of the dusky light shone in those beautiful eyes. "I'm on a business trip."

Lydia's eyebrows went up. "Is that what I am? Business?"

"Lydia," he said and nothing else.

"Go home," she said, turning away from him. "To your pregnant wife." She started to walk back to her cottage.

Ryan caught her hand and said, "Wait. Wait."

She waited, because while she'd ended things with him two weeks ago, and he'd promised she'd never see him again, here he stood. Here she stood. There they'd kissed.

"Come to Long Island," he whispered. "My grandfather is in Europe for the summer. We can just…" He trailed off, because Lydia knew what they'd just do there. Talk and laugh. He'd scramble her eggs in the morning, and tell her how good she looked wearing gardening gloves. He'd make love to her in the morning, the afternoon, and the evening, and it still wouldn't be enough for Lydia.

Nothing felt like enough for her. No one, and nothing.

Except maybe Ryan Harper.

She'd met him a few times in Long Island this summer

already. She knew the way, and she yearned to go even now, when she had two strapping men waiting for her in her bed.

"Why do you have to be married?" she whispered. He hadn't said he'd leave his wife. Lydia hadn't asked. The woman was pregnant—noticeably pregnant from a distance—and while she liked having fun with all the boys on Nantucket, she wasn't going to pull apart someone's family. Not right when their first seams were getting stitched.

"I'm sorry, Lydia," he said. He pressed a paper into her hand. "I'll be there on these dates." He nodded and looked to her cottage. "Greg's here."

"Yes," she murmured, staring at the slip of ivory paper, along with the money, in her hand and not the car parked in front of her cottage.

"I hate that you're with him," Ryan said, his voice hovering on the outer edge of anger now. "I can't stand thinking about you with him." His breath washed over her cheek, and she looked up into his eyes.

"You're married."

He slid his hand up her back and into her hair, taking a fistful of it and holding her still, right where he wanted her. Her heart raced with anticipation. With a thrill only Ryan Harper ever gave her. "Tell me you think of me when you're with him."

Lydia pressed her lips closed. She didn't have to admit that to anyone, least of all the married man she'd been sleeping with and falling in love with for the past year. And he'd been married all that time. All of it. Her chest ached where her heart sat.

"Lydia," he warned.

"I hate you," she whimpered, and he released her hair, almost stumbling a step away from her. "I hate you, Ryan Harper. Go home to your wife." She stomped away from him then, the last word she'd flung in his direction nearly a shout. If he was smart at all, he'd disappear into the night.

She stepped her way through the sand, shoving the slip of paper and wad of cash into the back pocket of her cutoff shorts.

"Lydia?" someone asked, and she turned toward Rick Fry as she made it past the last swell of sand dunes to the road. He walked toward her, concern in his eyes. "Are you okay?"

"Yes," she said, feeling wild and desperate and completely out of control. "Were you coming to see me?" She put a flirty smile on her face, hoping he'd be distracted enough to forget anything he'd heard her shout.

His expression shifted, but he did glance past her one more time before she reached him. She knew how to get a man's full attention on her, and for some sick reason, she didn't want Rick to see Ryan out on the sand. He shouldn't be here, and she wanted to protect him.

She ran her hands up Rick's chest, and that did the trick. She tipped up onto her toes and pressed her lips to his. He kissed her back hungrily, his hands landing on her hips and lifting her up and over the hardness of his length. He growled in the back of his throat, and Lydia broke their kiss so he could nip at her neck.

"I didn't know you'd be on the island this weekend," she whispered.

"Here with my family," he said back, his voice hardly his

own. *"We're staying at the inn, but I went for a walk, hoping to run into someone."*

She grinned up to the moon as he continued to kiss her. "Come inside," she said, her breath coming quick. "Greg and Dale are here too."

"All of us?" Rick asked, and Lydia slid down his body to her feet.

She laced her fingers through his, looked up at him again, and said, "I can handle all three of you." At the top of the steps, she indicated that Rick should enter the cottage first. Then she turned and looked out over the moonlit sand in the direction of The Lighthouse Inn.

Ryan had disappeared.

Chapter 16

Janey woke on Saturday morning, her temples throbbing with a splitting headache. An alarm sounded, and she realized she'd forgotten to turn it off last night. "Sorry," she muttered as she rolled over to get to her device. She silenced it, noting how the darkness still lingered outside, and then rolled back into Sean's side.

He'd been staying with her at Viola's this weekend, though that had come about by accident and had been the first time. She'd stayed with him plenty of times, but Viola was more old-fashioned than Janey, and she hadn't wanted any "strange men" creeping through her house at night.

Sean was a well-respected lawyer in Nantucket, so he certainly wasn't strange, but Janey had followed Viola's wishes. The storms that had hit the island the past few days had made it more necessary for him to stay in Wainscott rather than driving all the way back around the island to his place downtown, and Janey had enjoyed having him in her bed.

She moved easily into his side, and he lifted his arm around her shoulders. "Is it six?" he asked.

"I forgot to turn off the alarm," she said. She'd gone shopping early yesterday morning with McKenna and Rachel, but they'd all agreed to sleep late this morning. The beach just beyond the mansion awaited them this morning, and then they had several paddle boards and canoes reserved for the afternoon at Light-house Beach.

Janey was doing everything she could to cram in years of experiences and memories with her children. They were both leaving tomorrow, and then she'd be on Nantucket alone again.

She told herself she wasn't alone. Her sister lived here, but her mind whispered *half-sister* over and over again.

She had Viola, but Janey didn't have the same bond to her as she did her son and daughter. They meant so much to her, and they'd become more impor-tant since she'd discovered that Gregory Clarke had not been her biological father.

Ryan had gone back to Southhampton yesterday, and Janey had texted him a goodbye. She saw no reason to make anything harder for him or his wife, though she did yearn to spend more time with him too. Just sitting on the beach, sipping a drink, would be nice. They wouldn't even have to talk.

Her hand drifted down Sean's chest to his stomach, then lower. He chuckled and said, "Do you want to make the most of our early-morning wake-up call?"

"If you do," she whispered back.

He did, and as Janey let him make love to her, she completely erased all of the other garbage from her mind. She didn't have to worry that she'd be alone soon enough. She didn't have to think about Tessa's somewhat aggressive texts that said she could've at least stopped by the inn yesterday morning for breakfast. That she'd missed all of the Seashell Promise stuff, and she wasn't doing a very good job of keeping her friends in her life.

Janey thought about none of it, and once they'd finished, she lay in bed with her phone while Sean went to shower. She didn't have a defense for Tessa, though they'd fought plenty in their lives.

She simply thumbed out, *I'm sorry. What are you doing today?* and then she sent an apology to both Maddy and Julia. They had fed her and her entire family for free on Thanksgiving, and Janey hadn't even taken her own plate back into the kitchen.

It's 100% fine, Julia said. *If my boys were here, I wouldn't have been there either. What are you doing today?*

Beach, Janey typed out. *Lighthouse Beach, if you want to come.*

Maddy, Tessa, and I are going to The Glass Dolphin for lunch, Julia said before Janey could hit send. *You're welcome to come. Bring all the kids. Annie will be there with her girls.*

Janey hesitated before sending her message. She quickly added, *We'll come before we go get our canoe rentals. There will be six of us. Is that okay?*

Absolutely, Julia said. She sent a smiley face, and Janey found herself smiling at her device. Julia was her half-sister also. Her kids had more cousins, even if they weren't full-blood relatives. Janey had known this, but the meaning of the information cascaded through her.

She sat up and sent a text to her kids, telling them that they'd be going to The Glass Dolphin for lunch. She'd been there several times, and it was a more upscale restaurant. *So bring something you can wear to some-place nice. Everyone will be there.*

She hadn't heard back from Tessa yet, so she quickly sent her a message that said, *I'll see you for lunch at The Glass Dolphin,* and she started to make the bed. Her phone chimed a few times in the few minutes it took her, and she wasn't expecting to see her children's names on the screen.

When she picked up her phone, she didn't. *Wait,* Julia had said. *Tessa might be going out with her new boyfriend today.*

Then another text: *Forget I said that.*

Janey's pulse leapt over itself in some weird game of leapfrog. "Tessa has a boyfriend?"

"What, hon?" Sean came into the bedroom, a towel around his waist and one in his hand as he dried his hair.

Janey looked up from her phone, feelings of betrayal sliding down her spine. She wasn't even sure why. Tessa was a grown woman. She was divorced. Able to date. Why shouldn't she?

"Tessa has a boyfriend," she said.

"Oh, good for her," Sean said. Janey frowned at him, and he lowered his hand. "Not good for her?"

Janey looked back at her phone. "She didn't tell me." Not only had she *not* told Janey, but she *had* told Julia. Probably Maddy too. Definitely Helen.

Something pinched inside Janey, and she didn't like it. There were a lot of things she didn't tell her sister; they weren't exactly the closest they'd ever been right now, despite everything they'd been through this year. Why did she feel so left out of everything happening around The Lighthouse Inn, when she actually worked hard to not be around the inn all the time?

"You're asking her about it?" Sean asked as he crowded over Janey's shoulder.

She turned away from him, her thumbs flying.

"Janey," he said. "I don't think that's a good idea. You sound upset."

"I am upset."

"Then you shouldn't be texting her."

Frustration filled her, and she tossed her phone on the bed. "She texted me about how I should've been at breakfast yesterday. She did it upset."

Sean looked at her steadily, and she did like that he wasn't afraid of her. She liked that he was rational when she wasn't, and that he thought clearly almost all the time. "She misses you," he said. "At the same time, she doesn't feel connected to you. She does to Julia and Maddy, so she's going to tell them, and she'll tell you when she thinks you'll listen to her."

"I listen to her." Janey folded her arms, and Sean turned away from her. He didn't say Janey didn't listen to Tessa, but he didn't need to. Janey sometimes didn't like hearing what her younger sister had to say.

"Julia invited us to lunch at The Glass Dolphin today," she said, some of the fight leaving her body.

Sean pulled on his pants. "And?"

"We're going to lunch at The Glass Dolphin today." His eyebrows went up, and Janey chose to ignore that. "I texted the kids. We need to bring clothes we can wear there."

"Okay." Sean tugged his shirt over his head and bent to pick up his shoes. "I'm sure I have something I can wear there." He sat on the bench at the foot of the bed to put on his shoes. "I'm going to walk down to the shore. Did you want to come?"

Janey hadn't gotten dressed yet, and she looked down at her silky nightgown. She loved flowy, free fabrics, and this fit the bill. If she owned Viola's huge mansion near the water, she'd only wear muumuus and shapeless dresses in a variety of colors and patterns. She'd be the eccentric woman clipping her rose bushes in silk and cashmere, and she'd be able to walk down to the shore with Sean every day.

She sat next to him on the bench. "I'm...sorry I'm who I am."

He sighed, and Janey studied her hands. "You don't need to apologize to me." He pressed a kiss to her forehead and stood up. "If your alarm hadn't gone off, you'd still be asleep."

"Probably, yeah."

He chuckled and said, "Then go back to bed, sweetheart. I know how to walk by myself." He ducked out of the bedroom then, and Janey emitted the sigh this time. She didn't want to drive Sean away, but he'd put up with a lot in the short time they'd known one another.

She'd been in a psychiatric unit for six days not that long ago. He'd picked her up. He drove her to whatever beach she wanted, and he waited in the car while she walked along the shore, thinking. Grounding herself. She knew she didn't deserve him, and yet, she couldn't make herself give him up.

She too got to her feet, but instead of crawling

back under the covers, she went over to the huge windows. This bedroom faced the street, and Janey had stood or sat here for hours since she'd moved in with Viola. Especially in the beginning, she'd just stay here and watch the street.

It was a quiet street, with few cars traveling it, and even less foot traffic. So when Sean and Cole appeared down in the driveway, they stuck out. They would've anyway, the two of them taller than most people. Janey smiled to herself as she wrapped her arms around her middle. Sean was easy-going and casual, and that was exactly the type of man Janey needed right now.

He'd taken to her kids, and they both liked him. Tessa liked him. Everyone liked him—except Viola, it seemed.

They went down the road and disappeared from her sight when they turned to take the beach access path. She drew in a deep breath, found the pause at the top of it, and then exhaled. Her eyes had drifted closed during the brief meditation, and when she opened them again, a dark blue car eased itself down the street.

Janey watched it, unsurprised that she hadn't seen it before. She worked in Sean's office, and she didn't spend her days cataloguing the vehicles in the neighborhood. A woman drove from what she could see, and Janey watched her until she made a right turn at the corner and left the area.

Her phone pinged at her, and Janey turned back to the bed to get it. Rachel had confirmed they'd have appropriate attire for lunch, and Janey migrated back to the window.

Great, she said. *Cole, I know you're up. Confirm that you and McKenna will have proper clothes for a nicer restaurant.*

She'd always had to make Cole confirm. As a teenager, when she'd launch into one of her lectures— usually about one of three things: girls, grades, or getting home on time—Cole zoned out if Janey spoke more than three sentences, and once she got going, she could lecture for a while.

At the end, when she realized her son's expression had glazed over, she'd bark, "Confirm," at him, and he'd confirm.

Just like then, right now, he sent, *Got it, Mom,* and Janey looked up from her phone.

The same navy blue car crawled past Viola's house. This time, it went in the same direction Cole and Sean had gone, like the woman had turned the corner, flipped around, and then came back.

Janey's pulse ricocheted through her body. Who was that, and why were they here? She clutched the throat of her nightgown, her worry growing by the second. The car was barely moving, and it came to a complete stop right where the pedestrian beach access path met the road.

Janey stepped closer to the window, her eyes riveted

to the car. They seemed to be waiting for someone. "They could be on the phone," she said. "Or lost." There were a dozen reasons someone would be in this neighborhood on a Saturday morning.

Maybe not this early, as there were no retail shops over here, but maybe that woman was trying to find a friend who lived in the neighborhood. Janey had been trying to give everyone more grace. The benefit of the doubt. Her therapist had said that most people did exactly what she'd done at Riggs's house—they reacted the situation they were in. It didn't make them inherently good people or bad people if they acted good or bad.

Sometimes a situation was so bad, a person could shut down.

Sometimes the situation was so tense, a person could say things they didn't mean or that weren't true.

Sometimes the situation was so confusing, a person could discharge a weapon.

Janey was just about to turn away from the car when her son—*her son*—approached it. He wasn't with Sean anymore, and he went right up to the blue car, opened the door, and got in. The car moved onto the road and drove away at a much faster pace than it had moved previously.

"Cole," Janey whispered, her breath fogging the window in front of her because she'd moved so close to it. "What are you doing? Where are you going?"

She thought of McKenna, his long-time girlfriend, here in the house. Did she know about this morning outing?

Did Sean? Was that why he'd "gone for a walk" to the shore?

Distrust ran rampant through Janey, and she stayed at the window for several long moments. Then she blinked her way back to reality, realizing she'd just fallen into the very situational reaction she'd been thinking about.

She dialed her son, knowing full-well he had his phone. His line rang, and rang, and rang. "Cole," she said after his voice mail had picked up. "It's your mother. Where are you?" She turned away from the window, not quite knowing what to say next. Sean might know about this. He might not. Best not to use him.

In reality, Janey should be straightforward. Her son was an adult. She didn't have to tiptoe around him, and if he was cheating on McKenna, there would be bombs thrown, no tiptoes in sight.

"I saw you get in a blue car just now, and I'm worried about you. Please text or call me." She hung up, not knowing what else she could do. She dialed Sean too, and when he answered, she heard the roar of the surf. This side of the island had rougher waters, with rocky ledges, and at least he was where he'd said he'd be.

"Hey," he said easily.

"Hey." Her voice definitely radiated tension. "Where did Cole go?"

"I assume back to the mansion," Sean said. "His phone rang, and he answered it. I didn't hear much of what he said. Then he turned back to me and said he had to go meet McKenna."

Janey's blood turned to chilled gelatin, and she once again fell to a seated position on the bed. "He got in a blue car by the pedestrian walkway down to the beach. He didn't come back to the mansion."

Sean said nothing, but his breath came through the line. "I'm on my way back," he said.

"You didn't hear anything he said on the phone?" Janey asked. "A name? Something?"

"Uh." Sean let a few seconds pass. "He turned his back on me, but I think I heard him say the name Claire…or Catherine…something like that."

Claire. Catherine. Caroline.

Janey pressed her eyes closed, a prayer zipping through her. "Caroline?" she asked.

"Yeah, that's it."

Janey's phone slipped from her fingers, Sean's voice saying, "Janey? Who's Caroline? Hello?" as it clattered against the hard floor in her bedroom.

Chapter 17

Tessa's phone vibrated against her leg, and this time it was more than a text. She told herself to be a window and let the irritation at being interrupted when she didn't want to be flow right through her. If she had truly wanted to disconnect, she could've left her phone in the cottage.

At the same time, being out on the beach without a way to get in touch with someone should she need help brought fear right into her gut. So she'd brought the phone, determined to ignore it.

She'd succeeded so far, but she tugged the device from the pocket on the side of her thigh and found her sister's name there. She frowned at the letters, then swiped on the call. "Hey, Janey," she said though she didn't really feel like talking to her sister. She'd apologized and asked Tessa what she was doing that day already this morning, and the non-aggressive message had unnerved her.

"Cole got in a car with Caroline," she said, her voice rushing over itself. "Where is she? Do you know? Have you heard from her?"

Tessa's steps slowed to a stop. "No," she said slowly. Her brain buzzed, trying to make dots connect that seemed impossibly far apart. "Why would he get in a car with her?"

"I don't know." Janey made a noise Tessa couldn't classify instantly, and then it became more like a sob. "Sean said he got a call, said her name, and then only a minute or two later, I saw him get in her car."

"How do you know it was her?" Tessa asked. Janey hadn't met Caroline.

"Sean heard him say her name!" Janey shouted at her, and Tessa pulled the phone from her ear. She didn't need to go deaf on such a glorious morning.

"All right," Sean said through the scuffles coming through the line when Tessa put the phone back to her ear. "Tessa, we're sorry about that."

"Why do you put up with her?" Tessa asked, and she wasn't sure if she needed to answer or if she'd asked Sean.

He ignored her and said, "Did you ever see Caroline's car?"

"No," Tessa said, her lungs filling with cement. It was so dang hard to breathe, and she hated feeling like she needed a box of wine and all the silence in the world. "She came on foot through the squall, knocking doors, desperate for help, remember?"

"No," Sean said. "I haven't heard a word about this Caroline Fyfe woman until this morning." His voice lowered with every word he spoke. "Janey's freaking out."

"She always freaks out," Tessa said. She wasn't sure why she felt so…discompassionate toward her sister today. She didn't usually, but she was also ready to stand up for herself. She had needs and cares too, and Janey had never given any thought to those. Even when they were together, Janey spent much of her time on her phone, talking to someone more interesting than Tessa, or looking at something more interesting than conversing with Tessa.

"This is real, Tessa," Sean said. "We're worried about Cole."

"Doesn't she track his phone?" Tessa asked.

"Janey, do you have a tracker on his phone?"

"He's twenty-four years old," her voice sniped from somewhere beyond the speaker of the phone.

"Ask McKenna," Tessa said. She got moving again, as she still had the whole length of the beach to go before she'd get back to the blue cottage where she lived full-time now. "He might have shared a pin with her. He works on boats. Surely they have a way for her to know where he is, in case there's trouble."

Sean relayed the information to Janey, and then silence came through the line. Tessa's guilt grew, doubled, and then choked her. "I'm sorry, Sean," she said. "Of course I'm concerned about Cole. How did she know it was Caroline, again?"

"She doesn't," Sean said. "We're trying to get some confirmation of that, but Cole isn't answering texts or calls."

"How would Caroline know about him?" she mused. "Or how to contact him?"

"She said you're the expert on Caroline," he said. "What can you tell me about her?"

Tessa didn't want to rehash all of it, and she said, "I really thought she'd tell you, Sean. I didn't mean to hide anything from you."

"I know, Tess." The way he spoke so softly, so real, made Tessa's heart bloom to life again. She didn't have feelings for Sean, but she'd been walking this stretch of beach every morning for a couple of weeks—since she'd started seriously talking to Abe.

She felt a restless itch beneath her skin, and she wasn't sure of its source. She was nervous to meet Abe, she knew that. Talking to him via her phone was so different than actually dressing up, putting on makeup, and trying to talk to someone face-to-face. At this point in her life, she honestly wasn't sure she could handle the rejection.

Maybe a year ago, she would've been fine. Right

now? She needed all the tender loving care she could get.

"I can put up with her, because she needs help," Sean said.

"Sean," Tessa said. "She's not your responsibility."

"I know that."

"Do you?" she challenged, as she'd been trying to be braver when it came to her relationships. She had to be, which was why the squall forcing her into a panic attack had been so emotionally draining.

"Yes," he said, his voice still very quiet.

"Are you in love with her?" Tessa asked.

"I care for her," he said. "And I don't think those of us who do should abandon her right now."

"I haven't abandoned her," Tessa said. "She's the one who's really good at that."

Sean sighed, but it didn't feel too exasperated. "I know, Tess."

Tessa wanted to warn him that Janey could turn into a tropical storm at the drop of a pin, and then she'd cyclone away from Nantucket. From Julia, Maddy, and Tessa—and Sean. She wouldn't even look back. There'd be destruction here that would require months of clean-up, but Janey would already be doing something else, living her life somewhere else.

"She doesn't look back," Tessa said, because Sean was a level-headed lawyer. He knew Janey, and he knew he had the very real possibility of getting hurt by her.

"That she does not," Sean agreed. "I'm sorry you're hurting, Tessa."

"Thank you," she murmured.

"McKenna has a pin for him," Janey said, her voice completely out of breath.

"What's going on?" McKenna asked, and Tessa realized the call had been switched to speakerphone. "Why is he at a gas station on the east side of the island?"

"We have to call the police," Janey said.

Tessa's nerves frayed, and she wished she wasn't almost a mile away from her house. She needed to get in her car and get to where Cole was right now.

Janey's mama bear had come out, though, and if there was one thing that spurred Janey to action, it was someone hurting her children. She simply wouldn't stand for it, and she'd go to the ends of the earth for Cole or Rachel.

"I'm calling the police," Janey said. "I'm not waiting."

"He got in the car willingly," Sean said.

"Then I'll tell them he didn't," Janey said. "Yes, hello, my son has been kidnapped, and I have his location on a pin on his girlfriend's phone."

Tessa suddenly felt the earth moving through space at a million miles an hour. Involving the police was serious, but she didn't know what Caroline wanted with Cole. She didn't want to ever see Caroline Fyfe again, and just knowing that she was here on the island unnerved Tessa.

"I'm going to let you go," Sean said. "We'll stay in touch, Tess."

"Thanks, Sean."

He ended the call, and Tessa walked numbly for several steps. A quarter mile. Maybe more. She simply kept moving, because if she stopped, she'd drop to her knees and start sobbing.

The roof on the blue beach cottage came into view, and Tessa did slow her steps once more. "I have to move," she said aloud. Those four words became like beacons of truth and light in her mind, and Tessa did not want to spend another night in the cottage here on Nantucket.

Too much had happened there. Too many ghosts lived in the walls. Too much heartache emanated from the very rooftop.

She couldn't go there. The Lighthouse Inn was full. There wasn't another hotel on this side of the island, and it was a holiday weekend. The squall had damaged several hotels downtown, and as Tessa ran through her options, they dwindled.

She'd have to go inside and pack a few things. She had plenty of money from her mother's estate, and she could find somewhere else to live and work. She glanced at the creamy exterior of The Lighthouse Inn, her heart shriveling in her chest. She couldn't leave behind Maddy and Julia. How could she just move somewhere else and start over completely?

"You can," she told herself. "You have plenty of friends in Pennsylvania. You're a nice person, and it's not here or nothing."

She'd heard nothing from the emergency number Riggs had left for her. She still didn't know if he had a sister or not. She wondered if her message had been too vague. Maybe he wasn't in a place where he could connect to data or power, and his phone didn't work. Perhaps he'd passed away since she'd seen him last. Anything was possible, and Tessa was honestly tired of having so many thoughts rotating in her mind.

She went past the inn and started across the sand. More of the house came into view, and then more of it, until she saw a man coming down her front steps. She froze for a moment, and then realized who she was looking at.

"Abe?" she called as she went past the last swell in the sand.

The man looked up as he reached the patch of sidewalk in front of the house. His face split into a smile, and he came toward her.

It *was* him. Abraham Sanders. They weren't supposed to meet until lunchtime, a date she'd moved up to alleviate the anxiety currently streaming through her.

"Tessa." He laughed as he jogged the last few steps to her and wrapped her in a hug. "It's so great to meet you in person."

She carefully, slowly wrapped her arms around him too, and having this very real, very warm, clean-shaven and cologned man hold her brought everything dormant inside Tessa to life. Tears stung her eyes, and she squinched them closed. She let her mind drift, because it was far too difficult to hold onto thoughts right now anyway.

When Abe finally pulled away, he'd sobered. Tessa never had laughed, and she still hadn't spoken. She looked up to him. "Am I late? I thought we were meeting for lunch."

"We were," he said. "I just..." He toed the sand along the edge of the road where they stood. "I got a little excited, and I thought I'd just come see if you wanted to spend the morning together, and then get lunch."

She very much did, as now that she stood in front of him, being face-to-face wasn't so bad. "Okay," she said. "I'm obviously not dressed or ready, but...okay."

"You look perfect," he said, his eyes sliding down to her tennis shoes. He wore a pair of dark jeans, a black jacket with a poke of red showing at the throat, and a pair of cowboy boots. She wasn't expecting those, and as she raised her eyes to meet his, her heartbeat fluttered.

She couldn't remember the last time it had done that—well, at least not when she wasn't in a life-or-death situation or hadn't just been injected with something.

"Let's go inside," she said, gathering all of her courage and wits about her. "I'll change, and we can... I don't know. Go to the bakery. Go for a walk."

"We could just sit on your porch."

Tessa eyed the house. "I'd rather go somewhere else," she said. "My sister might call at any moment too," she added as she took the first step toward the cottage. "And I need to find somewhere to stay at some point today."

Abe turned toward her with surprise. "Somewhere to stay? Why can't you stay here?"

Tessa swallowed, her nerves once again running rampant. She'd been talking to Abe for a few weeks now. Fine, almost three. Not quite a few. But she trusted him, and she reached over and slid her hand into his. She looked down at their fingers, her heartbeat blipping strangely.

"I don't want to stay here," she said. "My house doesn't feel as...safe as it once did."

Abe said nothing as the crossed the narrow road and went up the steps. Tessa led the way inside, and she said, "Make yourself at home. I'll change and pack a bag quickly."

"I can make a couple of calls," he said. "Maybe help you find somewhere for tonight."

She looked at him, pure gratitude filling her. She wasn't a very forward woman, but she also wasn't the same person she'd been when she'd first come to this cottage. "Thank you, Abe," she said. Feeling completely unlike herself, Tessa moved into his personal space, took his face in both of her hands, and kissed him politely on the mouth. "I'll be so fast."

Abe looked like he'd just run face-first into a brick wall, and he blinked, everything else of his perfectly still and straight. Tessa dropped her head and smiled at the floor.

With that, she almost skipped down the hall to her bedroom. Once there, she had no idea how to pack what she needed for an undetermined amount of time in an unknown place. Waves of overwhelm rocked through her, but she took one long, calming breath.

Her phone vibrated, and she pulled it out, expecting to hear from Sean or Janey a lot today. *The police are on their way*, Sean said. *We'll call when we know more.*

Thanks, Sean, she typed out. *I'm not staying at the cottage tonight. It doesn't feel safe. I'll let you know where I end up.*

Stay safe, Tessa, he said.

You too, she sent back. *Keep Janey safe.*

"You have a purse and a phone," she told herself. "Pack a few clothes and go." With those instructions from herself, she did exactly that, and she and Abe left the blue cottage she'd once loved but which now felt so very much like a prison.

She said she'd follow him as she needed her car, and he said, "Want to get coffee?"

"Coffee sounds amazing," she said, sure she could order tea somewhere.

"Wait," he said. "You don't drink coffee." A smile touched his face and lit up those dark eyes. Tessa could see herself falling down, deep into them easily. "I know the perfect place."

"I'll follow you." She got behind the wheel and sent a quick text to both Julia and Maddy, letting them know she wouldn't be at the cottage that day or evening, and she'd keep them updated about her date with Abe and where she'd be staying that night.

They also told her to stay safe and to call if she needed anything, and Tessa put her phone in the cup holder, feeling more tethered to people and reality than she had in a long, long time.

She kneaded the steering wheel as she followed Abe down the street. He made a left turn, and Tessa did too. As she got further and further from the blue cottage, everything from breathing to thinking became easier.

Chapter 18

Annie put on her blinker and eased off the road and into the parking lot at the gas station. "Coffee?"

"Definitely," Paige said. Annie counted her blessings that her daughters had gotten up early with her this morning to do the sunrise ocean tour. Maddy had given them three spots on the yacht, and Annie had enjoyed the cold, crisp breeze coming over the water as the sun had lifted into the sky. Maddy spoke with such knowledge about the sea, and Annie could see why her tours booked out weeks and months in advance.

Once she and the girls had returned to The Lighthouse Inn, they'd decided to head out for breakfast, as Maddy then had to go from boat captain and tour guide extraordinaire to chef.

The place Annie had looked up online was seasonal and closed for the winter, so she, Paige, and

Bri had been driving down the road leading around the east knob of the island for a few minutes, scoping out the scenery for another hotspot that served pancakes and bacon.

They'd found nothing yet, and Annie thought this gas station might be their best bet. There were plenty of cars here, and as she drove slowly around the building, trying to find a place to park, she realized there was a restaurant attached to the convenience store.

"We can eat here," she said. This was obviously where the locals came on Saturday mornings, as she couldn't find a single parking spot.

They had plans to eat lunch with the crowd at The Glass Dolphin that afternoon, but since it was still early, Annie had plenty of time to get hungry again. She finally found a place to park way down at the end of the row, and she pulled in and turned off the ignition. "Ready?"

"Ready," Bri confirmed from the backseat.

"Yep." Paige was extraordinarily chipper—and had been since the Seashell Promise session yesterday. Something had definitely switched in her, but Annie didn't know what. She looked at her eldest as Bri got out of the car.

"Are you okay?" she asked, hating the words as they came out of her mouth. Paige hated being asked if she was okay.

Today, though, she simply smiled and said, "Yeah,

I'm okay."

"What's going on?" Annie asked as she gathered her purse from behind her knee.

"Just…" She exhaled. "Boys are really stupid sometimes, you know?" She got out of the car, and that left little choice but for Annie to do the same. She did, and she looked over the roof of the car to her daughter.

"I think I've been telling you about boys for five years now," she said with a smile.

Paige returned the smile, her head cocked. So she didn't entirely appreciate the alternate version of "I told you so."

"What did Logan do?" Annie asked.

"It's not Logan," Paige said, coming around the car. They all stepped up onto the sidewalk, and Annie positioned herself between her daughters. Bri was fourteen, boyfriendless, but not disinterested. She'd have boy troubles soon enough, and she didn't need to be shielded from conversations like this.

"Who is it then?" Bri asked. "If you say Griffin…"

Paige threw her a look, but Annie didn't know who Griffin was. She told herself not to jump in with questions. In radiology, she waited for the doctor to ask the questions. She wrote down answers and notes. She didn't read x-rays or exams. Doctors did that.

Here, she was the nurse, doctor, and specialist, but that didn't mean she had to rush in, sword raised, bellowing questions.

"He asked me out," Paige finally said. "He knows I'm..." She cut a look at Annie out of the corner of her eye, but Annie only saw it in her peripheral vision, because she had her eyes on the line out the door at the restaurant's entrance up ahead. They might be here for a while.

It's okay, she told herself. They had nothing else to do today, and Paige was talking.

"He's your boyfriend," Bri said, and Annie was just glad she hadn't had to. She'd said the same thing to Paige before, who'd denied it and then accused Annie of always accusing her of things that weren't true.

It had been a circular argument, and none of them had come out winners. Still, Annie adored her girls, and she wanted them to feel safe with her, with themselves, and with the world.

"Logan is not my boyfriend," Paige said very quietly, her own head dipped down now. "I just want him to be. I'm just waiting for him to realize he should be."

Annie looked at her daughter and felt the yearning inside her. She reached over and took her hand. "I'm sorry, baby. He...doesn't get it?"

"He kissed her," Bri blurted out.

"Bri," Paige snapped. "Not your news to tell."

"Well, he did." Bri shook her hair over her shoulders and held her head high. "And now he's acting like

222

he didn't, or that it was a big mistake. He's just as dumb as Griffin."

Paige said nothing, and that was Annie's cue to stay silent too. She could see everything clearly now. Paige and Logan had been best friends for many years now. He'd been there for her when Donovan had come out. She'd attended every single one of his rowing tournaments, shouting for him from the shoreline, where he couldn't possibly hear her.

And now, he'd kissed her. She liked him. She wanted him to be her boyfriend. He obviously felt something for her too—or else he was playing with her. Then he'd backed off, leaving her wondering why she was best friend material, but not girlfriend-worthy.

Then entered Griffin…

"Do you like Griffin?" Annie asked. "I don't know him."

"He's just this boy in my ancient history class," Paige said. "We did a project together this term. He's nice. He's cute. I could go out with him."

"He lives right next door to Logan," Bri said. "It would make Logan jealous maybe."

Annie didn't need Paige playing two boys against each other, and she shot Bri a dirty look. "What?" Bri asked. "It would. Or it would wake him up to how awesome Paige is, and that she's totally in love with him, and that he should get over whatever he's worried about and go out with her already."

Annie shook her head, a small smile coming to her lips.

"She has it all figured out, doesn't she?" Paige asked, clearly teasing Bri.

"Sounds like it," Annie said.

"You guys make everything so complicated," Bri said. "You won't even tell Logan you want to be more than friends."

"It's not that simple," Paige said, and that about summed up life in general. Relationships too. They were never as simple as they seemed on the outside, Annie knew that.

They arrived at the end of the line, and she craned her neck to see past the people there. "Excuse me," she said, and the man in front of her turned toward her. "Do I check in somewhere and then wait? Or are you guys waiting to check in?"

"You go inside first," he said with a smile.

Annie nodded her thanks and turned to Paige. "You two stay here. I'll go get us on the list and find out what kind of wait we're looking at." She hitched her purse higher on her shoulder and prepared to enter the fray.

With her petite frame, she made it inside okay, and the path to the hostess table was clear. "Hello," she said, and the woman looked up. "There are three of us. How long?" She scanned the surface in front of the woman, but the colors, lists, and numbers meant nothing to her.

"It's probably going to be about thirty-five minutes."

Annie nodded and said, "That's fine. My name is—"

"Aunt Annie," a man said, and Annie turned toward him. The voice was familiar, and it matched up with the tall, skinny image of Cole Forsythe standing a few feet from her. Surprise shook through her, especially as her brain caught up to what he'd called her.

She was not his aunt. Not really. Maybe she was?

She and Janey did share the same father. Could someone be a half-aunt?

"Cole," she said, torn between putting her name on the list and finding out what he was doing here. She didn't see McKenna, or anyone in his family. Definitely not Janey or Sean. He seemed to be here alone.

She held up one finger and turned back to the hostess. "I'm Annie."

She handed her a buzzer and said, "This will go off when it's your turn."

"Thanks." She tucked the buzzer into her purse and stepped away from the table and toward Cole. He froze and shook his head in tiny bursts of movement.

Annie paused too, confused and suddenly scared. She felt like someone had turned a spotlight on her, and even though there were probably over a hundred people already seated in this restaurant or waiting to be admitted, she felt very alone. Like someone could snatch her and even with the huge spotlight on her, no one would notice.

"What are you doing here?" she asked, though everything about Cole told her to leave.

He turned away from her just as a woman brushed by her. "Sorry," she said, and Annie caught sight of the side of her face. She had long, dark hair, streaked with gray at the hairline. She wore black from head to toe, which wasn't that unusual in the winter.

Her coat fell all the way to the floor, and the scent of brine and fish moved by Annie a moment after the woman did. She went over to Cole and stood in front of him, but he didn't look at her either. He stayed in a perpendicular stance to her, everything about him radiating tension and discomfort.

Annie didn't know what to do. Make a scene? Go join him and get a better look at the woman? Demand to know what was going on and where his mother was? He was an adult, and not just by a few months. By several years.

She swallowed and fell to the side too, moving so she could see the woman better but be out of the way for the party the hostess had just called. She took out her phone and texted Janey.

Your son is at a restaurant called The Pearled Wharf. It's on the east highway. He seems to be alone. Is everything okay?

226

She looked up, and the woman stood directly in front of her now. Her dark eyes glinted, and Annie startled, gasped, and stepped away. She shoved her phone in her back pocket, but she suspected the woman had already seen it.

"Annie, right?" she asked.

Annie said nothing, but she also couldn't look away from the woman. She was probably twenty or thirty years older than her. Maybe more. Her age was very hard to tell with the layers of black clothing and the long hair. Most women over seventy didn't keep such long hair, and Annie's eyes flitted all around her face, trying to find lines and wrinkles that could add up to years.

"Where are your lovely daughters?" the woman asked, and a creepy chill ran down Annie's arms. She prayed with everything she had that Paige and Bri would stay outside. They had no way of knowing what it was like in here, and they would probably give her plenty of time to get their name on the list.

The unknown always caused the most fear for people, Annie included.

"I'm sorry," she said. She took a deep breath. She peered more closely at the woman. "I don't know you. Have we met?"

"Yes, just now." The woman smiled, but it felt predatory, like the kind of grin an evil stepmother would give in the cartoons her girls used to watch.

"Then how did you know my name?" she asked.

"Your nephew." She indicated Cole, who stood in the exact same spot. Annie looked over to him, noting how white his face had become. The woman in front of her, however, didn't seem bothered at all.

Annie's skin crawled. "Cole," she said as if she hadn't seen him before. She stepped past the woman. "What are you doing here? Is your mom here?" She made a show of looking around and then back to him. She linked her hand through his arm. "Come with me. You can sit with us."

"He's with me," the woman said, and she did move to block Annie from leading Cole out of the restaurant.

Annie scanned her down to her shoes, her heart-beat getting louder and louder with every millisecond that passed. There were a lot of people here. This woman couldn't do anything and not have three dozen witnesses. Why she'd brought Cole here, Annie had no idea, but she knew something was very wrong, and that she needed to keep Cole with her if at all possible.

"Who are you?" she asked.

"Caroline Fyfe," the woman said proudly, with a smile to match.

Annie's blood ran cold, and she increased her grip on Cole's arm. She didn't know what to say, and she looked past Caroline to the exit. A couple went through it, and then a pair of police officers entered.

Relief sagged through her, and Annie lifted her

hand. The cops were already looking in her direction, and one of them pointed at her. Caroline turned, and Annie pushed Cole toward the crowd. "Go," she hissed.

He went, and the people waiting there shuffled out of the way to make room for them. Annie didn't think she could run from cops; she wasn't trying to run from cops. She simply wanted more distance between her and Cole, and Caroline.

One man went to Caroline while the other deviated toward her. "Ma'am," she heard him say, but Annie kept pushing Cole toward the front corner of the restaurant.

A commotion started, and Annie's adrenaline allowed her to keep moving and listen and see everything.

Caroline reached out and pushed the cop backward.

He announced in a loud voice that she was under arrest.

The crowd had gone silent, and several of them had their phones out, recording.

The man who'd come toward her and Cole turned to help his fellow officer.

Another man dressed in a suit and tie appeared and started moving the bystanders back and out of the way. A manager, from the looks of the name tag.

Annie's ears caught everything, but only in a huge

wave of noise. She saw everything, but only in small clips of time. She and Cole reached the front window, and she pushed him toward the door. "Go," she said, but her voice sounded like a whimper in her ears.

Cole went though, and they made it outside. Annie hurried past all the people standing on the sidewalk, most of whom were trying to see what was happening inside. She reached Paige and Bri, who both wore confusion on their face, and she said, "Back to the car. Now. Right now."

"Mom—what?" Paige started.

Annie glared at her and said, "Now," one more time before the girls turned and went. She followed them, moving as quickly as she could with her short legs. She did not let go of Cole for even an instant. He said nothing. No explanation. No protests.

In the safety of her car, Annie sagged against the seat. Her adrenaline still pumped, making her fingers twitchy. She didn't think she could just run away from this. Cole had to talk to the police.

She met his eye in the rearview mirror. "Did she kidnap you?"

"Sort of," he said.

"What does that mean?" Bri asked. It was a valid question, in Annie's opinion, and she raised her eyebrows.

"She called and said she had the necklace I wanted to buy for Mickie," he said, his voice hardly his own. "I went up to meet her from the beach this morning. She drove me to her shop—but it wasn't a shop. It wasn't anything. She wouldn't let me out. She just kept talking and talking and talking about my mom and my grandfather and how she was going to make sure someone paid for all the things that had gone wrong in her life. Her son, her daughter, all of it."

Annie couldn't keep up with him. He fell silent, and she reached back and patted his leg. "Did she say who she was?"

He shook his head. "She never gave me her name. Well, she did. The person I bought the necklace from was named Nina. Not Caroline."

"She used a false name." And she'd come after one of Janey's children. That meant no one was safe, and true fear sliced through Annie.

"Mom," Paige said, and Annie saw her nod out the windshield.

Annie turned to face the front again, and two cops stood there. Different people than the two who'd entered the restaurant. The woman stepped off the curb and indicated that Annie should get out of the car. She wore no smile, and she meant business.

Annie told herself she was the adult here, and she'd done nothing wrong. She said, "Stay in the car," and then got out. "Caroline Fyfe is dangerous," she said. "She kidnapped my nephew, and I just happened to be here with my girls." She folded her arms and pressed her back into the car.

"We need to talk to Mister Forsythe," the woman said.

"He needs someone there with him," Annie said. "He's upset and shook up, as he's a kidnapping victim."

"His mother is here."

Annie's heart leapt. "Okay. I'll get him out, and I'm going with him until he's safely with his mother."

The policewoman nodded, and Annie turned back to the car. She bent down, met Cole's eyes, and he got out of the car. "Your mother is here," she said.

He nodded and looked from one police officer to the other. "She took my phone," he said. "Nina. Caroline. Whoever. That woman. She took my phone, and I need that back. My clients are in that phone."

"We'll get it back," Annie told him, though she knew she couldn't guarantee him anything. She gathered him into her side and tucked him there. She looked at the woman. "My girls are minors. Can one of you stay with them, just to make sure they're okay?"

"We took Miss Fyfe into custody," the woman said. "She's not a threat anymore."

"She's a threat, no matter what," Annie said. "Don't underestimate her."

The policewoman nodded and came to Annie's side to escort her and Cole to his mother. Annie wanted to tell her not to underestimate the power of mothers either, or women who cared for a person who'd been threatened. She'd only met Cole a couple of times now, and yet she'd put herself between him and danger without even thinking about it.

A trio of police cars sat in front of the entrance of the restaurant, all three of them with lights flashing. Annie didn't like parading past all the onlookers, but she had to do it. She thankfully didn't see Caroline in any of the cars either, and when Janey appeared at the back of a big, black SUV, Annie released Cole so she could continue with the police officer toward her.

She brought up the rear, and she stood out of the way as Cole hugged his mother, then his girlfriend, and then his sister. Then every eye came back to her, and she flushed, sure her face steamed in the cool morning air.

"Thank you, Annie," Janey said, embracing her and holding her tightly.

"It was nothing."

"Let's take this somewhere else," a man said, and everyone faced him. Annie faded into the background, her stomach growling at her for food.

She met the policewoman's eyes. "Am I needed?"

"Give me your number," she said. "I'll call you if they need you."

"Who's 'they'?" she asked.

"The Sheriff called the FBI," the woman said, and

she flipped open an old-fashioned notebook the size that would fit in her pocket, just the way Annie had seen cops do in movies and TV shows growing up. She wrote down Annie's number, and she returned to the car to get her girls.

"Come on, girls," she said as her purse started to rumble. "That's us. Our table is ready." How she could just waltz into the restaurant and order bacon and eggs, she didn't know. The world felt different now, but she couldn't pinpoint quite how.

Paige and Bri got out of the car, and Annie drew them both into a hug while the cop who'd been standing guard on the sidewalk retreated. "I love you both," she whispered.

They clung to her, and Annie liked how strong she felt. She was their anchor, and though she'd have weak moments in her life, she could be tall, strong, and steady through any storm that came.

She glanced to the cop cars as they dispersed. They'd gone by the time she and the girls entered the restaurant, and it looked normal inside. Like nothing had happened.

Annie knew that wasn't true, though, and she knew there'd be more activity as questions got asked and the case progressed. But for now, she sat in a booth and picked up her menu, hankering for some chicken fried steak and eggs.

Chapter 19

Janey led the way into The Glass Dolphin, sure the day was going to get better from here. She wasn't quite certain they'd still go pick up their canoes and paddle boards, but part of her really wanted to. They couldn't hunker down when the sun shone as brightly as it did, she knew that.

If they didn't keep living, Caroline had won. Janey would not allow that.

It was one reason she'd insisted they still meet everyone for lunch today. She didn't want to type everything out with her thumbs. She didn't want to explain it four separate times—or even once. She didn't want to answer the same questions more than once. This way, she wouldn't have to.

The scent of something brown and seared met her nose, and Janey started to relax. She knew she'd have to talk a lot today, and she glanced over to Cole. He put a smile on his face, and he'd been through a lot in his lifetime, short as it was.

Nothing compared to being stuck in a moving vehicle, without a phone, with someone ranting about a murder from almost fifty years ago. He was shaken, and Janey could see it plainly.

"Maybe we should go," she said.

"I'm fine, Mom," he said. "We have to eat, and I'm starving." He tucked McKenna into his side. "Mickie is too. We're fine."

They'd been at the police station for a few hours after the arrest, but once the story had been told, there really wasn't anything else to do. They'd gone to the grocery store for drinks and ice for their afternoon at Lighthouse Beach, but Janey didn't even have any of her clothes. She'd left the mansion in such a rush.

"Janey."

She turned at the sound of Maddy's voice, and then the blonde wrapped her up into a tight, tight hug. Janey gripped her back too, and while she hadn't been as diligent about making friends with the two women at the inn, she still felt the bond between them solidifying and running through her hotly.

She pressed her eyes closed as they filled with tears, and a single sob escaped her throat. "It's so good to be here," she said, because Maddy just accepted her how she was. Janey wasn't sure she'd acknowledged or even known that before, but she did now.

"Oh, Janey." Julia flew toward her, and she barely had time to release Maddy before her half-sister arrived. She had been better about trying to build bridges between her and her newfound family, even if they only shared half of the blood.

Julia cried openly, and Janey wept only a little. "You're okay?" She gripped her by the shoulders and looked at her.

"Yes," Janey said.

"Cole." Julia moved over to him, and Janey straightened her clothes.

"We should go sit down," Sean said. "There are people watching." He scanned the restaurant and put his hand on the small of Janey's back.

"We have a table over here," Maddy said, her eyes still locked on Julia. They held some malice she wiped away as she blinked, but Janey had seen it. Or maybe she'd imagined it.

She went with Maddy, her group following her. A man already sat at the table, along with Annie…and Tessa.

Janey swallowed, because she didn't think Tessa would be here. Her sister rose, and she too took Janey into a hug. "I'm so glad you're all okay," she said. Nerves poured from her too, and Janey could probably attribute some of them to the man she'd brought to lunch. It had to be her new boyfriend, a person Janey still hadn't heard a word about.

Everyone started to sit, and Janey noticed Cole take a place right next to Sean. She started to pull out the chair beside Tessa, but her sister stayed standing. "Janey," she said. She glanced at the man sitting there, and he dropped his napkin on the table and stood. Next to her, he looked…good. Really good.

"I joined a dating app," Tessa said. "I met Abe a few weeks ago, and we've been talking." She offered him a smile, but her eyes barely left Janey's face. "We just met this morning, actually. I wanted to be here for this, and I hope it's okay that I invited him along."

"Of course it's okay," Janey said. She reached out and shook Abe's hand. "It's great to meet you."

"You live over in Wainscott, don't you?" Sean asked, and Abe nodded at him.

"No, I actually have a place downtown," he said, his voice clipped and probably a bit too polite. Janey cut him some slack, as he was meeting a lot of people today, not just Tessa. "But I work in Wainscott. I own the deli on Fifth Street down there."

"Yes," Sean said with a smile. "That's it. Remember we went in there on Wednesday night, right before they closed?" He looked up at Janey and patted her place. She sat, because she hadn't gone inside the deli. Sean had, while she'd stayed in the van.

"Hmm," she said, because she didn't want to say she hadn't gone in. She glanced across the table to see Julia and Maddy glaring at one another. They seemed to feel the weight of her eyes at the same time, and they both looked at her. False smiles sprang to their faces.

Janey knew what fake looked like, because she'd lived a lot of her life behind such a mask. She looked between the two of them, but she didn't ask them anything.

"Tell us everything," Tessa said. "Annie's updated us all, but what happened after you went to the police station?"

"It started when I found a necklace from a local artist here on the island," Cole said. "I started messaging them, because I wanted the piece for Christmas for Mickie." He swallowed and looked at his girlfriend. "I thought I was talking to a woman named Nina. She said she'd come pick me up this morning and take me to her shop, which is in Wainscott, and I could be back on the beach before anyone knew I was gone."

He reached for his glass of water and took a long drink. Everyone waited, menus down. Janey hated the tension, and she rolled her neck from side to side. Cole's intentions were good. Normally, messaging someone about a piece they had for sale was good. Easy. Nothing to worry about.

Getting in the car with them? She wished he hadn't done that.

"So I get in the car, and she immediately takes off. I knew something was wrong right away, but I'm in the car at this point. She starts down the highway, and she tells me to put my phone in the cupholder or she'll drive us into the ocean." He swallowed and glanced to Janey. She'd stayed with him during the interview, and she knew all of this. It didn't make it easy to listen to, but she managed to stay dry-eyed.

"So I do, and she grabs the phone and puts it under her leg."

"She should've turned it off," McKenna said. "Because his pin still worked."

"She's ranting about murders and missing children, her kids, all of it," Cole said as he laced his fingers through McKenna's. "I just let her talk, but I knew I needed to get out of the car. So I suggested breakfast. She pulled off, and while she went to the bathroom, I saw Annie."

"We'd already found his pin," Janey said. "We called the cops. Sheriff Cochran called the FBI, because the case is so old. They'd already turned over the evidence they found in the inn to their cold case department."

"This is the murder that just won't die," Maddy said, her smile prevalent but not happy. Janey returned it, because she did appreciate a good pun.

"We debriefed with the Sheriff and the lead FBI investigator," Janey said. "His name is Bill Cartright." She exhaled and unwrapped her silverware. "And now we're here, and we're going to Lighthouse Beach this afternoon for anyone who wants to join us." She looked around the table at everyone, hoping they could feel her love for them. She'd never been very good at saying how she felt. She was more of a doer. A woman who put things in action for those she loved and cared about.

"Are you ready to order?" a woman asked, and she had a young man with her.

Janey smiled up at both of them. "Yes," she said. "Let's start with drinks and appetizers. This will be just one bill."

"Janey," Tessa said, and their eyes met. They had plenty of money. After a beat of time, Tessa nodded.

"I'd like a glass of merlot," Janey said. "And we're going to need two orders of the burrata and two of the fried calamari." She glanced around the table, not truly looking at anyone else. "Anyone want something besides that?"

No one said anything, and the waitress went around to get all the drink orders. Janey then picked up her menu and said, "I'm feeling like seafood. What did we get here that one time that I liked, Sean?"

The talk surrounding Cole's ordeal that morning was clearly over, and Janey was relieved when Tessa said, "So Abe and I went on a little hike this morning," and the conversation moved to outdoorsy things to do around Nantucket.

Later, once lunch finished and everyone retreated back to their own places of refuge for an hour or two, Janey set up her beach chair while Sean pounded an umbrella into the sand. It wasn't hot today—it was almost December—and the wind had picked up. But they could still wear wetsuits and get in the shallow water.

Janey wouldn't, as she had her phone and her e-reader fully charged. She just wanted to sit back and relax. She'd enjoyed lunch once all the talk about the attempted kidnapping had ended, and she only had one more night with her kids before they returned to their regular lives. Before she had to go back to work too.

She looked out across the Sound, wondering where Caroline Fyfe was, and where she'd go next. She wondered who she was, because it didn't make sense for her to show up out of nowhere and start demanding that her brother's name be cleared.

"Afternoon," Julia said, and Janey turned toward her.

"You came," she said.

"Maddy's handling dinner alone." Julia's tone cooled, and Janey tilted her head.

"What's with the two of you?" she asked.

"Nothing," Julia blinked rapidly and wouldn't look at Janey.

"Uh-huh, right." She laughed lightly and moved her chair into the shade created by the now stable umbrella. "That sounds believable."

"We're just...at odds right now." Julia unclipped the straps keeping her camp chair bunched tight and she shook it open. She set up right next to Janey. "I have to tell you something."

"Is this one of your Seashell Promise things?" Janey asked. Apparently, they'd all shared a secret and something they were afraid of now. Janey had missed both of those sessions, and part of her ached to be included. Another part of her paid a therapist, and she talked about her secrets and the things she was afraid of all the time. And paid someone else to listen to her.

"No," Julia said. "But we can do that if you want." She wore hope in her eyes, and Janey just smiled at her and shook her head. Julia deflated slightly and she crossed her arms. "It's windy today."

"It's picked up," Janey said. "For sure."

Cole called to Travis, and the two of them grabbed paddle boards and headed for the water. Rachel plunked her bag down beside Janey. "We're going to use a canoe, okay?"

"Yeah, fine," Janey said, smiling up at her. "It's not as warm as yesterday."

"Yeah, I don't want to get wet," she said.

She and McKenna each lifted one end of the canoe and started carting it toward the water's edge. Janey watched them, her heart swelling with love. They got along so well, but that could've been from how chill and easy-going Rachel was. Even this morning, with her brother missing and cops and FBI swarming, she'd been rational and calm. She was about the complete opposite of Janey, and she had no idea where Rachel had come from.

"Our dad was on the island when Louisa went missing," Julia said, and Janey actually flinched.

She swung her attention away from the girls and to her half-sister. "What?" Her mind repeated the words Julia had already said. She didn't repeat them.

"He told you that?" Janey asked.

Julia pressed her lips together and nodded. "I couldn't find any evidence, though, so it probably isn't a big deal."

Janey didn't know what to say. She didn't know Ryan Harper as well as the woman seated beside her, obviously. She'd only spent time with him a handful of times now. Of course he was going to be on his best behavior with her.

She cleared her throat. "Do you think he…could've had anything to do with it?"

"No," Julia said firmly. "I don't. I just don't want there to be any suspicion." She met Janey's eyes. "He lied. He said he went back to Manhattan permanently

two weeks before Louisa disappeared, but he came
back for just one night."

"Why'd he—?" Janey cut off her question. She
knew why he'd come back. Her mother. The pull of
the sweet and sexy Lydia Merrill. Janey had often felt
so much like her mother, but now, she felt like she'd
hardly known her at all.

"I don't know when they broke up," Julia said.
"Dad won't talk about Lydia at all."

"Even to you?"

"Especially to me, he says."

Janey looked away, hearing the underlying sentence
between Julia's statement. *Maybe you could ask him, Janey.
It involves you.*

She watched her kids and their loved ones
splashing and calling to one another. Rowing and
paddling and laughing. Cole had been with McKenna
for five years now, and they had no diamonds in sight.
Rachel and Travis were engaged now, but they'd been
together for three years, and the wedding wasn't for
another several months.

She knew she'd brought her own views of marriage
and relationships to her children, and they'd absorbed
it all. She'd never told them outright not to rush into
marriage, but she'd done it twice now, and it felt like
every relationship she had went from zero to sixty in
only a few days.

"I'll talk to him," Janey said without looking at

Julia. "If you tell me why you and Maddy aren't getting along."

"Because of Dad being on the island that night," she said. "She overheard me on the yacht, and I maybe went in her room without asking to find the scrapbooks and guest logs."

Janey said nothing, because she'd been judged so much in her life, and Julia already felt stupid. She heard as much in her voice.

"Was he on the island during the day? Or just at night?"

"He said he came in the evening," Julia said.

"Louisa disappeared in the morning," Janey said quietly. "He couldn't have done it."

"You're right," she said, her voice lifting with light and happiness. "You're absolutely right." She laughed, and Janey managed to smile with her.

"Did he say anything else about that day or night?" she asked.

Julia sobered and shook her head. "He said he came in on the evening ferry. He never went by Lydia's until after dark, he said, so he found something to eat and tried to get a room at the inn."

"Did he?"

"No," she said. "But he said he signed in before he found out he really couldn't have a room. So I was looking for that sheet. We don't have it."

"And Louisa disappeared the next morning," Janey said. She had the timeline for Louisa's disappearance memorized. She and Tessa had gone over it and over it.

"Yes," she said. "Dad said he left in the morning too."

"My mom must've told him something. Didn't he usually come for the weekend? Or at least more than one night?"

"Yeah," Julia said. "All I can figure is that your mom broke up with him. He won't say much more."

Janey hated talking about her mother in this way. She'd been shocked to learn of her mother's...free ways regarding sex, and it reminded Janey a little bit too much of herself, if she were being honest.

"But we know they didn't really break up," she said. "Mom went to Long Island a lot that summer."

"After July?"

"Yes," Janey said. "She went all the way until she and Dad—Greg—got married." They'd been married in late August, and Janey had been born in late March. It wasn't quite the right timing, but she'd also come three weeks early. So anyone doing the math didn't really have all the facts.

She pulled in a breath, which caused Julia to ask, "What?"

"I just realized that maybe I wasn't born three weeks early," she said, looking at Julia. "I've told everyone for my whole life that I was born three weeks early, but I don't think so all of a sudden."

"I don't think so either," Julia said. She reached over and squeezed Janey's hand. "Do you think Lydia found out Dad was married? Maybe that's why he stopped coming to Nantucket."

"But she didn't stop going to see him. Wouldn't it be easier for him to come to her? Where did they even meet?"

"I don't know," Julia said, her voice soft and far away. Janey understood that, because her mind drifted in the same way.

"I'll talk to him," Janey said, already thinking of a way she could bring it up. "See what he says."

Julia nodded, and then she said. "I can't stay for much longer. I should go talk to Maddy and set things right."

Janey didn't tell her she should or shouldn't. She did say, "When are you guys doing the Seashell Promise again? I'd like to come."

"Tonight," Julia said, her smile widening. "That would be great if you came. We're going to do it later, after the dinner and dessert bar. Probably closer to eight-thirty or nine."

"I'll be there," Janey said. She'd gotten up early that morning, and honestly, everything that had happened that day felt like it had taken place in another lifetime.

"Great," Julia said. "We're going to do the last two, because Annie has to get back to Chatham tomorrow." She grinned as she stood and collapsed her camp chair again. "Oh, what did you think of Abe?"

"I liked him," Janey said casually. "He sure seems to like Tessa, and he was kind and personable."

"I liked him too," Julia said. "She's been so nervous about meeting him, but she said it's been a great day." She smiled. "And she's at The Swinging Lantern, so she's happy about that."

Janey looked up at Julia. "Why is she staying at The Swinging Lantern?"

Anxiety crossed Julia's face as some color drained from it. "Uh, she...didn't tell you?"

"No."

"Probably because you had so much going on this morning," Julia said, her words rushing over themselves. "She doesn't feel safe at the cottage. She doesn't want to stay there anymore."

Surprise darted through Janey. "At all? Like she's going to move?"

"I don't really know," Julia said. "She didn't go into detail. She said she was going to find somewhere else to stay on the island, and Abe helped her get in at the Lantern. They're full, like everywhere else, but they found her a room."

Janey nodded, and because she didn't want to put Julia on the spot, she said, "I'll call her."

Julia nodded and left, and Janey flipped her phone over and over on her leg. She glanced to her left, where Sean had set up, but he snored softly in the chair beside her. Lunch with Tessa at her side had been easy and effortless, because they had plenty of other people around them.

Just the two of them, though, and Janey felt so much pressure and tension between them. Over and over her phone went, and Janey didn't call. Maybe it was time to toss up all the cards and then let them land wherever they may.

Chapter 20

Julia smiled at the two guests coming down the huge staircase that led up to the rooms. No one stayed on the main floor of The Lighthouse Inn; all five guest rooms sat upstairs. She and Maddy lived downstairs, in two separate rooms. They had closets and a tiny room to house supplies, and the laundry facilities took up some space down there too.

She didn't know who was here in the inn and who'd gone out for the day. Everyone was checking out tomorrow, and they only had two rooms booked for Sunday night. The inn would be full again by Monday at three p.m. She needed to plan her tours for next week. She knew the schedule, but she liked to review her notes and make sure she had everything she needed. Props, clothing, old books.

Right now, Julia needed to find Maddy and clear

the air. She looked toward the office, as they often worked in there together during the slower moments of the day. No one was checking in today, so neither she nor Maddy needed to be out in the lobby. Maddy had said she'd handle everything that evening, because she wanted tomorrow afternoon and night off. Ben was returning to Nantucket.

Julia went into the office, and Maddy looked up from the desktop computer there. They both used it for various reasons, but she didn't know what Maddy was doing that afternoon. She could be checking the weather, ordering more oil for the yacht's engine, or checking her personal social media.

She pressed her palms together and stood at the edge of the desk. Maddy wore surprise on her face, which Julia expected. They'd fought yesterday afternoon, and she hated the queasy, gnawing feeling she'd had in her gut since.

"I'm sorry," she said, though she'd apologized before. "I just didn't want my father to be in even more trouble."

Maddy's eyebrows went down, as did her shoulders. She seemed to accept Julia's apology, and she swept her hand toward the pair of chairs situated in front of the desk. "Tell me about it."

Julia stepped and sat down, her stomach still shaking. "He called me and said he actually *was* on Nantucket the night before Louisa disappeared. So he was here that morning, and I got really nervous there might be some evidence that could be twisted to implicate him." Her fingers wrapped around one another, over and over again.

"You went in my room without my permission."

"I didn't go through anything," Julia said. "I went in and got the scrapbook, and I left."

"It broke our trust." She'd said this yesterday too, and Julia had brushed it off.

Today, she hung her head and nodded. "I know. I'm so sorry."

Maddy got up and came around the desk. She moved the chair beside Julia and sat down. "What's next in the Seashell Promise book?"

"Maddy." Julia rolled her eyes. They weren't in college anymore. Janey's son had been *kidnapped* earlier that day. Her fantasies about an amazing Thanksgiving Day weekend had gone up in smoke when her mother had texted and asked if she could come to Nantucket for the feast.

"What's next?" Maddy asked.

Julia looked at her. The two of them stared at one another, both of them blazing with energy. Maddy had never been one to back down from a challenge— except for that one time when Julia had stolen Alan from her. Why she had then, Julia still didn't understand.

"A big, scary dream," she said.

Maddy nodded and sighed, looking up toward the ceiling and then out the window behind the desk. "Honestly, at this point, it would be to put all of this chaos behind me. Nothing with the inn. Louisa. Riggs. None of it." She sank back into her chair and glanced over to Julia again. "Sometimes I wonder what I'm doing here."

Julia's eyes widened. "Do you?"

"It's…I don't need the money. I don't think you do either. So why are we here?"

Julia opened her mouth to answer, but nothing came out. She didn't know.

"Where would you go?"

"My dad is here," Maddy whispered. "I like being close to him, but honestly, Jules, this inn…Louisa…it doesn't feel like it's going to stop. I don't like living in fear. I don't like looking up to the balcony and wondering what happened, and who did it, or any of it." She shivered.

Julia's arms broke out in gooseflesh. "Me either."

"So my big dream would be to…I don't know." Maddy sighed, a smile filling her face. "Buy a nice house on the water, where I can live with Ben and my dad can have a private space too. I can do boat tours like I do now. I like that. But I wouldn't have to do so much cooking, or worrying about guests, or trying to figure out if I can or can't paint the walls in my room."

Julia smiled too. "You can, Maddy. This place isn't haunted."

"Isn't it?" Their eyes met again, and Julia started to doubt that The Lighthouse Inn wasn't haunted. "What's your big dream?" she asked.

"Uh, I don't know," Julia said.

"Come on," Maddy said. "We're hosting the meeting tonight, and you don't know? You at least get to know the topic before the rest of us."

"I thought you'd say you wanted your own restaurant," Julia said instead of laying out her dream. It sounded stupid inside her own head. "The Glass Dolphin is opening a new branch in Five Island Cove."

"I know." Maddy got up and went around the desk again. She sat and fiddled with the mouse.

"You're thinking of doing it," Julia said, a touch of fear pouring through her, as well as wonder. She shut that emotion down, because why shouldn't Maddy do what she wanted to do? She could, and Julia could too.

"Maddy," she barked when her friend refused to look at her and hadn't said anything.

"Yes," she said. "I've spoken to Teresa about it." She finally looked away from the screen. "Okay? I'm thinking about it."

"I don't want to run this inn with anyone but you," Julia blurted out. She hadn't thought of those words before she'd said them, but they were true. "It could be a complete nightmare." Images of a tall, gangly woman wearing all black ran through her head. "Maddy, promise me you'll tell me the moment you decide."

"I will," Maddy said.

"What about Ben? Your dad?"

"I don't know." Maddy sounded irritated and frustrated, and Julia told herself not to ask another question.

She stood and looked at Maddy. She continued clicking around for a few seconds, and then she met Julia's eye. "I'll support you," she said. "No matter what, okay? If I have to help you pack your dad and move the two of you to the Cove, I'll do it. If I have to go over to the Coast Guard station and console a heartbroken Captain Gorgeous, I could probably do that too." She grinned at Maddy, who smiled, rolled her eyes, and shook her head.

She stood and came to embrace Julia. "Thank you," she whispered. As she pulled back, she added, "Don't think I didn't realize you didn't share your big dream." She put a hooked eyebrow up, and Julia would never think that she'd gotten something past Maddy.

"Tonight," she promised. She just had to figure out how to put into words what she'd been dreaming about.

"CAN YOU HEAR US?" she asked later that night. For some reason, she leaned closer to the screen, as if the laptop would be able to transmit the sound better that way.

"Yes," Tessa said. She sat at a desk, clearly in a hotel. She hadn't wanted to make the drive from downtown to the inn tonight, because the wind had picked up again. Maddy and Julia had already called Vivian once that day, when a gust had taken off one of the shutters on an upstairs window.

"I'm here," Helen announced, and she plunked down a pink pastry box in the middle of the dining room table.

"Ouch, that was loud," Tessa said, and she disappeared from the screen.

"Helen," Julia said.

"Sorry," the older woman said. "I didn't think it would land that hard."

"What are these?" Janey asked, standing up and reaching for the box.

"Oh, Janey's here?" Tessa asked. Julia looked over to her half-sister to judge the reaction. She had the very real inkling that Tessa and Janey weren't getting along right now, but Janey only smiled.

"I'm here, Tess," she said. "Is The Swinging Lantern nice? It always looks so posh from the outside."

"Yes," Tessa said, her video coming back on. "Sorry, I had to adjust some settings."

"Everyone's here," Julia said, glancing over to Annie too. "My nieces as well, so we better keep it clean tonight."

Maddy scoffed. "As if we've ever gone into something dirty."

Julia picked up the book. "Tonight, we're going to do the last two things. Annie has to leave tomorrow, and I want her to do it if she wants." Annie gave her a smile, and encouraged, Julia went on. "So I think Maddy can start with the first one, which will give us all time to think. It's one of your big dreams. What do you want to do? Or what's a dream of yours?"

"The biggest dream," Maddy said, meeting Julia's eyes. "Not just any old dream. Right?"

"Right," she said. "The last one is a truth you've been holding back on admitting." She flipped the pages in the book. "It could be something you have to admit to yourself, or something you should admit to someone else, present or not present." She focused on the screen again and then looked at Annie, Janey, Helen, and finally Maddy.

Silence filled the dining room, where they'd finished serving their cookie and hot chocolate bar only twenty minutes ago. The scent of chocolate, whipped cream, and mint still hung in the air. Warmth blew in from the ducts, and Julia had always adored this new color palette she and Maddy had chosen and implemented in the inn.

Tessa had been there to help paint plenty of times over the autumnal months, and Helen had brought pastries and good company continually. Julia's heart grew in size as she waited, and then she decided she better start.

"One of my biggest dreams," she said, clearing her throat. "Is to paint. Draw. Do art." She dropped her gaze back to the book. "I love drawing. I used to do it every single day. I want to come up with this amazingly brilliant idea and then paint it. It'll be huge, and take up an entire wall in someone's house, and it'll bring them so much joy."

She could almost see the colors on the canvas. Almost smell the oils in the air. Almost visualize the sunlight as it came through the windows and lit the painting in authentic, natural light.

She looked at the screen, and Tessa was smiling. "You should do that," she said, her voice a little robotic over the video chat.

"I agree," Maddy said, linking her arm through Julia's and resting her head against her shoulder. "I'll go next."

Before she could speak, a terrible crash filled the inn, causing all five women gathered in the dining room to shriek. Maddy exploded to her feet, as did

Julia, and they didn't waste another second before streaking out of the dining room.

"What was that?" Tessa asked.

As Julia followed Maddy through the doorway, Helen said, "It sounded like a window breaking. They'll be back in a minute…"

Chapter 21

What else can possibly go wrong this weekend? Maddy couldn't help the poisonous thoughts in her head. But seriously. A squall. Julia's parents at dinner. A kidnapping. Now a windstorm causing damage to the inn twice in the same day?

She exited the hallway to a blast of cold air, and she flew down the steps toward a man standing in front of the now-shattered entrance to The Lighthouse Inn. He looked up, his eyes wide as the wind now whipped through the lobby, tickling the picture frames and making the tassels on the pillows waver.

"I'm so sorry," he said. "I was just coming in for a minute to get out of the wind, and it just…" He looked behind him. "Snatched the door from me."

Julia crowded in behind Maddy, as did Janey and

Annie. The four of them stood in a huddle, looking at this stranger.

"Who are you?" Janey demanded, taking a couple of steps and putting herself between Maddy and the man. "Are you a guest here?" She spun back to Maddy and Julia. "Is he a guest here?"

"No," Julia said.

Janey turned again, her hands going right on her hips. "Only guests can come in here."

"I was just trying to get out of the wind," he said, holding up both hands. He had a pair of light brown eyes that seemed honest. Maddy didn't really know, and she hated that Janey's default was to question who he was, why he was there, and what he wanted.

To be honest, Maddy had been thinking the exact same things. "Janey," she said, and the woman faced her again. Her eyes seemed a bit wild, but she'd been through something terrible that day. Earlier this year too. Several things.

"I'm Michael Forrester," he said. "I live a couple of streets over." His eyes moved behind the crowd of women, relief painting his features. "Helen. It's so windy out there."

"Mike," the older woman said as she came down the few steps from the hallway. "What's going on?"

"I was down at The Holiday House with my sister when the wind kicked up," he said. "Her kids are at my house, so I said I'd run home to sit with them so they wouldn't be afraid."

Sister. Kids. Volunteering to take care of them. Maddy wasn't sure she believed him. *Stop it*, she told herself. W*hat's he going to do? Come in here and make up a story so he can…what?*

She didn't know how to answer herself, and Helen moved past her and Janey and drew Michael out of the pool of broken glass. "Come in, come in," she said. "Ladies, we've got to get this door covered."

"There's one downstairs," Julia said, and she turned to go down the steps only she and Maddy used.

"Can we help?" another man asked, and Maddy faced the two guests coming down from their rooms on the second floor.

"Yes," she said, regaining control of her emotions and her faculties. "Julia went to get a door, but she won't be able to carry it far. Could you help her, Hector?"

"Yes, ma'am." The Southerner turned and went down the steps. He'd come to the island with his brother, and Maddy met Walter's eye.

"Then maybe you can help us hold it while we get it in place."

"Absolutely."

"I have a toolbox in the kitchen." Maddy made the dash to go get it, and when she returned to the lobby, Hector had brought up the door. He, Walker, and

Michael stood in all the glass and covered the gaping hole.

While they worked to nail it all in place, Maddy went to get the broom. Julia stood in the office, her phone pressed to her ear, so she'd probably called Vivian. A missing shutter was nothing, but their main entrance blown wide open? That was serious.

Finally, the last of the wind got shut out, and everyone got out of the way so Maddy could clean up the glass. Annie went into the kitchen and came out with several wet cloths, and she, Janey, and Julia got down on the floor to catch any teeny tiny shards the broom bristles had missed.

"I'm so sorry, really," Michael said. He tugged a card free from his wallet and handed it to Julia. "I'll pay for it."

"Michael Forrester," Julia read from the card. She looked up at him, and then back at it. "You're the manager at The Holiday House?"

"Yes," he said. "My brother owns it. Well, his wife does, but she's been really sick lately. I've been managing this branch for years."

"Mike is amazing," Helen said, smiling at him fondly.

He ducked his head, and Julia sighed. Shock moved through Maddy, and she turned in slow motion to look at her fellow caretaker. Julia smiled at Mike like she'd fallen into a dreamland, and Maddy's heart beat out several big, booming beats.

She *liked* him.

Maddy shifted and gave her a tiny nudge with her foot, but Julia startled like she'd been shaken by an earthquake. She met Maddy's eyes, her face flushing red. "We'll be in touch, Mister Forrester."

Maddy hid her smile as Julia faded back into the group. "You can stay until you feel safe enough to get back to your place," he said.

"We can take 'im," Hector said. "The wind won't push our truck around." He grinned at Walter. "We're gonna be out at the Shipwreck for a while, ladies." He tipped his ball cap at Maddy, his smile wide.

She preceded him to the door still standing and pushed it open for him. "Hector," she said in her best Mom-voice. "If you're in trouble tonight, you call me. Do you hear me?" She couldn't pull off "ya'hear?" the way she'd heard him say, but the message was the same.

"Yes, ma'am," he said. He was a few years older than her son, but Maddy could still easily mother him, and she nodded to him and then Walter.

"Are you drinking tonight?" she asked.

"No, ma'am," he said.

"Take care of each other," she said, and then she nodded at Mike as he followed the brothers outside.

When she turned back to the lobby, only Julia waited for her. Maddy wanted to throw questions at her for what had just happened, but she didn't. "Come on," she said. "Tessa and Janey have both had a long day, and we need to get this Seashell thing wrapped up."

She led the way back into the dining room, ready for bed. They served breakfast later on the weekends, but Maddy would still have to be awake and upstairs by six-thirty in the morning.

"Anyone want to share their biggest dream?" Julia asked. "Or the truth. We don't have to go in order."

Maddy didn't want to do the last one, so she raised her hand slightly and said, "My dream is to open and run my own restaurant." She skipped her gaze past Julia's, because she hadn't said as much that afternoon.

"I can see you doing that," Janey said with a smile. "I think my dream would be to feel mentally well."

The room sobered, but Helen only let it stay that way for a moment. She said, "My dream is to die before my body gives out. Or before I can't enjoy raspberry fritters anymore." She lifted one from the box and saluted with it.

Maddy laughed with the others, her eyes falling to the laptop where Tessa sat, then over to Annie. "My dream," Annie said. "Is to switch departments and work with mothers and babies." She wore a soft expression on her face. "I met this woman yesterday at

The Holiday House, and she was pregnant. There's just something about babies, you know?"

"Can you do that?" Julia asked. "Just move around in nursing?"

"I think so," Annie said. "I'm a registered nurse. I can get any nursing job."

"Look into it," Tessa said, and Annie nodded. She practically glowed, and Maddy reached over and patted her hand.

"My dream is kind of like my truth," Tessa said, and everyone leaned closer to the laptop. "I'm not happy here, on Nantucket. I'm not sure I've admitted that to anyone, but I'm not. I want to be happy. That feels like my dream."

"Tess," Janey said, but she didn't follow it up with anything else.

Maddy's pulse bounced against her ribs. Tessa wasn't happy here?

Of course she isn't, Maddy chastised herself. *She's staying in a hotel because she doesn't want to be in that cottage.*

Maddy wouldn't want to be there either. Tessa had been kidnapped there. A strange woman had come inside and made threats there. So much revolved around that cottage too, and Maddy's skin chilled the same way it did when she thought about The Lighthouse Inn.

"My truth," she said when no one else spoke up. "Is similar. I'm thinking of leaving the inn and the island and going to Five Island Cove. The Glass Dolphin is opening a new branch there, and I've been talking to their manager about…well, about being the manager over the new branch."

"Thinking about it?" Janey challenged. "Or is the truth that you're going to do it, and you just haven't admitted it yet?"

Maddy met her eyes, the words clogged in her throat. She drew in a breath, trying to clear them away, but they wouldn't go. She looked at Julia, her promise ringing in her ears. "I want to do it," she said. "It feels a little silly, because Julia and I just opened this place, but yes."

She lifted her head and nodded. "I'm going to call Vivian on Monday and schedule a time to talk to her about my exit from The Lighthouse Inn."

"Wow," Annie said, and Maddy caught Helen nodding wisely. Julia looked like she'd just been hit with a wall of ghosts, and Maddy leaned toward her and drew her into a hug.

"It's okay," she whispered.

"Maybe I'll go with you," Julia whispered back.

Maddy smiled at her and shook her head as she pulled away. "No, because you just met that handsome Michael Forrester, and he's going to need someone to make him pay for that door."

"You met who?" Tessa asked, and things spiraled from there. After the truths had been shared—nothing too earth-shattering besides what Tessa and Maddy had said—Julia closed the laptop. They walked their friends to the non-broken door.

Julia looked at Maddy and said, "I really could go to the Cove too. There are art studios there. Lots of rich people who need big paintings for their big walls." Hope streamed from her face, and Maddy's heart filled with love for her best friend.

"What about Janey?" Maddy linked her arm through Julia's, and they headed for the stairs that led down to the basement.

"Janey has Sean." She looked at Maddy. "What about your dad? Ben?"

Maddy's mind grew heavy, and she blew out an exhausted breath. "There are a lot of things to work out."

Dad would be easy. It was Ben who wasn't mobile. Ben who could be moved to another Coast Guard base at any time as it was. Ben who might be her biggest dream yet...one she might never be able to achieve.

She put a smile on her face, though, and said, "I'll talk to them both tomorrow. Then Vivian on Monday, and I'll call Teresa too."

"This scares me," Julia admitted. "It feels fast, and I can't run this place without you."

"The Glass Dolphin isn't set to open until spring," Maddy said. "I'll be here for a few more months at least. I know that much."

Julia nodded, slipped her arm away, and turned toward her room. Maddy watched her go, new things shifting in her life. Different pieces coming forward, and ones she'd been so focused on drifting away.

She hadn't expected her life on Nantucket to be easy, but she hadn't anticipated it to be this...chaotic either.

Maddy turned and went toward her room. Inside, she glanced first to the closet, the constant reminder of Riggs's notes to his sister right there, just beyond the door.

She didn't want to stay here, and she'd admitted it. Now she just had to complete a few hard conversations...starting with Ben tomorrow night.

<hr />

MADDY PRANCED like a fourteen-year-old out with her first boyfriend. "It's beautiful," she said as he laughed. "Look at the lights."

Downtown Nantucket had been transformed into a winter wonderland for the holidays. It hadn't snowed—praise the heavens—but every shop had hung snowflakes, lights, and garlands to create a festive atmosphere. Nantucket entertained tourists year-round, and the holidays were no exception.

Ben had met her downtown about five minutes ago, and Maddy couldn't get enough of him. He said,

"I'm starving, sweetheart," but he didn't take her toward any restaurants. The lampposts downtown were the old, whimsical kind, and he stopped by one of those and reached up to touch the red, tinselly bow above his head. He couldn't quite reach it, and he smiled down at her.

He lowered his head to kiss her, and Maddy gladly met him halfway. She didn't care that there were other people on the street, though she and her ex-husband had never participated in any public displays of affection. Her standing behind him was enough.

Maddy barely recognized herself here on Nantucket, and she liked that. She didn't think she'd been herself in the city, and the woman who wore skinny jeans and a dark brown duster, held her boyfriend's hand without gloves, and let him kiss her in public was more of who she really was.

"Mm, I feel better already," he said, grinning as he pulled back.

Maddy returned the smile. "Ben," she said. "What would happen to us if I wasn't on the island?"

His grin hitched and slipped. "Are you leaving?"

"I'm thinking about another job," she said, not able to hold his gaze now. They hadn't gone to dinner. They had the whole evening in front of them. Why had she brought this up now?

She told herself she was done enduring events with a sick stomach because she didn't want someone to be upset. She had to talk to Ben about this, and why not now?

"It's in Five Island Cove," she said. "It's a thirty-minute ferry ride from here."

"Yeah, I know the Cove," he said. "We share patrol there."

Her eyebrows went up, and she tugged him toward Pier and Piedmont, one of the best places to shop here on Nantucket. "Do they have a Coast Guard Station there?"

"Yes," he said. "It's the furthest east parcel of land in the US. You land there, you're in the country. They've had some drug problems in the past year or so."

Maddy didn't say he could be stationed there. He was a captain. He could ask to be transferred, and maybe he'd get it. He'd told her a bit about how transfers worked, and sometimes he got what he wanted, and sometimes he didn't.

Maybe, she thought, but she didn't dare expand the dream from there.

They wandered down the street, the silence between them nothing too harsh. Ben didn't say what didn't need to be said. So when he did say, "Tell me what you've been thinking about, beautiful," Maddy opened her mouth to start talking.

Chapter 22

I don't have a sister. Tessa stared at the text that had come in five minutes ago. Or had it been ten? Twenty?

She didn't know. The world had shifted with just a handful of words. For her, it had been doing a lot lately.

Your mother died.

Only three words, and everything she'd ever known had been dumped out, stomped on, and crushed to pieces.

I want a divorce.

Also life-changing, especially when she hadn't known her husband was so unhappy with their suburban life in Pennsylvania. Tessa hadn't been.

My father is Ryan Harper.

Those words had ripped her sister from her, and Tessa had honestly not realized it until very recently.

Tears gathered in her eyes, making the text she'd gotten from Riggs's emergency number blur.

I don't have a sister.

Caroline Fyfe wasn't his sister.

Deep down, Tessa had already known that. She'd sent him the text specifically to confirm her suspicion. Why it had taken him three days to answer, she didn't know. She felt like she'd lived three years in the past seventy-two hours.

A light knock on the door had her jumping to her feet, her phone skittering across the table in the hotel room where she'd stayed last night. It was far too nice for her, and she'd deliberately kept almost all the lights off last night during the video chat with her friends at the inn.

She'd told them the truth—and she'd admitted it to herself. She wasn't happy here, and she did want to be happy. That meant she had to do something different. Go somewhere else.

Unfortunately, the person on the other side of the door would be Abraham Sanders, and Tessa had enjoyed getting to know him, meeting him, and spending her day with him.

He'd gotten this room for her, as he knew a lot of business owners on Nantucket. The huge penthouse suite here at The Swinging Lantern hadn't been rented for the weekend, and Abe had secured it for her at a deep discount.

She didn't know how long she'd be staying here. She didn't have to work until Tuesday, and a ferry ticket to Five Island Cove cost twelve dollars. She could go there for the next couple of days and just…wander.

Just see how she felt.

She went to the door and hesitated. "Abe?"

"Yeah," he said. "It's me, Tessa."

She opened the door to find him standing in the hall with a large brown bag in his hand, the top rolled down as he gripped it. "I brought breakfast. You didn't order room service, did you?" A twinkle beamed from his eyes as he teased her.

She smiled and backed up. "Not yet, anyway."

He entered the room, and Tessa suddenly felt shy with him. They'd spent all day together yesterday, literally from morning until nearly midnight. He hadn't kissed her, but he had held her hand. They'd talked and talked and talked.

In her heart, she knew if she relocated—*when*, she thought. *When, not if*—she'd have to break-up with Abe. He owned a generational business here on Nantucket. He wasn't leaving.

He walked the length of the room to the big dining room table situated in front of the wall of windows. They faced east, and the sunrise this morning had painted a picture for Tessa she'd long remember. Abe sighed and said, "Wow, it's beautiful from up here."

She moved to his side, and the two of them looked

out across the world. At least it seemed that way to her. The sky had come blue today, and it blended almost seamlessly into the water. "I got up early to watch the sun come up," she said. "You should've seen it. Glorious."

He reached over and threaded his fingers between hers. "I'll bet."

The spell they'd entered stayed for a few more seconds, and then it snapped. He took a breath and said, "I got the sausage and cheese kolaches, and they're best hot." He released her hand and opened the bag. "How was your girl talk last night?"

"Good," she said, adjusting the chair she'd been sitting in before his arrival and lowering herself into it. "How was your house?"

"Oh, I didn't go home." He gave her a smile. "I had to talk to Damon about the shop, so I stayed with my brother."

"So he knows about me."

"He does." Abe gave her a smile. "He's known about you since the very first time I messaged you." He put a napkin down in front of her, and then a white, crinkly bag with her kolache in it.

Tessa's eyebrows went up, and she kept her focus on him. "Really?"

"He was with me," Abe said. "Damon practically dared me to do it." He chuckled as he sat down, his own breakfast in front of him now. He was so...

sparkly. So good. So fun, and he laughed like he'd never really endured anything hard in his life. So far, Tessa hadn't heard any stories to indicate he had, and she hadn't told him about her own kidnapping yet.

He took a bite of his kolache, his eyes rolling back in his head as he groaned. Tessa grinned at him, feeling some of his spark rub off on her. It had yesterday too, and honestly without him, she wasn't sure she'd have survived the past twenty-four hours.

She put her phone on the table and swiped it open. "Look at this text," she said. Then she picked up her kolache and took a bite. The dough was fantastic, almost a bite of sourness on her tongue from the salt. The sausage wasn't too spicy, and the cheese balanced it out anyway.

"Who is this?" Abe asked.

"Riggs," she said. "Rick Fry." She'd told him about Louisa Fry, her mother, and a lot of the twisted details. Maybe not everything, but she'd be shocked if he didn't already know. Nantucket wasn't that big of an island, and locals knew all the gossip.

Abe frowned. "I thought he was in jail."

"His wife is," Tessa said, swallowing though she'd already eaten her bite of food. "She kidnapped me last summer."

"What?" Abe looked up, the laughter on his face drying up when he realized she wasn't kidding.

"They're a large part of why I don't want to stay at the cottage."

"I talked to a realtor," he said. "By the way. I mean, the realtor is my brother, so." He shrugged one shoulder, back to his good-natured self. "He'll help you list the cottage, if you and Janey decide to do that."

"Thanks," she murmured.

"I'm sorry about the summer," he said, sobering too. "I know you've said it's been a difficult time for you since you came here."

She nodded, because she had said that. She was tired of wallowing in it, to be honest. "I need a change, Abe."

He said nothing, as he was also very good at hearing the unsaid words behind statements. "Where are you going to go?"

"The Cove," she said. "To start with. I mean, I have to work on Tuesday, but I thought I'd go this morning, and just...see how I feel."

He covered her hand with his again, and Tessa looked into his eyes. His were a color she'd not seen before on a human, almost gray, but definitely brown at the same time. The lines around his eyes told her he'd spent a lot of his life laughing, and she ran her fingers down the side of his face, the softness of his beard tickling her skin.

"I feel stupid," she whispered. "Starting this with you and then leaving."

"Oh, don't feel stupid," he whispered back. The
paper beneath his hand crackled as he moved it, and
he cupped her face too. "I have sausage breath, but I'm
willing to risk it." He grinned at her, and Tessa's heartbeat started pounding. He'd just asked if he could kiss
her, right after she'd told him she wasn't going to stay
on Nantucket.

She leaned closer, letting her eyes drift closed. He
touched his mouth to hers, and sparks flew from the
point of contact. They filled the whole suite in less
than a moment, and then Tessa breathed in sharply
through her nose, pulled away, and then kissed Abe
again.

Her pulse settled the longer he kissed her, and
Tessa didn't let her mind wander. She stayed right
inside the moment, relishing the feel of his breath, the
taste of his mouth, the scent of his skin.

When he finally ducked his head, Tessa felt starved
for air, and she took another long breath. She looked
up at him through her eyelashes. "I don't suppose you
can skip work for the next couple of days and go to the
Cove with me, can you?"

Abe nodded without a moment's hesitation. "My
son's fine at the deli."

Tessa smiled, hope filling her soul for the first time
in a long time. If she had someone, it wouldn't matter
that she'd lost everyone this year. She pulled back on
the thoughts, because they felt somewhat dangerous.

She didn't want to be with just anyone. A random *someone.*

She wanted to be with someone who helped her see the best in herself, who inspired her to be the best person she could be, and who truly understood her.

She wasn't sure if that person was Abraham Sanders or not, but right now, in this moment, it felt like it.

———

A COUPLE OF HOURS LATER, she and Abe disembarked from the ferry that had brought them the twelve miles from Nantucket to Five Island Cove. It had been a quick trip, and she reasoned she could easily get to Nantucket to visit him. He could get to Rocky Ridge—where they currently stood—in under an hour from his house or the deli.

"So this is Rocky Ridge," she said. "One of the five islands here."

"Yes," he said. "It's the least inhabited."

"No hotels here."

"Nope," he said. "They're going to be more centralized. Diamond Island—the big one in the middle of the chain—has an airport. Most tourists and visitors come that way, and it's easier to stay on Diamond."

She nodded and then tipped her head back to take a deep breath of the air here. "It feels clean."

Abe chuckled. "I don't know what that means, but it sounds good."

Tessa smiled at him. "It is good." She already held one of his hands, but she now sandwiched his between both of hers. "What is there to do here?"

"Eat," he said.

"We just ate," she said.

"Shop," he said. "Hike, especially on this island. The beaches are fantastic here. They have a couple of festivals, but not right now."

Tessa had picked up some brochures at the ferry station on Nantucket, and she'd read them on the ride here. "So shopping and dining for us," she said.

His phone zinged, and he took it out of his jacket pocket. "Oh, this is Tom," he said. "He's only got one room at the Lotus." He looked at Tessa, his eyebrows up. "Two queen beds."

"That's fine," she said coolly. She wasn't going to sleep with Abe, but she didn't have to say it. His raised eyebrows already knew.

"I'll let him know." He needed both hands to text, and he quickly sent the message back to his friend. Her phone chimed while he did, and she checked it.

I'm on my way to Nantucket to sort this out.

The sun went dark for a moment, and a chill washed over Tessa. Her lungs stopped functioning, and she stumbled. Abe said something to her, and everything rushed back into her life. Color, sound, light.

"He's coming," she said, tilting her phone toward Abe. Then she simply shoved it into his hands and walked away. She didn't want to deal with this anymore.

She never wanted to return to Nantucket, and as Abe called her name and came running up behind her, Tessa just wanted everything and everyone to go away.

The moment she thought that, she changed her mind. She spun back to him. "I need my phone," she said.

"Yes." He handed it to her. "What are you going to do?"

"I'm going to call the Sheriff," she said. "This ends right now."

Chapter 23

Summer, 1974:

Lydia woke in the morning with no one in bed with her, but the scent of coffee coming down the hall from the kitchen. She wasn't sure how long Riggs had stayed last night, because Bobbie had knocked on the door after midnight, and he'd...well, she wasn't sure what Riggs had done after that.

Dale wasn't anywhere to be seen, but as the floorboard creaked outside her bedroom, Greg poked his head around the corner from the kitchen. His grin could light cities. "You're up," he said.

"Barely." She gave him a smile. "I'm going to shower."

"Dale went to get doughnuts, and there's coffee."

"Okay." Lydia's stomach recoiled at the thought of doughnuts. All that sugar this early in the morning actually made her heave. She dashed into the bathroom and closed the door behind her. She bent over the toilet, but nothing came up.

She sure felt sick, with a thin layer of sweat beading up on her forehead almost instantly. She clung to the colder porcelain and took several quick breaths in and out, in and out. Her mind raced, because she'd not been sick in the morning before.

Yes, you have, *a voice in her head whispered.* Only a couple of days ago.

She'd thought it had been the clams she and Greg had gotten at The Wharf. Even he'd been a little off the next morning.

When she felt like she could, Lydia stood up. She looked at herself in the mirror, noting how dark her hair was against her fairer skin. She spent plenty of time in the sunshine, but her skin didn't tan the way other people's did. She usually tried to play it up by painting her lips a bright red and spending some of her allowance on hair dyes to make her strands even darker. She hadn't done that for a while, though, and a certain numbness moved through her.

In almost robotic motions, she opened the very bottom drawer. Bobbie had had a pregnancy scare earlier this year, and she'd bought a few tests. When the first one had come back negative, and she'd started to bleed a day later, she'd put them in this drawer and left them there.

Lydia bent to pick one up, and she simply stared at it. She already knew what it would tell her, but she went through the motions and got in the shower. She stayed in for a long time, the steam rising and rising but not taking her cares with it.

If she was pregnant, her father would be livid. He ran most of Newark, and the one thing he'd told her not to do was get pregnant. He gave her money for her life here. He constantly threatened to cut her off if she didn't do what he wanted, so she'd gone to college. She wore the right clothes at the right times.

Here, on Nantucket, she'd been able to be herself. Finally free, and yet the fear her father still held over her suffocated her.

When Greg knocked on the door and called, "Lydia, hon, are you okay?" she switched off the water and stepped out of the tub. She didn't tell him to come in, but he did anyway. When he saw her standing there, dripping wet and naked, he quickly darted inside and closed the door behind him.

"Hey," he said, so much kindness in his voice. "What's wrong?"

She hadn't looked at the test, but her eyes dropped to it now. That simple wand sitting on the counter. Greg looked at it too, and he picked it up. His eyes widened, and his gaze flew back to hers.

Lydia started to cry, and Greg wrapped her in his arms in an instant, catching her before she crumbled to the floor. "Hey," he soothed though she was soaking his dry clothes with her wet skin. "It's fine, honey. I love you. This is fine."

She didn't know what to say. He had to know the baby could be anyone's. She didn't have to say anything. He knew. He'd been there for all the fun. He pulled back and bent down, both hands holding her face. "I love you. I'll marry you. I want to marry you. This is fine."

She hiccuped and shook her head, her long, wet hair sending splashes of water flying. "We'd have to get married fast for him not to know."

"Then we get married fast." Greg smiled at her. "I've been

in love with you for a year, Lydia. It won't be a surprise to anyone that we're getting married."

She looked right into those dark eyes. "The baby might not be yours."

"If you're mine, the baby is mine," he said fiercely. "Okay? That doesn't matter to me. I'll love it as much as I love you."

"What if Dale or Ry...Rick says they want the baby? What if they think it's theirs and they cause a problem?" She couldn't believe she'd almost said Ryan's name. Greg knew about Ryan, but he also thought she'd broken up with him weeks ago.

"They won't," he said. "How long? I mean, when do you think you'll be due?"

"I have no idea," Lydia said. She also knew next to nothing about how to be a mother, other than to not abandon her child with an ex, a hug, and a head held high as she walked away. Lydia could still see her mother doing that, could still hear herself wailing for her to come back. She never had.

Greg kissed her, but it wasn't one of their rough, passion-filled unions. He kissed her sweetly, almost chastely, and said, "I love you, okay? We'll get married fast, and this isn't a problem."

She nodded, because when Greg assured her of something, she believed him.

━━━

LATER THAT MORNING, Lydia looked up as someone called a name she recognized. "Louisa!" She got to her feet, because she knew the voice too.

"Rick?" she asked, but he didn't look her way. He ran across the sand, fully dressed, down the beach, away from the inn. She didn't know all the details of his trip to the island with his family, because they didn't really talk about personal things in bed. Especially Rick.

He'd been upset, though, and Lydia scanned the beach, trying to find something out of place. A lot of people had come today, and colorful umbrellas, towels, and swimsuits assaulted her vision everywhere she looked. Nothing seemed out of the ordinary—except for Rick in shorts and a T-shirt. He hadn't even been wearing beach attire.

The crowd had swallowed him, and she didn't see him coming back. She gathered her towel and beach bag, shouldered everything, and turned back toward her cottage. She'd walked this path so many times, she could do it in her sleep. She knew every detail of her house, as she'd been taking care of it since her grandmother's death.

As she neared it, something caught her eye to her right. Movement.

A woman ducked behind the garage, and a moment later, a child cried out. The sound muted quickly, and Lydia's heartbeat lodged somewhere in the back of her throat. She turned back to the beach to see if anyone had heard that, but the nearest visitor slept at least twenty yards away.

She faced the garage again—her garage—and called, "Hello? Do you need to use the bathroom?"

Sometimes tourists would knock on her door with an urgent need, and Lydia's free spirit always invited them in.

No one answered, and Lydia dropped her bag by the footings of her porch and walked toward the garage. There was no fence between her yard and the sand, and she went across the lawn, beneath the trees, and around the corner of the garage.

Only an empty patch of overgrown grass stared back. No movement. Not even a whisper of wind. Certainly no people.

"Lydia."

She spun toward the voice to find Greg's step-sister there. "Bobbie," she said, pressing one hand to her chest.

"What are you doing?" Bobbie came toward her and peered into the backyard too.

"Nothing," she said. "I thought I saw someone back here."

Bobbie frowned. "Really? Just now?"

"Yeah." Lydia waved her hand out across the beach, indicating it all. "Did you see Rick running?"

Bobbie's interest piqued. "Rick was running?" She grinned and bit her lower lip. "Like jogging on the beach, shirtless?"

Lydia giggled and shook her head, her laughter not feeling right today. "No," she said, thinking maybe the increased hormones due to the baby were meddling with her mind and emotions. "Like, he looked like…" She didn't know how to finish. "Like he was chasing someone."

Bobbie frowned and took a few steps out from under the trees. "I thought he was going home today."

"Maybe he was late." Lydia joined her friend, her toes digging into the hot sand. "Where did you two…I mean, he left last night and I'm not sure he came back."

Bobbie slid her a look out of the corner of her eye, her smile growing. "We went over to the cabanas."

Lydia kept her smile in place, but she'd never go be with a boy in public. "Were there other people there?"

"Only one couple," Bobbie said. "Way down on the other end from us."

Lydia nodded, and she didn't have to tell Bobbie she found that behavior trashy for her best friend to know. She said nothing, and after a few seconds Bobbie said, "You know, you could be happy for me."

"I am," Lydia said, turning to look at Bobbie. She'd been a good friend—the best Lydia had—and she linked her arm through Bobbie's. "Of course I am, but you know, the cottage has two bedrooms right on the main floor. If you want to be with Rick, just use one of those."

Bobbie's anger melted away, and her jaw tightened. "He's in love with you."

"Oh, he is not," Lydia said with a laugh. "Besides, your brother proposed this morning, and I said yes." He hadn't, not really. She hadn't said anything like the word yes. She hadn't even told Greg she loved him.

Bobbie squealed and began jumping around in the sand. That got the closest people to look their way, and Lydia laughed as she tried to shush her. Bobbie wanted all the details, but thankfully, Lydia had never kissed and told, so she simply zipped her lips and threw away the imaginary key.

"Hello," a woman said from behind them, and Lydia gasped

as she spun around. She grabbed onto Bobbie again, but her friend was just as petite as Lydia.

A dark-haired woman walked across the back lawn. She looked a little…dazed, her ponytail a bit pulled out on one side.

"Can we help you?" Bobbie asked.

"Did you say the name Rick a moment ago?"

Lydia looked at Bobbie, the same fear riding in her best friend's eyes that she felt deep down in her soul. "No," Lydia lied, facing the woman again. "I don't think so."

"My son's name is Rick," the woman said. "He didn't come back until very late last night."

Lydia refused to look Bobbie again. She didn't know what to say. The woman wore a bright blue caftan that billowed around her legs as she walked. Underneath that, she wore a black swimming suit, and she didn't have shoes on her feet.

She blinked, and a smile burst onto her face. "Well, I'm late getting packed to leave." She transformed right in front of Lydia's eyes, startling her. She walked past them, and Lydia couldn't look away.

"Ma'am?" she called, and the woman froze. She turned back to Lydia, who nodded with her head. "What were you doing back there? That's my property."

The woman's face paled for only a moment, and then her eyes grew angry. They glinted in the sunlight, but not in a happy way. She took a step toward Lydia, who tightened her hand on Bobbie's arm, and then stopped.

"Nothing," she chirped. "My son had thrown a ball and we were trying to find it, but it was in the yard behind yours."

She turned again, but Bobbie called, "Is your son Rick Fry?"

The woman seemed to roll her whole head along with her eyes as she faced them again. "Yes, now, can I go? We have to catch a ferry and a flight today."

Lydia increased the pressure on Bobbie's arm. Don't say anything, *she thought. Bobbie and Rick's relationship was still new, and she might not know that Rick had to sneak around as an adult. He certainly hadn't been throwing a ball that went into her yard, and as far as Lydia knew, he only had the one sister. Louisa. Far younger than him, as his father had remarried.*

Bobbie licked her lips and nodded. "What's your name?"

"Caroline. Good-bye." The woman turned and left, and once she'd gone all the way past Lydia's cottage, past Farrah Garry setting up the rings for something at the inn, and out of sight, then Lydia took a decent breath.

"She's scary," she said. "No wonder Rick doesn't do anything out of line." She shivered and looked at Bobbie. "Were you seriously going to tell her you slept with her son under the stars last night?" She giggled even as Bobbie's eyebrows drew down. A moment later, she scoffed and started laughing too.

"He's a good time," Bobbie said as they started walking along the property line. "Again, you should be happy for me."

"I am," Lydia said, stooping to pick up her towel and beach bag. "Now come on, Greg's taking me to lunch, and I have to look absolutely perfect."

Chapter 24

Two days later, July 18, 1974:

Lydia paced in the living room of the cottage, her hands shaking as she held the paper in front of her. Bobbie hadn't answered her phone. Greg was packing and getting ready to move back to college. She'd cut off personal contact with Dale. She and Ryan never talked about the other people she hung out with here on the island.

Not only that, but her marriage to Gregory Clarke had been announced, and she hadn't been to Long Island to see Ryan yet at all. She wouldn't go again once she and Greg got married, but she'd been planning one more trip—a farewell extravaganza—for next weekend.

But she needed to talk to someone right now.

The headline read: 7-YEAR-OLD GIRL MISSING FROM NANTUCKET POINT.

Louisa Fry, Rick's sister. The article said he was wanted for questioning in relation to the disappearance of his younger sister.

She pressed her eyes closed, releasing the tears to track down her face. She heard him yell, "Louisa!"

She saw him run past her, kicking sand up and onto other tourists.

She'd seen his mother behind her house.

Lydia dropped the paper and screamed. Every muscle in her body went rigid, and she stayed locked in position for several long moments. Then, just like she'd turned numb and gone through the motions of moving and breathing and showering when she'd taken her pregnancy test, she turned and left the cottage. She went down the driveway and past the garage. Past the patch of back-yard behind that to the tree line.

Caroline had been back here. Lydia had heard a child. Had she hurt her own daughter? How could she do that?

"How did your mother drop you off at a complete stranger's house and never come back?" she asked herself right out loud. Some people were cruel. Some were sick. Twisted. Heartless.

Lydia had no idea what she was looking for. None at all. She didn't know what kind of evidence one left behind when hurting a seven-year-old.

She couldn't find anything in the bushes or behind the trees. The backyard of the house behind hers was across a drainage ditch, and Lydia could only stare at it. And stare at it.

Had Caroline been dirty when she'd come wandering from this direction? Lydia pressed her eyes closed and relived the whole conversation. Every detail she could remember. There had been no dirt.

She couldn't tell if someone had been down in the ditch recently or not. There were no distinguishable footprints. There was nothing.

Lydia turned around, the silence here when the beach and so many people were just yards away unnerved her. She drew in a deep breath and blew it all out. She looked up into the sky, petitioning the Lord for help, as she'd often done when she felt so scared and so scattered.

A flash of pink caught her eye, high up in the treetop.

Lydia moved instantly to the base of the tree. They didn't grow very tall here on the island, due to wind and poor soil conditions, but this was higher than she could reach or climb. "It's a flag," she muttered to herself. The breeze shifted, and the pink fabric billowed out.

It wasn't a flag.

It was a swimming suit.

Perfectly sized for a seven-year-old.

"DO YOU HAVE TO GO?" *Greg asked the following weekend.*

Lydia looked over to where he lay in her bed. She picked up the tank top she'd worn the day before. "Yes, silly," she said. "My step-sister is expecting me." She tossed the shirt into her suitcase and then climbed onto the bed with him. His grin grew and grew, and he received her into his arms.

Gregory Clarke kissed her, and Lydia wondered—not for the first time—if she could be happy with him. He was an excellent lover, and a good man. A smart man. He went to college in Maryland and would be a successful surgeon one day. She could be happy with him, and he'd take care of her.

"You have to stop," she murmured as she pulled away. "What am I to tell Virginia? That I can't come because my secret summer boyfriend won't let me leave the bedroom?"

He chuckled and had the audacity to look ashamed. "Dale's coming in this weekend."

"Oh, you two will have fun without me then." Lydia gave him a mock pout and slid off the bed again. "I'll be back on Monday night."

"Lydia," he said, and he spoke in that serious voice he'd used a time or two with her.

"Hmm?" She didn't like serious, and Greg knew it. She picked up a pair of shorts from the floor and folded them.

It wasn't until she looked at him again that he spoke. "I want to marry you. I'm in love with you." He pushed himself up onto one elbow. "We'd have to give up Dale, but I could do it."

Lydia blinked at him. This wasn't the first time he'd told her he loved her. She sighed and went to sit on the edge of the bed in front of him. He didn't touch her, and the man really was the most intelligent male she'd ever met.

"Do you really love me?"

"Truly," he whispered. "Why do I have to stay a secret? If

I was your fiancé, we could go to Long Island to see Virginia together."

"She's a recluse," Lydia said quickly, another sigh following. She turned her head and looked at Greg. Something blipped through her, and she whispered, "I love you too."

A smile split his face, and his laughter boomed up to the rafters. "It's about time, Lydia Merrill." He grabbed onto her then and hauled her back into bed with him. Lydia giggled, and she only mildly protested when he lifted her shirt and unhooked her bra.

"I'll be late," she whispered, claiming his mouth immediately afterward.

"Mm." He pulled away and slid his mouth along the length of her neck, sending goosebumps down to her toes. "Yeah, you'll be really late, because what I want to do to you is going to take a while." He grinned at her, and she smiled back, and then she kissed Greg like she really could be with only him.

———

LATER THAT NIGHT, *the cab she rode in pulled into a beautiful driveway with a pale yellow house sitting at the end of it. "Here you go, lady," the man said.*

Lydia slipped him a handful of cash, collected her suitcase from the seat beside her, and stood from the car. A light beamed through the front right window, and Lydia went quickly up the steps to ring the doorbell. It had barely sounded before Ryan opened the door.

He stood there wide-eyed and said, "I thought it was you, but the hat made it hard to tell."

Lydia put a smile on her red-painted lips, tipped up onto one toe, and nudged the brim of her huge beach hat up a little bit to see him better. "Looks like I found the right place."

"I didn't think you were coming." He looked to his left. "It's almost eight-thirty. You must've been on the last ferry off the island."

Lydia positioned her suitcase in front of her. It was Friday evening, and they had three whole days before Greg expected her back on Nantucket. "Am I too late?" Perhaps he didn't want her anymore.

"Not at all." He stepped back and swept her into the house with his arm. He took her suitcase as he closed the door behind her, and the satisfying click of the lock told her they might not even make it into the bedroom.

She turned back to him and found him staring at the suitcase. "What did you pack?" he asked.

"Clothes," she said. "I'm going to be here until Monday, Ryan." She took a step closer to him and took the suitcase. She then took both of his hands in hers and moved her fingers up his arms and along his shoulders. He stood very still in front of her, his eyes searching her face. "When do you have to get back to the city?"

He swallowed. "Whenever I want."

Lydia smiled at him. "Have you eaten dinner?"

"Not yet," he said. "I was going to order take-out."

"Order it," she said. "Then, you can tell me if I'm going to need any of these clothes or if we're going to spend the next three days in bed."

He smiled at her, a familiar spark entering his eyes. "Honey, I can already tell you that you don't need any of those clothes." His arms deftly went around her, and he easily slid the zipper of her dress down. "In fact, we've got to get you out of these immediately. It's far too hot to be wearing dresses and pantyhose."

Her dress puddled on the floor, and Lydia stepped out of it. She'd chosen her undergarments carefully, and she knew they were Ryan's favorite. "I have one rule for this," she whispered as his fingers slid down the band keeping her pantyhose in place just above her knee.

Ryan cocked his eyebrows, because he always made the rules for their sleepovers together. All of the men in Lydia's life did, and she liked it that way. She knew she was really the one in charge.

She let them dominate her physically, because it made the sex so much better. But she knew she dominated them. She could bring any of the four men she was currently sleeping with to their knees, and they all knew it.

"You have a rule?" Ryan asked.

She nodded, one finger sliding down his chest. He tensed as she neared his waistband, and she followed the path of her finger with her eyes. "This first time, I get all of you. I get everything you've got, Ryan Harper." She raised her gaze to his. "Heart, body, soul. You can do whatever you want, but I get all of you along with that."

"Heart, body, and soul," he repeated.

"And I'll know if you don't," she said, her fingers working the button on his pants. "If you can't follow the rule, this will be the last time you ever get to touch me." She watched a flush work its way up his neck and into his face, his eyes pressed closed.

"Is that a yes, you'll abide by the rule?" she whispered.

"Yes," he whispered.

"I'm not sure I heard you." He'd said the same thing to her the last time they'd been together. She'd whimpered her answer to his rule, and he'd made her repeat it. Oh, how she loved him.

He opened his eyes, that fierceness there that told Lydia if he said yes again, she'd get everything he had. She'd get his heart, his body, and his soul. Every cell in her body trembled with want for it, and he said, "Yes," in a loud, clear voice, and then kissed her in a way that told her he'd definitely be keeping his promise.

Need pulled through her too, and she decided she could marry Greg if she could have all of Ryan at least once.

Hours later, she lay in Ryan's arms. He'd given her all of himself twice now. His breaths were long and even, as he'd fallen asleep.

He'd wake when she wanted him again, but for now, she let him sleep. They had more time together, but Lydia wasn't sure she'd see him again after this weekend.

"I love you," she whispered to him. She didn't need him to say it back to know he loved her too. Their time together tonight had been no different than any other time in the past year. She knew now that he'd always given her all of himself, and Lydia loved him all the more for it.

"I'm pregnant," she said next. "The baby could be yours, but I'm going to marry Greg. It's going to be his."

The baby could be Rick Fry's too. Or Dale Harton's. Lydia had been with all of them in the past month. Greg the most. Greg was her boyfriend-boyfriend. He loved her, and he'd take good care of her and the baby.

A tear rolled down her face, because everything in her life was about to change. Once she told Greg about the baby, he'd want to get married quickly. She did too, because she didn't need her father asking questions about what she'd been doing in Nantucket. It would be obvious what she'd been doing.

Bobbie, Greg's half-sister, had told her to go visit her step-sister, figure things out, and come back to Nantucket ready to be a monogamous and faithful wife, and Lydia was going to do exactly that.

She could and would, because she already loved this life growing inside her, and she wanted to provide the best she could for the infant she'd welcome to the world in several months.

She sniffled, hating the weakness inside her that craved so much male attention, and then she wiped her face and nose with the back of her hand. She'd been using sex as a distraction from her terrible life since the age of thirteen, and with Ryan Harper in her bed, she saw no reason to change that now.

Chapter 25

Janey clicked to open a new tab, her mind trying to come up with possibilities for the inconsistencies she'd found.

One, Riggs Friedman had no other sisters besides Louisa. Nowhere could Janey find any birth certificates or records of such a thing.

Two, the name Caroline Fyfe did not show up in any genealogical database Janey had searched over the past two days. At least not one roughly the same age as the woman who'd taken Cole.

"You're still at this?" Sean asked as he came into the kitchen.

"Mm." She reached up and rubbed the back of her neck. "Rick Fry's mother's name was Monica, right?"

Sean just quirked his eyebrows at her, his silent way of saying, *We went over this last night.*

Yes, it was Monica. She was currently still in the assisted living facility in New Jersey. Janey had been on the phone for an hour that morning to confirm it. Truth be told, no one had come right out and confirmed anything. Legally, they couldn't.

Janey had explained the situation twice, dropped words like, "life in prison," and "FBI case number," and finally the woman on the other end of the line had said, "If one of my patients wasn't here, ma'am, I would know it."

She started to go through the headlines again. Sean moved around her, doing the dishes and then sitting down with his laptop too. They had three weeks between Thanksgiving and Christmas, and he had two court appearances and other cases to work on.

Janey didn't see anything else in the pictures Tessa and Maddy had taken of everything they'd turned over to the police. She finally stood, her lower back twinging in pain. "I'm going to go for a drive," she said. "Clear my head."

Sean looked up, and he was incredibly sexy with his reading glasses perched on the end of his nose. "Do you want me to take you to the beach?"

"No." She gave him a smile and leaned down to kiss him. "I'm just going to drive around the island and come back."

"Turn on your pin," he said.

"It's on." She held up her phone, which was almost

all the way charged, as it had been plugged in while she looked through everything she'd already been through multiple times.

She left his house and got behind the wheel of her car. She couldn't just sit back and do nothing anymore. She felt more centered when she did something, even if that something didn't yield any results.

She drove, the morning light bright today. The weatherman had called the past several days of atmospheric activity some of the more unusual he'd seen, and he was predicting snow before Christmas. Janey didn't mind, as she loved the magic a white Christmas brought.

Her kids weren't leaving until evening, and she'd meet them for lunch and a send-off in a couple of hours. That was more than enough time to drive the island and get her head on straight.

Janey didn't just circle the island, though. She found herself making familiar turns and then parking in front of the blue cottage she'd first returned to months ago. It sat serenely in the weak sunshine, like nothing bad had ever happened there.

Janey knew better. She gazed down the driveway to the front part of the garage she could see poking out from behind the house. She'd been attacked back there. Tessa had been kidnapped from this house. Threatened.

Her head pounded, and she got out of the car,

ignoring her phone as it chimed with Tessa's notification sound. She and her sister had been through everything in this house. Every drawer. Every cupboard. Every closet.

Janey wasn't sure why she was here. Maybe because Tessa had done most of the work, and she'd kept out anything she thought might interest Janey. She glanced next door as she closed the car door, but nothing stirred at the Friedmans.

She heard the explosion of a gunshot, and she winced. Her eyes clenched closed.

Pulling herself back to reality, Janey took a steadying breath. "You're better now," she said. Instead of going toward the cottage, she took slow, measured steps toward the one next door.

She'd shown up with the gun just as Rick had told Tessa why he'd come back. Well, he'd come back for two reasons. One, to verify that the bones they'd found in the inn were his sister's. And two, to find something Bobbie had told him she had.

Proof that his step-mother had killed Louisa.

She hadn't believed him then, and to be honest, Janey still wasn't sure what she believed. She was tired of all talk, though, and when she reached the Friedman's house, she took in all the garden gnomes that Bobbie had loved so much. Oh, how she'd hated coming here, but now, she walked down the sidewalk and right into the house.

She found it odd it was unlocked, but she kept going. No air moved here, and it hadn't for quite some time. The scent of stale heat met her nose, and Janey looked left and right, scanning the living room.

The stupid gnome Tessa had brought in during their last encounter lay over by the hearth, and Janey wondered why a beach cabin even needed a fireplace. Her mind moved down such odd paths, and she let it, because she didn't want to second-guess herself.

"You're not the same person you were last time you were here." Her therapist would be so proud. Janey detoured into the kitchen and found it disheveled, like the last person to have been here had been going through drawers and cabinets.

Janey touched nothing but picked up a drinking straw wrapped in paper and started pushing things around. Receipts. Bills. Useless retirement statements. Paperwork for something. She rounded the counter and looked into the drawer.

Newspaper clippings sat there, all of them about the sports the Friedman children had once played. Janey couldn't believe how many there were, and she nudged one aside to read another.

On the fourth or fifth nudge, the headlines weren't about soccer and lacrosse anymore, but the disappearance of Louisa Fry. She pulled in a breath and held it.

The house was so, so silent, and even her breath sounded loud like a bomb. The window rattled in the wind, and Janey jumped and looked up, expecting to see someone standing on the other side of the glass, watching her.

Chills ran down her shoulders to her hands. No one was there.

She took another steadying breath and peered into the drawer again. She moved article after article up and out of the way, pushing it toward the back of the drawer so she could see the one underneath it. She remembered her sister saying Rick had been in the news for almost two years. That was a lot of newspaper headlines for a small island community, and the paper on the straw started to wear down.

She had to be close to the bottom of the drawer, and as she pushed up one more weathered, nearly shredded newspaper, she found herself reading the breaking headline.

This had to be the very first article that had come out, as it was dated July 18, 1974. She closed her eyes against the terrible, tall letters.

7-YEAR-OLD GIRL MISSING FROM NANTUCKET POINT.

She'd just spent the morning reading through the items she and Tessa had amassed, and she knew Louisa had gone missing two days before this article. Even then, it was indicating Rick as a person of interest the police needed to find and talk to.

Janey didn't need to read the article, though she

hadn't before. She started to look away right as her eyes registered something in her head. She jerked her attention back to the newspaper clipping.

Someone had written on it, right under the headline. The letters were so teeny tiny that Janey had to lean closer to see them.

The name *Caroline* sat there.

Her blood turned into solid ice, and she gasped for air.

Immediately following that, in the dimmest pencil imaginable, someone had written, *Not her real name. Swimming suit photo.*

She looked up, once again expecting either a SWAT team to break through the glass or a whole host of monsters to come flying at her. Neither happened, but Janey couldn't breathe. She pressed her palm to her chest and took one long breath after another, her head feeling so light and so distant from the rest of her body.

She backed up until she met the range behind her, and she closed her eyes and focused on her breath going into her nostrils, and then she searched for the top of the breath. She struggled to find it, and she had to breathe out, so she did.

After a few breaths like this, Janey began to calm. She opened her eyes, and the light coming in through the dining room windows almost felt false it was so bright. The sky darkened as the sun went behind clouds, and new shadows formed and flitted around as the wind kicked through the trees.

Janey locked her eyes on the open drawer, wondering how long she'd been here. Would Sean have noticed that she'd stopped at the cottage? They both knew that Tessa wasn't here, and Janey needed to stop ignoring her sister. Tessa hadn't exactly been forthright with her either, and Janey pushed all the confusing thoughts about her relationship with her sister from her mind.

She edged over to the drawer again and looked down into it. "Swimming suit photo," she murmured. What did that mean?

Using the straw, she pushed that paper up to see if there was anything else there, but there wasn't. She had no idea where Bobbie Friedman kept her photos, and if she was anything like Janey's mother, they'd be in shoe boxes in every available space in this cottage. Janey didn't have time to go through all of them to find one called "swimming suit photo."

They lived on the beach. Wasn't every photo a swimming suit photo? Her mother had lived in her swimwear and beachwear, Janey knew that.

Her heart thudded strangely in her chest, and Janey decided she needed to leave. She was no amateur sleuth. She could call the police and say she'd found something in the cottage next door, and they'd handle it. Yes, she'd have to admit to entering the house, but right now, that was her best option.

She didn't want to end up bloody again, nor did she want to put anyone she cared about in danger. Not herself, Sean, her children, Tessa, Julia, or anyone else at the inn. She took the wrapped straw with her and picked her way out of the kitchen and then back through the front door. With it closed behind her, she turned to go back down the sidewalk and past the trees separating her cottage's driveway from the Friedman's front yard.

A man stood at the end of the sidewalk, and Janey yelped and backpedaled. Riggs Friedman held up both hands, and called, "I'm not armed. I'm not going to hurt you."

Her heartbeat raced around and around like a toy car on a tiny track. She blinked, and he blurred around the edges. She forced herself back into focus, and realized she'd dropped the straw. Not only that, but she now had both hands planted flat against the front door.

"What are you doing here?" she asked.

"Tessa texted and asked me if I'd enjoyed Thanksgiving with my sister." He didn't take a step toward her. "I don't have a sister, and I figured I better come find out what was going on."

"Caroline's here," she said, expecting the name to carry some weight. Anger rose in her, but Janey tamped it down, tamed it, told it to wait. Simmer, and wait. "She kidnapped my son, Riggs."

He didn't react to the name at all. He did if confusion and eye squinting counted. "Who's Caroline?"

"She said she was your sister." Janey pushed away from the door and put all of her weight on her feet now. She took one step toward him and stopped. "She threatened Tessa and the rest of us to find a way to clear your name so you could come back here."

Riggs frowned and tilted his head further. "Janey, you're not making any sense."

She'd left her phone in her car, and she held up both hands. "I'm not armed either."

"Okay."

"I left my phone in my car," she said. "I can show you." She took slow steps toward him, wondering how he'd missed this story. Maybe it hadn't reached him wherever he'd been. "She got arrested yesterday." It sure felt like longer than that, but it really had only been yesterday morning. "I can show you."

He pulled out his phone and shook his head. "Mine doesn't have Internet."

"I can get mine," she said. "Will you please back up?"

He did, and once Janey could go around the trees, she moved quicker. She retrieved her phone from her car, noting that she'd missed half a dozen texts from various people and three calls—two from Tessa.

She knows, Janey thought, but she didn't keep her eyes on her phone for long. She pressed her back into her car and swiped, looking up and over to Riggs every other millisecond. Her phone loaded so slowly, but the mention of the arrest out on the west side of the island finally came up.

With her phone held straight out in front of her, Janey approached Riggs. His hair had grown longer than when she'd seen him a couple of months ago, but he still had those bright blue eyes, and with a shower and a shave, he'd be back to the man she'd known next door. Hopefully, without the creepy vibes he'd put off this past summer.

Janey realized how powerful her mother was; she'd held Riggs and Bobbie at bay for decades, and she hoped she could be like her when it really mattered. She didn't think Riggs was a threat anymore, but Caroline certainly was, and Janey wanted to know who she was.

Riggs took her phone, and Janey danced back a step. "Who is that?" she asked. "She said her name was Caroline and that she was your sister."

He stared at the phone, his eyes getting wider and wider and wider. "This is impossible," he whispered.

Janey saw a sleek black car turn the corner down at the end of the road. She knew who that was: FBI.

Her throat tightened, and part of her wanted to warn Riggs to run. Just go and never come back.

Instead, she cleared her throat and said, "Riggs, the police are here. It's time to stay and deal with this."

He turned as the sound of the car approaching increased, and his body tensed.

"Riggs," Janey said again, her voice much more powerful this time. More vehicles made the turn, and she hoped she wouldn't get in too much trouble for going inside the cottage and digging through kitchen drawers. "Who is she?"

Riggs looked at her, the phone still clutched in his hand. A wildness existed in his eyes, and she held up both hands. "It's fine. Tell me who she is. What do you know about a swimming suit photo?"

The first car came to a screeching halt, but Janey didn't take her eyes from Riggs.

"This woman is my step-mother," he said. "And her name is not Caroline."

"Stay right where you are," Special Agent Cartright yelled. "Rick Fry, do not move."

"He's not going to run," Janey said in a calm voice. She moved to stand right beside him. She held out her hand, and he passed her phone back to her. "He has information about the woman calling herself Caroline Fyfe, as well as the disappearance of his sister, Louisa." She looked up at him, and appreciation shone in his eyes.

He held up both of his hands too, and he did not move as the police handcuffed and arrested him.

Janey stayed out of the way as much as possible, but she was right in the thick of things—again. Even Sheriff Cochran sighed as she approached Janey. She put her hands on her hips and said, "I'm so tired of talking to you," with a half-smile on her face.

"Trust me, I agree." Janey nodded toward the cottage. "I found something in there I think you'll want to see."

Sheriff Cochran looked at the cottage, sighed, and looked back at Janey. "What is it?"

"It's a newspaper clipping with my mother's hand-writing on it," Janey said. "It's a clue, and a big one." She started toward the cottage. "Come on, I don't want to get in trouble for touching something I shouldn't."

"Janey," the Sheriff said. "You're not going in there at all." She caught Janey's arm and made her stop. "You're going home. You're done here."

She considered Sheriff Cochran. "You promise me you'll call me if you need something? Maybe I can help. Or Tessa. She has the case memorized. There's a photo that's missing. Maybe our mother had it."

"Janey," Sheriff Cochran said. "If we have any questions at all, we'll call you." She nodded down the street, and Janey looked that way. Sean, Cole, Rachel, Travis, and McKenna stood just beyond the perimeter of police vehicles. "Go on."

Janey hesitated for only a moment, and then she

nodded smartly to the Sheriff and headed down the street to her family. She ran the last several steps and embraced both of her children. "Sorry," she whispered to them. "I'm sorry."

"I thought you were just going for a drive," Sean said dryly, and Janey pulled away from Cole to look at him.

"I was," she said, turning back to the two cottages at the end of the lane. "And somehow, I ended up here. I don't know why."

"Aunt Tessa's freaking out," Rachel said. "She's in Five Island Cove, and she wants you to call her immediately." She looked up from her phone. "I've been keeping her updated."

Janey smiled at her daughter. "All right, I'll call her on the way to lunch."

Chapter 26

Annie looked up from her phone at the sound of the police siren. It wasn't specific to the police, but a siren nonetheless. She couldn't see anything from her position along the railing of the ferry, near the back.

"Mom," Bri said, and Annie dropped her phone into her coat pocket. She glanced at her daughter and then out to the water again.

"Everyone please step back from the railing," a man said over the speaker system. "We'll be encountering a high-speed boat, and there will be increased water lift. Please move away from the railing immediately."

Annie's heartbeat sprinted through her chest, and she gathered Paige and Bri closer to her. They stepped back, but the ferry already felt unsteady. Still, Annie kept going, because she didn't need to be splashed with freezing ocean water today.

Before they'd made it too far, a Coast Guard boat sped past them, headed toward the island they'd just left, churning up waves and water into great whitecaps. Her throat tightened, and all she could think about was her sister and her friends on Nantucket.

"Hold onto something," the man said, but Annie only had her children to grip. She did, and Paige reached out and grabbed a pole to her left.

"Mom," she said.

"Just hold on," she said.

"Brace for wave impact," the announcer said.

Every muscle in Annie's body tensed, and she watched as the tide created by the Coast Guard vessel hit the side of the ferry. A huge plume of water shot straight up into the sky, and their boat got bumped —hard.

People's voices rose in a chorus of a cry, but Annie kept hers quiet. The ferry began to rock side to side, water splashed a good five feet onto the deck, and if Annie had stayed where she'd been, she'd be soaked.

Her stomach boiled, and she kept her eyes on the horizon. "Look to the horizon," she said to Bri and Paige. "Don't watch the water. Look at where the sky meets the water. You can almost see New York."

Bri whimpered at her side; the ferry turned; the violent motion subsided.

"We're evening out now, folks," the announcer said. "Thank you for your quick response."

Water ran off the sides of the ferry, disappearing as quickly as it had arrived. Annie released her breath and let go of her daughters. She first looked at Paige, who had her eyebrows as high as Annie's. "What do you think is going on?" she asked.

"I don't know." Annie looked back toward Nantucket. They'd left about ten minutes ago, on the second ferry of the day to get home. She hadn't seen any reason to stay, and this way, she'd be able to get some laundry done and relax before she had to go to work in the morning. Before the girls had to get ready to go back to school.

Her phone rang, and Annie pulled it out. "This is Aunt Julia," she said. She was almost afraid to answer the call, but she swiped it on anyway. "Hey."

"You're never going to believe this," she said, her voice half hushed and half…scared.

"What?" Annie asked, glancing between Paige and Bri.

"Caroline Fyfe? She's really Riggs's *mother*." Julia exhaled as if she'd been holding her breath along with the words. "She broke out of her assisted living facility and came to Nantucket."

"You're kidding." Annie blinked, but she didn't know what to think.

"Yeah, I guess Tessa had a number for Riggs, and

she texted him about his sister. He said he didn't have one, and he came to the island too."

Annie's pulse leapt into the back of her throat. She had a very serious thought about jumping off the ferry and swimming back to Nantucket to help Julia.

"Tell her they arrested him," Maddy said, her voice further from the speaker.

"I was going to," Julia bickered back.

"She'll worry about you," Maddy said. "Lead with the stuff that keeps you safe, that's all I'm saying."

"They arrested him outside his cottage just a few minutes ago," Julia said, the wind now scratching at her speaker. "Janey was there with him. He identified his mother. He went without a fight. They're looking for some evidence he claims his wife and Tessa's mom had and have been hiding for years."

Annie took a few moments to absorb. "I don't understand," she said. "If his wife had evidence to exonerate him, why didn't she use it?"

"I...don't know," Julia said. "We're standing on the sand, just watching everything. They've got police tape everywhere, keeping everyone off the street. Tessa went to the Cove, so she's not here. They took Janey to the police station for questioning. The FBI agent called for more investigators to come help with the interviews, and there are cops going in and out of Riggs's cottage and Tessa's cottage. That's what we know."

"Wow," Annie said. "Just...yeah, wow." She didn't know what else to say. "I'm so glad I left this morning."

"Yes, they shut down the ferries," Julia said. "No one can leave until they've been cleared."

Annie swallowed, so glad she didn't have to go through any of that. Her, or her girls. "What are they looking for?"

"I don't know," Julia said. "I'll keep you updated. I just wanted you to know."

"Thanks," Annie said. "I do want to know. Janey and Tessa are good women." Good friends too, but Annie just held that in her heart.

"I love you, Annie," Julia said, her voice a touch strained.

"I love you, too, Jules." The call ended, and Annie lowered her phone. "Maybe now everyone involved in the disappearance of Louisa Fry can rest."

―――

LATER THAT NIGHT, after Annie had made it back to her home in Chatham, she'd done a load of laundry, and she'd ordered Chinese take-out, she put the last plate down on the table in front of Paige. "Girls," she said. "I do want to seriously consider moving some-where else."

Both Paige and Bri looked at her, and Annie sank into her seat. "Paige, I'm the most worried about you."

She cut a look over to Bri. "Not that I'm not worried about you, Bri, but Paige only has one more year of high school left, and it can be very hard to move right before your senior year."

Paige wouldn't want to do that, Annie already knew. To her daughter's credit—and as a testament to how much she'd grown in only a few short days—Paige said, "I could do it, Mom. I don't want to, but I could."

Annie nodded, and murmured, "I appreciate that, Paige."

Paige burst into tears, and Annie could only stare at her. She blinked, not sure what was going on. "I'm sorry," Paige said. "I've been so spoiled and difficult lately, and I'm sorry." She looked at Annie with pure agony in her expression. "I—things have been hard for all of us, but I seriously thought I had it the worst."

"It's okay," Annie said, though Paige had put them all through some trying times. "Life is confusing some-times, especially for someone your age."

Paige got up and wrapped her arms around Annie, holding her tightly. "I'm sorry," she whispered again. "I'll do better, I promise."

"You already are," she said. She hugged her daughter back fiercely until Paige was ready to let go. She grabbed a paper towel and wiped her face as she settled back into her seat.

"Bri?"

"I'll do whatever, Mom," she said, reaching for the

closest container of food. It popped open as she picked it up, revealing the white sticky rice inside. "If it's this year, I'll be starting fresh at a new high school. If it's next year, then I'll be a sophomore. It's fine."

Overall, Bri had far fewer friends than Paige. That would make moving easier for Bri, but Paige would be severed from all of her friends and popularity here.

Annie couldn't riddle everything out right now. "There's obviously a lot to do and consider," she said. "Jobs, a place to live, if this house will even sell." She reached for a container of food too. "I just want you guys to know I'm really considering it. I think it might be good for all of us to have a fresh start."

Paige picked up the white rice as Bri set it down. "I can't believe Dad moved and didn't tell us." She wore daggers in her eyes, and Annie had been on the receiving end of those. It wasn't that fun.

"I'm sure he had his reasons," Annie said.

"Don't, Mom," Paige said, back to her sassy self. The tears hadn't even dried on her eyelashes yet. "Why do you defend him?"

"I'm not—"

"You are, Mom," Bri said quietly. She looked at Annie, who had surprise cascading through her at the boldness in her younger daughter. "We don't need to be protected. We get to make our own judgments about Dad." She looked across the table to Paige, who nodded.

Annie lifted her head high. She spooned beef and broccoli onto her plate. "Sounds like you two have been talking behind my back."

Paige scoffed, but Bri started to giggle. Soon enough, a smile came to Annie's face too. Paige laughed, and that got her to do the same. The three of them released the tension in the room with their giggles, and Annie sure did love her family.

She didn't know what the future held. She didn't know if she'd stay here in Chatham or end up moving somewhere else. She didn't know when all of that would happen. She needed to call her ex-husband and work out some sort of schedule for his visitation, how they could get the girls back and forth now that he'd moved, all of that.

A million tiny little details needed to be worked out, but Annie could do it. She knew she could do it. And she knew her girls would be right at her side, and she knew that whatever happened, they'd find their way through it—and back to each other.

"I love you guys," she said as their laughter subsided.

"Love you too, Mom," Bri and Paige said in unison, and Annie smiled at them fondly.

She may have a lot of balls up in the air, but for the first time in a while, she was excited to see where they'd all drop.

Chapter 27

Maddy looked up as the front door to the inn squealed and squeaked. Someone had just come in. She got to her feet from behind the desk in the office and went to greet whoever had arrived. She was expecting three guests this afternoon, but it wasn't even close to check-in time yet. No one had contacted the inn to request an early check-in.

Ben was supposed to be stopping by today some-time too. He really didn't like giving a time for when he'd be by, as sometimes his job wasn't predictable.

She clipped her way out of the office, her heels making petite noises against the floor. She froze at the sight of two men in black suits, white shirts, and ties. They reached up and slid their sunglasses back as if they were one unit, and both of them looked at her.

"Miss Lancaster?" one of them asked. He had dark, rich skin to go with his deep, rich voice.

"Yes," she said as pleasantly as she could. She told herself this was just another politician. Someone to wine and dine, and heaven knew she'd done that many times in her life. "Can I help you?"

"We're looking for photos," he said while his partner migrated over to one of their larger frames on the wall. "Janey Forsythe said the inn had quite the collection."

"Yes," Maddy said, glancing between the men. "We turned everything over to the Sheriff's department when they found...the...before."

The man smiled. "I'm Agent Richards." He extended his hand for her to shake, which she did. "Did you ever see a photo of anyone in a pink bathing suit?"

"Or just the suit," the other man said. Maddy glanced at him, but he'd kept his nose practically pressed to the glass of one of the shadowboxes.

"A pink bathing suit?" Maddy couldn't remember seeing anything like that. "I don't think so, but we have all of the photos either on display here, or in our original scrapbooks. I can get them if you'd like?"

"Yes, please," Agent Richards said with a smile. He was clearly the Good Cop, and Maddy nodded before she headed for the stairs that led down to her room. She collected all of the albums, suddenly desperate to get rid of them. Perhaps the FBI would want to take them all into evidence.

She went back upstairs with her arms full, and both agents took volumes from her. "We're going to need these for a while," Agent Richards said.

"That's fine," Maddy said. "We pulled the ones we felt best represented the history of the inn and put them on the walls." She indicated them needlessly. "If you need any of those, just let me know."

"We will," the second agent said, and he turned to leave.

Agent Richards stayed, his smile steady too. "How well do you know Tessa Simmons?" he asked.

"Well," Maddy said. "Is she back from Five Island Cove?"

He shook his head, that grin slipping. "We find it a little odd that she hasn't returned."

Maddy frowned. "Odd? Why? She's not involved in this."

Agent Richards's eyebrows drew down too. "Yes, she is. She's a key player in all of this, and we don't have access to her."

"She's coming home today," Maddy said. "She has to work tomorrow."

"Mm." He nodded and headed for the exit, leaving Maddy to wonder why Tessa was so key. Janey was the one who'd gone through the cottage next to the one their mother had owned. Riggs had cooperated with the police. Surely they knew everything he did.

They had Caroline—or whatever her name was—in custody as well. Bobbie Friedman was still awaiting her trial, held in the jail here without bail.

Tessa…Tessa shouldn't be the "key player." She'd already turned everything over to the police that she knew about Caroline Fyfe, Louisa Fry, and Riggs Friedman.

Maddy returned to the office and picked up her phone. She dialed Tessa, concern spiking through her.

Tessa picked up on the third ring, "Hey, Maddy."

"Hey," she said, noting the rush of air across Tessa's speaker. "Are you on your way back?"

"Yes," she said. "The ferry just left. We should be there in less than a half-hour."

Maddy marveled that Five Island Cove was so close to Nantucket. It felt so far away, and she told herself that she could get to her father easily if he needed help. Thirty minutes was about what it took for her to get to him now, especially if she was in the middle of something at the inn. Fine, it didn't take that long, but Maddy wouldn't be halfway around the world. She'd be a thirty-minute ferry ride away.

In her head, she'd simply take her father to live with her on Five Island Cove. But her father had a stubborn streak, and he'd been in his place in Wainscott for fifteen years now.

"The FBI just came by," Maddy said, sinking into her desk chair. It rolled backward, and she went with it. She turned and looked out the window. "They're going to want to talk to you."

"I've been speaking with them," she said. "They know when I'm going to be back. I'd be shocked if they weren't waiting at the harbor."

Maddy nodded. "Okay. I figured you knew."

"What did they want?"

"The photos," Maddy said. "Any and all photos I had. They've been going through the cottage too."

"I gave them permission," she said. "Hopefully they find what they need."

"Hopefully," Maddy said. She drew in a deep breath. "So. How was the Cove? Are you going to move there?"

"It's gorgeous," Tessa said, her voice bordering on gushing now. "Yes, I'm definitely going to be relocating to the Cove. I went by the library this morning, and they don't have any immediate openings. But I've been talking to Helen, and we've got some ideas."

"Helen, huh?" Maddy smiled at the enthusiasm in Tessa's voice. "She's a firecracker."

Tessa laughed, and Maddy joined in. "That she is. She's also got a great mind for business, and she comes up with innovative things," Tessa said. "I don't know when I'll go. Probably after everything is over with...everything."

Maddy watched the wind blow a plastic bag along the beach. She wanted to go out and pick it up so it wouldn't make it to the ocean, but she stayed in her seat. "I have an appointment with Vivian tomorrow morning," she said. "I'm talking to Teresa tonight after The Glass Dolphin closes."

"Putting the pieces in place," Tessa said. "Good for you, Maddy."

She nodded. "Yeah." Good for her. She wasn't sure if it was good or not, but it did feel necessary. Once again, the door squealed, alerting her of an arrival, and she spun back toward the open arch that led into the lobby. "Someone's here," she said. "I have to go."

"I'll see you tonight," Tessa said, and she hung up.

Maddy rose to her feet, but she stayed where she was as Ben approached. He carried a bouquet of roses —white roses—that made Maddy's heart melt and her smile appear. "Hey," he said, his smile slow and sexy. "Did I interrupt you?"

She put her phone on the desk. "No." She nodded to the roses. "Are those for me?"

He came around the desk, but he didn't give her the roses. He took her into his arms and pressed them to her back with one hand. The other slid up her arm, then her neck, to the back of her head. He leaned down and kissed her, and Maddy really didn't want to leave him here on Nantucket.

He knew how to kiss a woman, and by the time he

pulled away, Maddy's pulse raced along all the fine veins in her throat. "These are for you," he said, finally handing her the flowers.

"Thank you," she murmured. She kept her eyes on them, not sure what else to say to him. He perched on the edge of her desk, his height a little less now, and watched her.

"What?" she asked.

"Did you get your appointment with your boss?" he asked.

"Yes," she said. "Tomorrow."

He nodded, his blue eyes firing that attraction at her that made her blood burn hotter. "That's great. I filed a transfer request today."

Maddy's eyebrows went up. "You did?"

"Yep," he said. "I don't know when an opening will come up on the Rocky Ridge Point Station, but I filed to be moved there if one does."

Maddy grinned at him and moved right into his personal space. He put those warm, big hands on her hips and held her in place. "You want to move to Five Island Cove with me?" she murmured as she lurked slightly above him.

"Yes," he whispered. "I want to move to Five Island Cove with you." His expression burned, because everything Captain Benjamin Downs did operated at a level-ten. "I'm falling in love with you, Maddy."

"Even if you don't get it right away," she said. "It's only thirty minutes on a ferry."

"From here to Brant Point is too far," he whispered right before he claimed her mouth again. Maddy was falling in love with him too, and everything in her life finally seemed to settle where it needed to be.

All she had to do now was meet with Teresa and figure out how to open a restaurant in an unknown place—hopefully without any decades-old bones in the ceiling or any mysteries to solve.

———

THAT NIGHT, Maddy pulled open the door at The Glass Dolphin and entered. The woman at the hostess station said, "We're not seating anyone. We're closed."

"I know," Maddy said, smiling at her. "I have a meeting with Teresa Skimm?"

The hostess looked dubious, but she picked up a radio and asked, "Name?"

"Madeleine Lancaster." She'd made the walk from the inn to the restaurant, as they neighbored each other. It was still about a two-block walk, and Maddy had bundled up in her trench coat. She tucked her hands in her pockets as the woman said she'd arrived.

"Send her to my office," Teresa said through the radio, and the woman nodded.

"Do you know where it is?" she asked Maddy.

"Yes," she said. "I've been here before." She hadn't changed out of her pencil skirt, heels, or blouse from earlier that day. She hadn't heard from Tessa after she'd arrived back on the island. She hadn't been out of Ben's sight until now.

He'd said to call him after the meeting, and he'd jumped on his bike and roared away while she'd began her walk down here. Her chest felt warm and everything in The Glass Dolphin was inviting. She loved the upscale atmosphere that was still functional.

She pushed into the kitchen, where several people turned to look at her. Teresa came out of the office, which sat in the corner, and said, "Maddy," as she laughed.

Maddy smiled and hugged her too, then followed the brunette into her office. Teresa closed the door with a sigh.

"Busy tonight?"

"For a Monday, yes," she said as she took her seat behind her desk. It held a variety of papers, folders, coffee filters, utensils, and assorted other restaurant gear. Maddy didn't know how Teresa operated in such chaos, but everyone had a different system.

Teresa smiled at her, her dark brown eyes full of happiness. "We got the building today."

"On Diamond?" Maddy asked, her eyebrows lifting.

Teresa nodded and laughed. "Finally. I've been trying to get this lease signed for two months."

Maddy said, "Congratulations."

Teresa nodded and pulled a blue folder toward her. "We won't open until spring. The goal is to be fully operational, staffed, and ready for summer tourist season. It happens about Memorial Day, though there are other high-traffic times earlier in the spring." She handed the folder to Maddy. "This has the timelines of things, including when I'd need my manager there."

Maddy kept her eyes on Teresa's even as she took the folder. "I just spoke to Vivian today."

"Oh? And?"

"She knows I want to quit, but I have a contract with her."

Teresa frowned. "How long?"

Maddy didn't want to say. She'd signed on to work at The Lighthouse Inn for a year, and then she had to give three months' notice so the Historical Society could find a replacement. "Three months," she said. "They require three months' notice."

"Did you give notice?"

Maddy flipped open the folder. She nodded. She couldn't be in Five Island Cove until March first, and that was only if Vivian managed to hire someone to replace her before then. Otherwise, Maddy had to stay until she did, or until the twelve months ran out, which wouldn't be for another nine months.

She and Julia had only been at the inn for three months, and Vivian hadn't been pleased by Maddy's call that day. She couldn't even imagine the tension that would be in the room when they met tomorrow.

Her lungs ached for air, and she took a long breath as she studied the first page. "I can't be in the Cove by February first," she said, looking up. She closed the folder, feeling like she might be closing the door on her future. "I'm sorry. Maybe this isn't going to work out." She extended the folder toward Teresa, holding it above a stack of what looked like paid invoices.

Teresa shook her head and waved her hands, refusing to take the folder back. "We'll make it work. You're who I want there." She nodded to the folder. "That has the contract for us. Your salary. Health insurance. All of it. It has the plans for renovating the building we got, but I have a construction manager on Diamond who will do that. He'll report to me and you. His name is Liam Randall, and his information is in the folder."

Maddy nodded. "Okay."

"Once you get there, you'll design the menu, hire staff, get the training done. We could probably still open by mid-April if you can't get there until March first."

Maddy swallowed her true confession. Instead, she prayed Vivian would be able to find a replacement for her before March first. She had to. *Please, Lord,* she begged silently.

"I'll go over all of it," Maddy said. "I think it'll be fine."

"If you have any questions, let me know," Teresa said as she stood. A knock sounded at the door as Maddy did, and Teresa yelled, "Come."

The door opened and a man stood there. "Teresa, the fish monger is on the line."

"Perry or Laura?" Teresa asked.

"Perry."

"He is not cutting off my supply of swordfish," Teresa said, and the aggressive nature of her tone would've terrified Maddy. She watched the shorter woman stalk away with the man who'd come to get her, and Maddy tucked the folder under her arm as she made her way to the exit.

She made the walk back to the inn, and she dialed Ben. "So?" he asked instead of saying hello. "How did it go?"

"I start March first," she said. "If Vivian can get me a replacement." She sighed, because while she wanted to burst with excitement, the dream still sat on the horizon. It hadn't come all the way to her yet, and she didn't have it in her grasp.

"She'll get someone," Ben said.

"I'm a little worried." Maddy paced toward her closed bedroom door and then turned to go back to the bed. "What if she doesn't, and I'm stuck here for nine more months?"

"I think you'll have to cross that bridge when you come to it," he said.

She sighed and sank onto her mattress. "Aren't you so wise?" she teased.

He chuckled. "I'm not wise," he said. "I'm wishing I'd stayed at the inn. You weren't gone long."

"No," she said. "I didn't realize it would be so fast." She looked at the folder of information Teresa had given her.

"Maybe I could come back," Ben said, something suggestive in his tone.

Maddy knew why he wanted to come back. They'd shared the past couple of months together, and he'd kissed her passionately. She'd never allowed him into her private room here at the inn, and he lived on a Coast Guard base with dozens of other men. Their alone time was hard to come by, and usually happened at a restaurant, on a boardwalk, or the back of his bike.

Maddy heart beat out of control. "Where are you?" she asked.

"The Corner Shop in Wainscott," he said. "You want anything?"

"Yeah," she said, reaching up to unbutton her blouse at her throat. Maybe then she'd be able to swallow. "Why don't you bring me some of those candied pecans? You know the ones I like? With the craisins in them?"

"Yeah," he said, oh-so-coolly. "I know those. I'll get them and see you soon." He ended the call, and Maddy sprang back to her feet. She couldn't let him in here, could she?

Why not? a voice whispered in her head. Julia's room sat dozens of feet from Maddy's. Guests were all the way up on the second floor. She paced back to her door, chewing on her thumbnail.

She still hadn't decided if she'd meet Ben in the lobby and keep things chaste between them or if she'd let him come into her bedroom when someone knocked on her door.

A lightning bolt of adrenaline shot through her.

"Maddy?" Ben said, his voice low. "It's me."

She dashed to the door and opened it, suddenly wanting him inside so no one else would see him. He grinned at her and stepped over the threshold, just like that. Outside in one moment, inside in another.

Numb, she closed the door, locked it, and turned around. Every movement felt very deliberate, and her bedroom, which had served her just fine for the past few months, felt far too small to hold both of them.

He handed her the nuts. "Here you go."

"Thank you," she murmured, her eyes on the snack and not the man. Several seconds of silence passed, and Maddy felt stupider and stupider with each one.

"Well," Ben said. "I should go."

Maddy looked up then, the fog in her brain clearing. "Go?"

"Yeah." His expression blazed with pure danger. Fire. All things hot. "I'm not going to force this, honey. If you want me to stay, you have to say so."

Maddy stared at him, her neck pulsing with the throbbing of her pulse. She wanted him to stay. She took a step toward him, then another, and finally a third to reach him. He took her effortlessly into his arms and kissed her, no more questions asked.

His rough-around-the-edges style melted into passion after a couple of strokes, and Maddy pulled away only long enough to breathe, "Stay," before he lifted her into his arms and pressed her into the wall behind her, already kissing her again.

Chapter 28

Tessa cinched her arms across her chest as another box of photos got opened. She'd stayed out of the way in the cottage, hating every moment she had to be there. But standing in this sterile room with stainless steel tables wasn't much better. Watching strangers go through all of her mother's photos made Tessa's stomach ache.

They wore white gloves, and they handled every photo with care. Tessa hadn't looked through all of them. How could she? Mom had boxes and boxes of photos. She'd fancied herself a bit of a photog, and she'd snapped pictures of everything from birthdays to Easter dresses to a simple day laying on the beach.

The FBI agents wouldn't let Tessa sort photos with them. They'd asked her dozens of questions yesterday after meeting her at the south harbor. They hadn't let

Abe come into the interrogation room with her, and he'd ended up going home long before she'd finished answering everything.

She didn't know Janey's part of the story, other than what Julia and Maddy had texted. Janey had messaged several times too, but Tessa hadn't been here. She had no eyewitness testimony to give.

Janey had apparently found a newspaper article—the first one that had come out after Louisa had disappeared—with their mother's handwriting on it. Tessa had seen it beneath a layer of plastic, only to confirm that it was Lydia Clarke's handwriting.

It was. Tessa saw it all over the boxes and photos in Mom's cottage.

She'd written the name *Caroline* there, along with *Not her real name. Swimming suit photo.*

It was that photo the FBI was currently searching for.

A knock sounded on the door, and Tessa looked toward it. The three agents in the room did too. Just their heads, though. Finally, Agent Cartwright straightened. "Are we expecting anyone, boys?"

"I'm not," Agent Strickland said. Agent Ryder shook his head.

The door opened while they stood there, and Agent Cartwright darted around the table. "What do you want, Pennington?"

"Miss Forsythe is here," she said. "You said to bring her in when she arrived."

Tessa pushed away from the bookcase where she'd been leaning, her heart pounding in the back of her throat.

"Oh, of course," Agent Cartwright said. He moved toward the door in a couple of quick strides, and Janey entered the room. She didn't wear the frightened look of a mouse the way Tessa had seen before. Instead, she held her head high, her long earrings—made of black feathers—brushed her shoulders as she moved. She wore a flowing silk poncho-like jacket over a black tank top, a pair of wide-leg pants nearly brushing the floor. The only reason they didn't was because Janey wore a pair of ankle boots with a three-inch platform heel.

She met Tessa's eyes, and Tessa's first reaction was to wall off. Shut her out. Janey had done that this weekend, and Tessa would be justified in returning the favor.

Her mouth turned up, and she stepped toward Janey. Toward this woman who was so foreign and yet so familiar at the same time. She didn't have to say hello; Janey didn't either. It was like they were meeting one another for the first time. This new version of each of them, that was.

She opened her arms, and Janey flew into them. "They're looking for a photo," Tessa whispered.

"They haven't found it yet?" Janey asked.

Tessa shook her head as she stepped back. All three agents watched them. Janey grabbed the folds of her jacket and pulled it tight around her torso. That barrel torso they'd both gotten from their father—except Janey's father wasn't the same as Tessa's.

"Mom took all kinds of strange photos," Janey said.

"We're aware," Agent Cartwright said. "We need to find this specific one." He didn't say why, but Tessa knew. It seemed a single photo from forty-five years ago would exonerate or convict a man.

"Well, keep going," Janey said. "If you have some extra gloves, Tessa and I can help."

"No," Agent Cartwright said. The other two agents bent over the counter again.

"Then why are we here?" Tessa asked.

"In case we have questions about anything we see here," Agent Cartwright said. He went back to sifting through photos too.

Tessa drew Janey back to her side. "You went into the Friedman's cottage?"

Janey nodded. Then she lifted her shoulders in a slight shrug. "I don't know why. I'd been studying the pictures you and Maddy took months ago. Going over the case again." She exhaled in a long, nearly silent hiss. "I told Sean I was going for a drive, and I ended up there. Well." She waved one hand, and three of the five fingers wore a ring. "Our cottage. But I was drawn to the Friedman's. I remembered that Riggs had said he was there when we ran into him last time, looking for something Bobbie said she'd kept as evidence."

Tessa nodded, several pieces of the puzzle floating around inside her head too. "Mom and Bobbie were always best friends," she murmured. Their eyes met again. "Maybe they each had a piece of the evidence."

"She, the newspaper."

"Mom, the photo." Tessa turned her eyes back to the boxes on the chest-high tables. "They've gone through those on the left," she said. "They have those to do." She nodded to the four or five shoe boxes that hadn't been touched yet.

"Mom never sorted anything," Janey said.

A lightbulb went off in Tessa's head. "Yes, she did." She looked at Janey again, her mind racing down paths. "She did. I'd open a box of photos and go, 'oh, photos,' and set them aside. I condensed them into these boxes."

She took a step away from her sister. "Agent Cartwright?"

He turned toward her. "Hmm?"

"You need something from nineteen-seventy-four." He frowned, but Tessa went all the way to the counter where the agents stood. "I moved the photos around. The photos are mostly in order, but every once in a while, there was room at the back of a box, and I split up two or three—maybe four—boxes and put them with the others so I wouldn't have to store so many."

He searched her face, and Tessa could tell he didn't get the importance of this. "You need to start at the *back* of every box. I bet I split up nineteen-seventy-four."

The agents exchanged glances, and then they each moved over to the handful of boxes left and brought them all to the counter. Lids came off, and hands plucked stacks from the back.

"This one says nineteen-seventy-three," Agent Ryder said.

Agent Strickland lifted a photo that had Mom and Dad in it, smiling. It was their wedding day. "That's it," Tessa said, her pulse jumping. Her internal organs squeezed hard, and the room swooped. "That's my mom and dad's wedding day. That's nineteen-seventy-four."

All the agents reached with white-gloved hands for the photos in the back of that box, and they got spread out. Only a few seconds passed before a faded photo of mostly tree leaves…with a small pink swimming suit hung up in the branches.

"That's it," Tessa said. None of the agents spoke. Agent Ryder held the photo, and they all stared at it.

"Is that a swimming suit in a tree?" Janey asked.

Tessa flinched, because she hadn't realized that Janey had come up beside her.

"Yes," Agent Cartwright said slowly. "That's exactly what it is."

"Riggs said his sister was wearing a pink swimming suit," Tessa whispered. "When she went missing."

Agent Ryder flipped the picture over, and Tessa leaned in further to read what Mom had written on the back.

July 18, 1974. Found in the trees behind my cottage after a strange woman, who gave her name as Caroline, had been back there.

Her print was in black pen and some of it had warped and faded.

"That's my mom's handwriting," Tessa said.

When I saw the newspaper article about Louisa going missing, I went back there to search. I saw this swimming suit up in the trees. I think it's hers, but I had no way of getting it down.

Bobbie was with me. She met "Caroline" too. She said Rick Fry was her son, but his mother's name is Monica. We kept this picture and the newspaper article in case someone ever accuses Rick.

"This is incredible," Janey said.

The last line on the photograph said, *There's more in my journal, the pink one with the white flowers down the spine.*

All three agents seemed to finish reading the back of the photo at the same time, and six eyes landed on Tessa.

"Where is the pink journal with flowers down the spine?" Agent Cartwright asked.

Tessa swallowed, though she wasn't in trouble here. "All of my mom's journals are at the cottage," she whispered. "I put them upstairs in the bookcase by the window where she liked to sit and watch the beach. She'd write in them there, and it felt fitting."

Agent Cartwright nodded, and Agent Ryder left the room. "Why wouldn't your mother just call the police?" he asked.

"How are we supposed to know that?" Janey asked.

Tessa just shook her head and said nothing.

"You've never read her journals?"

Janey looked at her, because she certainly hadn't. She'd handled the cleaning out of the cottage poorly, and Tessa had done most of it. "No," Tessa said, a sob gathering in the back of her throat. "I couldn't." She took a deep breath. "It was too much. Too fresh. It would've made her too alive, and I...needed to figure out how to deal with her being gone."

Agent Cartwright wore sympathy in his eyes, and he squeezed Tessa's hand. "We're going to have to go through them."

Tessa nodded. "You're wearing gloves."

"We'll get them back, right?" Janey asked.

"In pristine condition," Agent Cartwright promised. "You have my word."

Chapter 29

Lydia sat in her burnt orange recliner on the second floor of the cottage, the view out the window absolute perfection. Blue sky. Golden sand. Brightly colored umbrellas, towels, people.

Her heart sobbed, and she blinked back her tears and focused on the ivory paper in her journal.

She'd tried to start this entry four or five times, and each time she'd failed. Each time, she'd put more and more blame on herself. Why hadn't she gone back and searched the trees the moment Caroline had left? Perhaps Louisa would've still been there.

July 18, 1974

Two days ago, I was coming in from the beach for a lunch date with my boyfriend when I heard someone behind my garage. I distinctly heard a child cry out. I called, but no one answered and no one came.

I went to investigate, but there was no one there. When I went back to the beach, I ran into my best friend, Bobbie Friedman. She asked me what I was doing, and I told her nothing. I sincerely thought it was nothing.

We gossiped about our boyfriends and were laughing and giggling when a strange woman came from my yard. She was dressed in a swimming suit and a bright blue caftan. She acted very strangely. She spoke in riddles and Bobbie and I were both quite confused.

Bobbie asked her for her name, and she said it was Caroline. She said she had to go get packed as she was leaving Nantucket that day.

People come and go from Nantucket every day. There are more tourists here than locals most of the time. It was a very odd experience, but I put it out of my head.

Today, I saw the paper saying that Louisa Fry had gone missing on the same day I ran into Caroline leaving my property. I'm terrified, standing in my own house, because I'd heard a child cry, and Louisa was only seven years old.

I went out to the yard and started searching. I couldn't see any footsteps. There was no blood. Nothing.

Past the trees, there's a drainage ditch, and I thought maybe I'd find her there. She wasn't there. Again, nothing. No footprints. No blood. Absolutely nothing. Part of me was relieved. Part of me absolutely furious. All of me terribly guilty.

I should've looked the moment she left.

Tears pooled in her eyes again, but Lydia blinked them back. She was almost done. "Finish," she told herself. "Just finish and get it out."

I looked up into the trees, and I saw the swimming suit up high. *I couldn't reach it, but I ran back to the house and grabbed my camera. I took a picture of the swimming suit and anything else I thought might help.*

Bobbie and I didn't know what else to do. We thought there was nothing to find, and we were very young. Scared.

Rick Fry is a friend for me. A good friend. Bobbie is his girlfriend, and she's my best friend. Caroline said she was Rick's mother, and the newspaper said he was a suspect. So I gave her the newspaper, and I plan to keep the photos once I get them developed.

If anything ever comes back on Rick, we'll have something to tell the police. That's the best we can do.

She lifted her pen and blew out her breath. Bobbie looked at her and held out her hand. Lydia passed the pink journal to her, and looked back out the window while Bobbie read.

"It's good," she said.

"Sign it," Lydia said, extending the pen toward her. Bobbie took it and added her name to the journal. She gave it back to Lydia, who signed her name below Bobbie's.

She snapped the journal closed and hugged it to her chest. "I feel so guilty." Her stomach clenched, and she never felt right anymore. That was probably due to her pregnancy, and not the disappearance of Louisa Fry, but Lydia wasn't sure.

"Don't," Bobbie said harshly. "This isn't your fault."

"He was right there," Lydia whispered, switching her gaze out the window again. "I saw him run by, and he was so close to her."

"*They'll find her.*" *Bobbie reached out and touched Lydia's knee.* "*What's really wrong?*"

Lydia sniffled and wiped her eyes. "*I'm pregnant.*"

Bobbie pulled in a breath, but Lydia smiled. "*Greg wants to marry me.*"

"*Oh, wow,*" *Bobbie said.* "*He proposed?*"

"*Not really,*" *she said.* "*I told him I needed to think about it.*" *She looked at Bobbie.* "*What should I do?*"

Bobbie's face turned tight, and she pressed her teeth together. "*Are you still going to Long Island this weekend?*"

Lydia's pulse bounced hard, skipping over itself and accelerating all at once. She didn't have to say yes for the answer to be in the room.

Bobbie sighed. "*Fine. Go one more time, Lydia. Last time. You get all of that out of your system this weekend, and then you get back here, ready to be a monogamous and faithful wife. Greg will take good care of you.*"

Lydia nodded, because Bobbie was right. "*He's so hard to give up,*" *she whispered.*

"*He's married,*" *Bobbie said firmly. She took the journal and set it on the windowsill.* "*If Rick ever comes back, I'd marry him in a heartbeat.*" *She smiled.* "*We'll be neighbors and best friends.*"

Lydia smiled at her and took her hand. "*You're right, Bobbie. You're always right. I hope Rick does come back to Nantucket, so you can get your happily-ever-after too.*"

Chapter 30

"So Rick did come back a few years later," Julia said, setting down a cup of coffee in front of Tessa. She sat beside her. "He and Bobbie did get married."

"They protected him," Tessa said. She reached for the sugar bowl, though she didn't drink coffee. "For decades, they protected him. He got a new identity. He lived here. He had Bobbie, and while he didn't know if Janey was his or not, he got to see her." She stirred in a couple of spoonfuls of sugar and then poured in a healthy dose of cream.

"That's wild," Julia said, glancing over to Janey. "And she never said anything?"

"None of them ever said anything," Janey said. "That generation, they know how to keep things under wraps. Viola's the same way."

"Are you like that, Helen?" Tessa asked, a smile touching her lips.

"Oh, yes," Helen said in all seriousness. It made Julia giggle. "I'm an expert at keeping secrets."

"Why are you like that?" Janey asked. "Why didn't you guys ever talk about *anything*?"

"You have to understand," Helen said. Her wrinkles added to her wisdom, and Julia loved her so much. "People in my generation kept all dirt behind closed doors. We didn't want anyone in the neighborhood to know about our dirty laundry. We were all expert secret-keepers. If you didn't talk about it, it didn't exist." She lifted a chocolate chip cookie to her mouth like this was normal Friday afternoon conversation.

Julia basked in the silence in the dining room. She'd have to go work the lobby in a few minutes, and that evening, she'd sit in on an interview for a new caretaker for the inn. Vivian would run the interview, but Julia had said she'd attend so she could offer an opinion on who would run this place with her once Maddy left.

Her throat narrowed at the thought of being here alone. She wanted to leave too, but she had a contract to honor, and she wouldn't leave Vivian high and dry. If, once September rolled around again, she still felt like she should be somewhere else, doing something else, she'd explore her options then.

"When are you moving?" she asked Tessa.

The brunette looked at her with sadness in her eyes. Also a hint of excitement. "I'm going to Five Island Cove again this weekend to look at houses. Abe is coming." She ducked her head, but Julia caught her smile.

She looked at Janey, and she'd seen Tessa as well. She smiled at her sister, and Julia marveled that the three of them could sit down together and talk like this. It felt like a lopsided triangle, with the two of them coming from the same mother, and her and Janey coming from the same father.

Maddy came out of the kitchen with a platter of cookies, the scent of chocolate and cinnamon coming with her. "It's almost time," she said to Julia. "You girls can stay if you want." She smiled at everyone, and no one moved.

"I'll be right out," Julia said. She waited for Maddy to exit the dining room with the warm cookies they served every afternoon for new guests and continuing vacationers. "I'm going to miss her."

"When is she leaving?" Janey asked.

"Depends on when Vivian can hire someone new," Julia said. She drained the last of her coffee and put down her mug. "If she hires someone soon, she'll leave by February first to start her new job on Diamond Island. If it takes longer, Maddy will have to stay until Vivian finds someone."

Julia honestly wasn't sure which to hope for. Of

course, she wanted Maddy to be happy, so she'd prayed the applicants for the job would be stellar. Plus, she didn't want to sit in on interview after interview. At the same time, Julia struggled to envision herself running The Lighthouse Inn with anyone but Maddy. The very idea brought tears to her eyes and a hitch to her lungs that she couldn't clear away no matter how hard she tried.

She stood. "I have to get to work." She started for the lobby.

"Julia," Janey said, and she turned back to her. "You'll be okay here. I'm going to stay on the island. Helen will be here."

"I know," she said. "You're right." She rotated her wrists, ready to start checking people in on the computer. "It's just...Annie might go there too, and I just feel like there might not ever be something like what we have now."

"There won't be," Tessa said as she stood too. She faced Julia and leaned back into the table. "But we have phones. We can call and text. Five Island Cove is a thirty-minute ferry ride. This isn't the end for us. It's just a new beginning."

Julia's heart warmed. "That's beautiful," she said as a smile curved her lips. "I'm going to think of it like that, Tessa. Thank you." She moved into her and hugged her tightly. "Thank you."

Chapter 31

Tessa held onto the railing as the ferry bumped against the dock. She was used to taking a ferry everywhere now that she'd been living in Five Island Cove for the past couple of months. She lived on Sanctuary Island, and she had to take a ferry out to Friendship Island every day for her job. She was incredibly blessed and lucky to have the job at Friendship Inn, where she was helping a couple renovate the inn and get it ready to open.

She felt like she'd just lived through a situation like this, although on a much smaller scale. And without any mystery or fear, danger or secrets, lurking over her head.

She'd moved here just before the Christmas holidays, alone. Maddy and Julia had been so busy with the guests and activities at The Lighthouse Inn, and

Janey had gone to Atlantic City to spend the holidays with her son. Tessa couldn't really say she'd done everything alone. Abe had helped her arrange for the moving of all of her furniture, and she'd had to get things from a storage unit in Pennsylvania, as the beach bungalow she'd rented didn't come with anything.

The moving event had taken her five full days, and Tessa never wanted to move again.

She walked toward the ramp to get off the ferry, expecting to see Maddy or Ben. They were both supposed to be on Rocky Ridge this morning, as Maddy was moving to the Cove to start her new job at The Glass Dolphin.

Tessa smiled as she saw the blonde waving from the dock, her smile huge. She waved back and suddenly couldn't wait to get off the ferry. She talked to her friends on Nantucket every day. She had a couple of neighbors she could call if she needed help. Abe came to the Cove a couple of times each week, and Tessa's heart plunked out an extra beat just thinking about him. He should be here on the evening ferry tonight, and she couldn't wait to see him.

"You made it," she said as she approached Maddy. They embraced, and Tessa pressed her eyes closed as Maddy held her tightly.

"I've missed you," she whispered. "Things aren't the same without you just across the sand."

Tessa smiled as she stepped back. "At least you don't have to make an extra tray of cookies just for me."

"Yeah, you know who I'm making them for now?" She cocked on hip and cast her eyes over to the tall, handsome man standing only a half-step behind her. "Him."

"Hey," Ben said, his smile solidly in place. He also gave Tessa a hug, but it was quick, and he immediately stepped back to Maddy's side. The Coast Guard Captain was transferring here to the Rocky Ridge Point Station, but not until the first of June.

Maddy would be here for all of March, April, and May without him, but Ben had told her he could commandeer a speedboat and come see her whenever he wanted. Everyone knew he couldn't really do that, but she suspected he'd do the best he could to see her.

Her replacement at The Lighthouse Inn had come in at the last minute, and Julia had been texting Tessa about the new caretaker, a woman named Sharon Winslow, since she'd come on a couple of weeks ago for training.

Maddy had been living in Tessa's cottage as she'd had to move out of the Blue Room in the inn to make room for Sharon, and Tessa reminded herself she needed to talk to Janey about listing the cottage for sale.

But do you? she asked herself. They owned the

cottage. No bank would come after them to pay the mortgage. Both she and Janey had plenty of money from their mother's estate. Janey worked in Sean's office, and Tessa helped at Friendship Inn to have something to do.

She went every morning and stayed until one o'clock, which gave her plenty of time to enjoy the beach, explore the five islands, and visit the therapist she'd found here. She went to Nantucket each week-end, and she felt guilty sometimes that she didn't tell anyone but Abe that she was there.

"Have you been by your place?" Tessa asked. Rocky Ridge wasn't the smallest island, but it was the least inhabited. Maddy wanted to live here, because the Coast Guard Station was here, located on the northern tip of the island. She'd have to commute via ferry to Diamond Island, the largest island in the center of the row of five, to work at the restaurant she was going to manage and open.

"Not yet," she said. "We got here on the ferry before yours and grabbed breakfast from that new Mexican place right over there." She indicated a building with colorful flags flying outside it, and Tessa nodded.

"Let's get a car," Tessa said. "Your containers arrived okay?"

"As far as I know," Maddy said. "I got the confir-mations a couple of days ago." She pulled out her phone. "This is the address." She'd come to the island to look for a place to live, and Tessa had met her to do that. If she had a car here, she could navigate them there.

She'd chosen not to bring a car to the Cove. The public transportation was stellar, and their paid Ride-Share network was the absolute best she'd ever seen. She paid a monthly fee and could go anywhere on any of the five islands.

They joined the RideShare line, and Maddy started talking about how she'd decided to leave some things at her father's. "He's going to move here when it warms up, so I'll have to move it all eventually," she said. "But for now, this move will be easier, and I don't need much."

"You're never going to be home anyway," Ben said. "You should've gotten a place on Diamond until I move here." They exchanged a glance, and Tessa looked away. She didn't know everything they said in their unspoken silence, but Maddy turned back to Tessa.

"How are things with Abe? You stopped texting the other night."

"That's because he showed up," she said with a smile. "Sorry. I should've come back to the conversation." The line inched forward, and Tessa went with it. She turned back to Maddy. "I think it's going good. He's...fun to talk to." She smiled, because she didn't know what else to say. She was forty-five years old; she didn't know how to talk about her relationship.

"I'm glad you like him," Maddy said. "He sure seems perfect for you."

"We get along really well," Tessa said. They got a car, and Maddy gave the driver the address. Only ten minutes later, he pulled up to a gorgeous house that overlooked the west beach.

Tessa turned toward Maddy and raised her eyebrows. "My ex-husband was a well-known politician," she said simply. "I maybe splurged a little bit."

"A little bit?" Ben peered through his window. "Maddy, this is huge."

"It's three bedrooms," she said, her voice a tad defensive. "I wanted something comfortable." She looked from Ben to Tessa. "I lived in that single room for several months. For some reason, it started to bother me. This place has a kitchen where I won't have to wash dishes in a sink the size of a bathtub, and I'll be making meals just for myself."

Ben took her hand and lifted it to his lips. "I'm excited for you." He opened his door and got out, then reached back for Maddy. Tessa got out on her side of the car, still a bit in awe of the house. She hadn't wanted somewhere very big, because then there were spaces she had to check to make sure no one had snuck in while she was out.

Irrational, she knew. Tessa was still working

through some things, and she smiled up to the blue sky as she followed Maddy and Ben toward the front door. "I think this is perfect for you," she said to Maddy, because she knew her friend had struggled at the inn for the past couple of months.

"How's Julia doing with the transition?" she asked. "I asked her last night, but she only said a few things."

"She's struggling," Maddy said. "But she's holding strong. Sharon's nice, and she'll do a good job."

She just wasn't Maddy, but Tessa didn't say that. She went inside the house, the floor a beautiful, deep, dark wood that felt like pure wealth. "Did you buy this place?" she asked.

"I'm renting it for now," Maddy said. "But the owners don't live here. We talked briefly about buying down the line."

"Look at those windows," Ben said, striding through the house to the huge wall of windows along the entire back wall. "Mads, you are going to *love* this."

"It has a private dock," she said. "So I can get a boat and go out on the water." She smiled at Tessa, and she returned the gesture.

"I'm so happy for you, Maddy." Their steps slowed at the same time, and they had their own silent conversation while Ben gazed out the windows.

"It feels right," Maddy said quietly.

"I love it here," Tessa said. "I really do."

"You're not too lonely?" Maddy asked, coming to a stop.

Tessa wanted to deny it instantly, but her throat tightened. "A little," she admitted. "Sometimes. When Abe's not here, and I've wandered the beach, and there's still a few hours of daylight left."

Maddy nodded. "Have you talked to Matt lately?"

Tessa nodded, a smile slipping across her face. "Yes, actually. I'm not sure why, but he's talked to me a lot more since I moved here." She thought of her son, who had plans for the summer to come visit her. She wasn't sure why he'd withdrawn from her last year, but she supposed everyone dealt with change in their own way.

She was glad she was more involved in his life, and she hoped to continue to rebuild and repair whatever had splintered between them.

"What about Kyle and Bea? Will you be able to go to the city for their wedding still?"

"Oh, yeah," Maddy said. "They're not getting married until June, and the restaurant will be open by then." She gave Tessa another smile and headed toward Ben. "I think we're both going to go, if Ben can get away."

He turned toward her and leaned down to kiss her forehead. "I put in for the time off," he said. "But it's only a couple of weeks after I start here, and I don't know what things will be like."

Tessa took in the kitchen to her right, noting that Maddy would be very happy here with the state-of-the-art appliances and the quartz countertop. The living room held no furniture whatsoever, but Tessa had walked past a large gray container in the driveway. Hopefully Maddy had a bed and a couch in there.

"There's a small grocer here on Rocky Ridge," Tessa said. "If you make me a list, I can go get you a few things while you use Captain Muscles here to get your bed set up." She smiled at Ben, who burst out laughing.

"Captain Muscles," he said, still chuckling. "I haven't heard that one."

Maddy giggled too, and she said, "I'll make you a list."

———

THAT EVENING, Tessa leaned forward and tapped her RideShare card against the reader. "Thank you," she said, and she got out of the car. Her bungalow sat beside several trees that provided shade in the mornings, and she smiled as the front door opened, spilling light out onto the porch.

She had a patch of lawn to get past, and then she'd be in her boyfriend's arms. "You're here," she said.

"I took an earlier ferry," he said coming down the

three steps to the sidewalk. "I just went inside with my key."

"It's fine," she said. "Why didn't you text?"

"I figured you'd be here soon enough." He received her into his arms and kissed her right there in the deepening dusk. He pulled away a few seconds later and gazed down at her. "How did the move go?"

"Good," she said, leaning into his chest. "Do you want to go out? There's a new place on Diamond."

He grinned at her, and Tessa's heart thumped in a beautiful way. "There's always a new place on Diamond these days."

"Yeah." She touched her lips to his again. "I met my boss's mom, and she told me about The Harbor Bistro."

"Is she the one who lived in the lighthouse?"

"Yes," Tessa said. "Then Clara said she'd go with us if we wanted to go."

His eyebrows went up, those dark eyes shining with stars in his pupils. "So we're going to go to dinner with your boss and her husband?"

"No," Tessa said. "Not tonight, at least. She said we *could* go together, not that I made a date and didn't ask you."

"Do you want to wait and go with her?"

"Not necessarily," she said. "What do you want?"

"I want those lobster rolls we had a few nights ago."

Tessa laughed and laced her fingers through his. "Okay, but I want to change first. I've been moving for a few hours, and I feel dirty and sweaty."

"You look amazing," Abe said, taking her hand in his as he turned back to her house. "I also noticed that you have a litter box inside now."

Tessa shot him a look. "Yes," she said. "I'm getting ready to adopt a cat."

"Just one?"

"Maybe two," she said, smiling at him.

"Of course," he teased.

"There's a pair of brothers at the shelter," she said. "They need a good home."

"I'm sure they do," he said. "When are you going to get them?"

"We're going tomorrow morning." She grinned at him and preceded him into the house while he chuckled.

Tessa changed her clothes and washed her hands, and she liked the coziness and quaintness of her two-bedroom bungalow, with one and a half baths, a small living room, the table which seated four, and the kitchen. She had a deck off the back of the house, which more trees shaded in the evening.

She stepped out there while Abe spoke on the phone with his son, and she took a deep breath of the sea air. She released it, letting the feelings of happiness fill her. "I *really* like it here," she whispered.

Abe came outside and to her side silently. She leaned into him, and he put his arm around her waist. "Any dreams come true today?" he asked.

"Yeah." She sighed. "Maddy's really happy to be here."

"For you?"

"Just a normal day," she said.

"That's not true," he murmured. "Now you're not here alone."

She laid her head against his chest and didn't look at him. She couldn't see the water anymore, but it continued to wash ashore, whispering against the sand as it did. "Yeah, it was a good day," she said.

"Any truths you want to tell me?"

Tessa thought about it for a moment, glad she'd incorporated the Seashell Promise into her relationship with Abe. He didn't seem to have any trouble talking about things in his life. Everything about him was so positive. So upbeat, like he'd been dipped in sugary gold as a baby and it still hadn't worn off.

"I can't think of one," she said.

"I have one." He cleared his throat, and Tessa stepped away from him a bit. She looked at him, but there wasn't much light coming from the house to shine on his face. She waited, then looked out across her backyard again.

Abe kept his attention in that direction as he said, "I'm making plans to come to Five Island Cove too."

She inhaled and held her breath. "When?"

"It might take a few months," he said. "But I want to be here with you all the time."

It wasn't far to Nantucket, but it wasn't right around the corner either.

"I have a new truth then," she said.

He smiled as he looked at her. "Yeah?"

"I want you to be here with me all the time."

Abe started to lean toward her, but Tessa tensed and he paused. "But I don't want things to be hard for you. You have your shop, and it's generational, and I don't want you to give up something that big for someone like me."

"My truth," he whispered. "Is I'm falling in love with you."

Tessa could hardly believe it, but he kissed her then, and she could *feel* it in his tender touch, in every stroke of his mouth against hers.

"I want to be here with you," he said again. "My son is ready to take over the shop, just like I did for my father. It's a slow process though, but I'm hoping to be here full-time by fall."

Tessa didn't know what to say, so she tucked herself into his arms again and vowed she would be completely mentally healthy by the time Abe made his move to Five Island Cove permanent.

Her mind wandered as they stood on the deck, and while the past year had been a roller coaster ride, with a lot of ups and downs, she felt reborn. She felt like she'd been refined through a fire she couldn't have walked through alone.

She hadn't. She'd had her sister with her. New friends in Julia, Maddy, Helen, and Annie. And now, she had a new place to continue to reinvent herself, with a new adventure with a handsome, kind man.

She thought of her mother, and all she'd done to provide for Tessa over the years. *I love you, Mom*, she thought, and then she was finally—*finally*—able to let her go.

Find out more about Friendship Inn, as well as Tessa's new boss and how the renovation is going - and see Tessa! - in REBUILDING FRIENDSHIP INN.

Read on for a sneak peek of REBUILDING FRIENDSHIP INN.

Sneak Peek! Rebuilding Friendship Inn Chapter One:

Clara Tanner knelt in front of her daughter, pressing the busyness of the airport out of her peripheral vision. "Lena," she said. "Look at Mom."

The twenty-year-old clutched her stuffed elephant, her eyes blitzing all over the place. This man. That woman. The television screen with the news playing on silent, the captions running along the bottom.

Everywhere but at Clara.

"Lena."

Her daughter had been born with Down Syndrome. She possessed the chubbier cheeks classic of those with the mutated gene, and she was lovable, bright, and still very much a child. So much of her world had been upended in the past couple of weeks, and Clara reached way down deep for her extra reserve of patience.

"Lena, we have to get on the plane soon. I need you to look at me."

Lena finally brought her hazel eyes to meet Clara's dark brown ones. She gave her daughter a kind smile and reached up to brush her bangs back off her forehead. "It's like going to see Grandma. Uncle Rueben and Aunt Jean will be at the airport to meet us."

"Dad's coming," Lena said, and Clara nodded encouragingly.

She refused to make her voice higher pitched. She'd never talked to Lena like she was an infant. She had a disability; she wasn't stupid. "Yes," she said. "Dad's getting the pretzels you asked for. He's coming this time too."

Their whole family was making the move from Montpelier to Five Island Cove. Clara had arranged with Jennifer Golden to rent a house on the island. It waited in a sleepy, old neighborhood that Jean told herself would be perfect for all of them. It would be away from the news crews, the cameras, and the rumors. The house would offer them far more than protection; the new location, with a new address, would give them anonymity.

Neither she nor Scott would be looking for a new job. They'd managed to get the sale of Friendship Inn to go through with her mother's generous donation for the down payment. Scott's only remaining friend in

Vermont had financed the loan. Otherwise, they never would've been able to do it.

As it was, he was probably putting their soft pretzels on a credit card right now. She'd have to figure out how to pay them off later.

Later.

The word ran through Clara's mind, as it had been one she'd been seizing onto for a while now. She'd be able to pick up the pieces of her life later, once she figured out where she'd be living.

She'd be able to provide a sense of safety and normalcy for Lena later, once they'd left Vermont and settled in the cove.

She'd be able to find a way to forgive her husband later, once all the dust had finally settled from the indictments, the bankruptcy, and the nervous looks from friends and neighbors.

"Here you go, Lena-Lou," Scott said.

Clara looked up at her husband and got to her feet, a pinch in her back telling her she was getting too old to crouch down. Her knees testified of it too.

Scott still made her world light up, and Clara turned away from him physically, almost wishing he didn't. His light hair made her think of California, and his blue eyes had spoken to her soul the first time she'd met him.

She clenched her arms across her midsection, feeling how much weight she'd lost recently. Only fifteen pounds or so, but it was enough to make her clothes baggy and her ribs a bit more pronounced.

Since she didn't have money to buy new blouses and shorts, she wore her old ones, the belt loop just one or two tighter than before.

Clara was a master at cinching everything tight. Life hadn't been horrible to her; she felt like she'd taken the good with the bad, rolled with the punches, and survived some of the worst storms. She'd been able to do so, because of the man at her side.

Scott Tanner had always given Clara strength. He was rational when she was emotional, and when he needed to vent, their roles reversed. He'd been kind and attentive to both Clara and Lena as the girl grew up, and heaven knew how many challenges the three of them had faced as they dealt with counselors, therapists, and doctors.

Lena's disability would challenge anyone, but when Clara had found out about the Down Syndrome, her first reaction had been peace. It would be okay. She and Scott could dedicate their lives to their daughter—who'd turned out to be their only child.

She'd felt like that *because* of Scott. The man had a larger-than-life personality, which had attracted Clara as well. From small-town Five Island Cove, where everyone knew everyone else, she'd been looking for excitement and adventure once she'd finally gotten out from underneath her father's thumb.

Scott had provided that. She'd fallen in love with him so fast, and she still loved him now, as she sat down in a hard airport seat a couple away from Lena. Their carryon luggage took up the space between them, and Scott sat to her immediate right, holding the cup of soft pretzel bites for their daughter.

Clara's thumb moved to her ring finger, where her wedding band should be sitting. She still hadn't put it back on. She wondered how she could learn to forgive faster. She puzzled through how to feel betrayed and broken and still in love with the man who'd done that to her.

She riddled through when she'd put the band back on, and how she'd feel when she finally did.

<hr/>

A FEW HOURS LATER, Clara's well of patience had dried up. They couldn't fly a car over from Montpelier. Couches and beds, all the Christmas decorations, the treadmill, even dishes had remained in Vermont.

Clara had the clothes, toiletries, and essential papers in her carryon, with more shoes, clothing, and other necessities in her checked bag.

Times three, that's what the Tanner family currently possessed. The rest of their stuff would arrive on a ship in four to six weeks, and that was only if Clara managed to find the funds to pay for it.

She couldn't look through couch cushions or strategically move money from one account to another. Not anymore. She had no couch, and the federal government had seized and frozen all of their bank accounts.

They'd gotten one back after the first couple of months, and without the help of a few kind souls in Montpelier who'd been Clara and Scott's closest friends, along with Scott's father, they'd survived.

Her phone chimed several times as Reuben maneuvered the SUV into the parking lot at the beachside condo where their mother lived.

The house which Scott and Clara had rented wouldn't be ready for another three weeks, and they'd been forced to ask for more help. A weight of exhaustion pressed against the back of Clara's skull, sending shockwaves of pain through her brain to her eyes.

She told herself over and over that it was okay. Everyone needed help at some point in their lives. She'd been there with meals, babysitting, and money for others over the years. Service brought her joy, and she needed to seize onto that word instead of the one that had been rotating through her mind lately.

"All right," Reuben said, pulling into an uncovered parking space. "This is as close as I can get you." He smiled at Scott in the front seat, his eyes moving to the rearview mirror to flash a grin in Clara's direction too.

She didn't want to seem ungrateful for the free ride, so she quickly curved her lips up. The cost to do so took the minute amount of energy she had left, so she moved just as rapidly to open the back door.

"Lena," she said across Jean, who sat in the middle. "Please come to the back and help with your bag."

The girl wouldn't, and Scott would have to ask her again. Jean would probably be the one to get Lena to do what she'd been asked to do, because Jean was gentle and powerful at the same time.

Clara glanced at her before she slid out, and she found the stress around her sister-in-law's eyes. Compassion filled her, making tears flood her eyes.

She couldn't hide them, so she simply let them fall down her face as she stood and faced her brother.

"Oh, come on," he said, his voice infused with kindness. He took her into a hug, and Clara clung to her big brother now as a forty-two-year-old the same way she had as a child.

"It's not so bad here," he said. "Especially in the summer."

They shifted out of the way as Jean exited the car, and Clara nodded as she stepped away from Reuben. "It's not that." She grabbed onto Jean and hugged her too. "Thank you guys for helping us. It means so much to me. To all of us."

She couldn't see what was happening on the other side of the SUV, and it didn't matter. Clara didn't say thank you enough, and she needed to do better at that. Heck, simply the fact that Reuben thought she'd been

377

crying about being back in the cove told her what her brother thought of her.

She told herself it wasn't a crime to be strong. She was allowed to have her own opinions, *and* to voice them. It wasn't her job to make anyone else feel good about their choices, though she could lend a listening ear.

"You're welcome," Jean said. "If you're dying here, come to the lighthouse."

"Or we'll help pay for a hotel room," Reuben said, his dark eyes filled with concern. He flicked a glance toward the back of the vehicle as the hatch opened.

"Mom," Lena said at the same time Clara wiped her face.

"Thank you," she said again. "We'll be okay. I'm okay." She took a deep breath, willing the oxygen to make the okay-ness she wanted simply appear.

She wasn't sure if it did or not, but she was able to step to the back of the car to help Lena and Scott with the bags. Reuben and Jean came too, and the five of them towed their six pieces of luggage across the lot and down the sidewalk.

"I'm sure Kristen will have coffee waiting," Jean said.

"She's been cooking for a couple of days, I know that," Reuben added.

A hot meal sounded like a slice of heaven to Clara, but she said nothing. What she really wanted was a room where she could be alone. Where she could cry as much as she wanted. Where she could scream until her throat ripped and all of the negativity inside her fled.

Then, she'd be able to rejoin her family with a better attitude and without tears.

They went past the dog park, where a couple of pooches played with one another while a man watched, and on to her mom's building.

She wasn't sure she could take another step, and then she did. One after the other, she did.

Reuben reached the door first, and he twisted the knob. Or tried to. "Huh." He looked down and then over to Clara. "It's locked."

He reached to ring the doorbell, and the *cling-clang-clong* of it reverberated through the condo, loud enough for everyone to hear outside on her porch.

She didn't come to the door. No one called from inside.

Reuben's eyebrows furrowed at the same time Clara's panic rose. "Where is she? She knew we were coming. I texted her."

Clara leaned closer to the door, trying to edge past a huge bag they'd checked. "Mom?" she called.

No answer.

Frustration piled on top of Clara's already frayed nerves, and the scream she needed to let loose migrated up her throat.

"I'll check the patio," Jean said, leaving behind the luggage she'd been carrying.

Reuben leaned toward the door too. "Mom?" He tried the doorknob again. "It's Reuben and Clara. Are you okay? We can't get in."

Clara dropped her carryon, her shoulder aching. Tears slipped down her face again, the thought of not having her mother for support as she transitioned her family from life in Vermont to life in Five Island Cove completely overwhelming.

And also selfish, she thought. But that didn't erase the fact that they couldn't get in the condo.

There was no relief from the heavy baggage and hot sun.

Her mother wasn't there, so that only left one question in her mind—and which she found in Reuben's eyes—where was their mom?

Sneak Peek! Rebuilding Friendship Inn Chapter Two:

Kristen Shields pressed the square of tissue she'd found in her pocket to the scrape on her knee. She hissed through her teeth, angry at herself for not watching the ground as intently as she should've.

Her and her bleeding heart—and now her knee. She'd just finished the appetizer tray for her children's arrival that evening when she'd seen the feral cat she'd been slowly taming over the past couple of months.

She'd grabbed the chicken cubes she'd cut up for her and dashed outside. Cats could move like ninjas, but with a little persistence and a lot of chicken, she'd managed to find the gray and white cat hiding out in the bushes lining the picnic area of the condo association, where Kristen lived.

She'd lured the cat down the decorative rocks to the beach and fed her the rest of the chicken. She'd even managed to give the cat a stroke or two before the feline had gotten startled and scampered off.

She hadn't been able to go through with getting the puppy she'd once said she'd take. She really was more of a cat person, and she'd been leaning feline for the past few months.

"Are you okay?" The male voice startled Kristen, and she very nearly stumbled again.

She looked up and away from her simple scrape—right into the navy eyes of Theodore Sands.

He lived in her community, and she'd seen him at a couple of the activities she'd managed to attend. She'd never spoken to him much, though sometimes their morning walks had her going out to the beach as he came in.

A nod. A hello. She knew him.

"Yes," she said with a sigh. "I was just feeding this cat, and my foot got caught in the rocks." As if a testament to what had happened, Kristen's ankle sent a spike of pain up her calf.

"I twisted my ankle and just went down on the one knee." She'd gotten up by herself too. No one had seen her, she was fairly certain of that.

Her chest heated, and she certainly hoped Theo had not seen.

Why? she asked herself. *Why does it matter if he saw you fall?*

Confused, she looked up at him. He was a handsome man, Kristen could admit that. The moment she did, her heartbeat stuttered in her chest.

"Let me help you back to your place," he said, extending his hand toward her. Feeling dumb, Kristen put her hand out too. That was what one did when offered help, wasn't it?

His fingers slid along hers, and he froze. She did too, not sure why her blood had started popping and fizzing and bubbling.

She quickly pulled her hand away. "I'm okay," she said. "My kids will be here any minute. I was just trying to stop the bleeding, so I didn't have it dripping down my leg while I walked."

Theo's eyes slipped down to her knee. "I think it looks okay now."

"Yes," Kristen said. "I'm okay." She straightened and wadded up the bloody tissue, quickly stuffing it back into her pocket. She offered Theo a wide smile, hoping that would let him know he could move along.

He gestured for her to go first up the steps that led back to the picnic area. Kristen couldn't think of a reason why she wouldn't go that way, so she went. His footsteps came behind her, a fact that sent her pulse into a whirlwind.

"It's Kristen, right?" he asked once they'd both reached the top of the steps. He gave her a smile that seemed genuine and kind.

"Yes," she said. "And you're Theo." She glanced over at him, finding him ducking his head as he smiled.

"Yes." They walked down the sidewalk together, and Kristen found herself taking in the glorious June evening. Somewhere in the distance, a dog barked, probably at the dog park on the other side of her building.

"Listen," Theo said. "I notice you go walking on the beach, same as me."

"Sometimes," Kristen said. Sometimes she went walking with AJ in the morning. Jean had been joining them this summer, as had Alice. Robin punished herself by running, and far too early for Kristen's liking. The older she'd gotten, the more sleep she'd needed. Especially since Joel's death, Kristen felt far older than she ever had previously.

"Maybe we could synchronize our walking schedule," he said, his silver eyebrows going up.

Kristen's mind screamed at her to say yes. Of course she wanted to go walking with Theo. He seemed interesting, and he was handsome, and she hadn't reacted to a man like this in a long, long time.

"There you are," someone said, and Kristen turned away from Theo, realizing she'd stopped walking. So had he.

Her son rushed toward her, pure panic on his face. He scooped her right into his arms, saying, "The door is locked, and we thought maybe you'd fallen inside."

He stepped back and held onto Kristen's upper arms, his eyes searching for injuries. "Are you okay?"

"Yes," Kristen said, somewhat surprised at his worry. Clara, Scott, and Jean came around the corner too, and Kristen's embarrassment doubled. "I just... saw that feral cat." She threw a look at Theo. "I'm fine."

He smiled, and his teeth certainly looked real. He ticked all the boxes for Kristen, especially as he kept her secret about twisting her ankle and scraping her knee. It was what toddlers did, and she really was fine.

"Clara's exhausted," Reuben said. "Do you have the key? I'll get the house unlocked and everyone settled." He focused on Theo for longer this time, his eyes harboring questions when he looked at Kristen again. "Then you can finish your conversation."

"We're finished," Theo said. "No intrusion." He waved his hand like Kristen's children's worry over her was nothing, but it sent a hot poker of embarrassment through her once again.

"I don't have my key," Kristen said slowly. Theo paused in his exit, and Rueben's eyebrows bushed over his eyes again.

"The door's locked," her son said. "The sliding door too."

"We'll have to call the front office," Kristen said. "I must've hit the lock in my haste to find the cat."

Reuben looked like he had something to say about

her chasing down feral cats, but he held his tongue. Thankfully. Kristen didn't want to get into anything with him in front of Theo, and she had no idea what that meant.

"I've got a key," Theo said, sending shock through her.

"You do?"

He started walking again, and she practically leapt to get to his side again. "Yeah," he said. "I work in the front office sometimes. I have can get in and get you a spare." He gifted her with another brilliant smile, and Kristen swore her muscles melted right off her bones.

"Mom?" Clara asked as they approached one another.

"Hello, dear." Kristen set aside her hormones, a bit surprised they worked after all these years. "I'm sorry about this. How was the flight?" She put one hand on Clara's shoulder while the other brushed the hair off her daughter's forehead. She looked one breath away from a complete break-down, and Kristen found Scott hovering back near the corner.

"It went well enough," Clara said.

"I'll only be a few minutes, Kristen," Theo said, touching her forearm. "Be right back."

"Thank you, Theo," Kristen said, and she watched him walk away for a few steps before she looked at her daughter again.

Everyone had gone silent, and a charge rode in the

air she hadn't felt in a while. Her gaze moved from Clara's narrowed eyes to Rueben's, which held a calculating look. Jean wore a bright smile on her face, and it looked like she might start laughing at any moment.

"What?" she asked just as Clara opened her mouth.

She stopped, breathed again, and asked, "Who was that, Mother?"

"Theo," she said.

"He's running off to get your spare key." Clara made it sound like a scandalous thing to do.

"He said he works in the front office," Kristen said, stepping past her. She couldn't look at Reuben, so she focused on Scott and Lena. "Hello, my family. Sorry I locked us out."

"The door is locked," Lena said, her voice loud and blunt.

Kristen grinned at her. "Yes," she said. "It sure is. Is that a new backpack?"

"Mom bought it for the plane." Lena looked down at the bright purple straps. She adored anything with purple and glitter, and Kristen wished she hadn't locked the sticker book she'd bought for her grand-daughter in the condo.

"Are you dating him?" Clara demanded, to which Jean burst out laughing.

Kristen almost twisted her compromised ankle,

but thankfully, it held her. She gave Clara the best withering look she could. "No," she said. "Of course not."

"Grandma," Lena said, whose attention had wandered somewhere else. "Come look at this gray cat."

LATER THAT NIGHT, Kristen finally entered her bedroom, the light off. She didn't reach to flip it on, because she needed the dark, quiet space. She closed the door behind her, glad everyone had found an acceptable place to sleep.

Scott had ended up going to the lighthouse with Reuben and Jean. They had an extra room on the second floor, and everyone could feel and see that Clara and Scott weren't really getting along.

That wasn't right. It wasn't that they argued or fought. They simply didn't speak to one another. Clara spoke *about* Scott, never truly looking him in the eye. Scott would say, "Clara has all of our important documents," and smile at her while she refused to look at him.

Kristen didn't know all the details and having Rueben and Jean living in the cove had taught her a boundary she couldn't cross when it came to her children's relationships. Scott and Clara got to decide how things functioned inside their marriage, and Kristen wasn't going to say anything about it.

Lena had taken the second bedroom, just on the other side of the wall from Kristen's, and Clara was once again sleeping on an air mattress in the formal dining room. Kristen had commissioned a barn door to section that room off from the rest of the condo to give her daughter some privacy, and it would be here in a couple of days.

Clara said she didn't mind. Kristen had seen so many changes in her already, and while she'd thoroughly enjoyed this evening, their dinner, the conversations, and presenting Lena with the sticker book, her emotions had been through a woodchipper.

She sighed as she sank onto the bed and removed her shoes. Theo had been fairly quick in getting the spare key to her condo, and she'd thanked him. He'd left without another word about synchronizing their walking schedules, but the thought hadn't left Kristen's mind, not even for a minute.

Her phone lit up the room, and Kristen looked at it. She'd put it on silent a while ago, and she hadn't bothered to check it. The only people who texted her were her Seafaring Girls—and any others they'd adopted into the group.

Jean was on the string, and Kristen had it on her list of things to do to ask the girls if she could add Clara. Her daughter would need the support this summer, and so many of Kristen's girls had been through hard things in the past several years.

Marriages, babies, divorces, new relationships, children graduating. The list went on and on.

She found over one hundred messages in the group thread from her girls, and she sighed as she tapped to read them. The arrow shot her back up to the last unread message, and she sucked in a breath as the words entered her brain.

Kristen was seen flirting with a very handsome older man outside her condo.

"Jean," Kristen murmured, stunned her daughter-in-law had tattled on her.

The thread had exploded from there, with everyone chiming in to know who it was, what was said, done, the whole nine yards.

"My goodness," she said, reading something she wished she could scrub from her eyeballs. "Alice."

Her thumbs started flying across her screen. *None of this is true. Yes, a man helped me after I twisted my ankle on the beach. It was and remains nothing.*

She sent the message and pressed her fingers against the corner of her phone to take off the case. There, a slip of paper fluttered to her thigh, and she shined her phone on it, the blue light illuminating the numbers there.

The name.

Theo.

She'd spoken true—she had twisted her ankle on the beach. A man had helped her. It was nothing, and it remained nothing.

At least until she got up the nerve to text him to let him know what time she liked to go walking on the beach.

Another message came in, and Kristen started typing again. This text would settle things once and for all, and nervous excitement fluttered through her stomach.

⸻

Rebuilding Friendship Inn is now available at all retailers!

Books in the Nantucket Point series

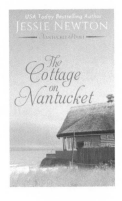

The Cottage on Nantucket, Book 1: When two sisters arrive at the cottage on Nantucket after their mother's death, they begin down a road filled with the ghosts of their past. And when Tessa finds a final letter addressed only to her in a locked desk drawer, the two sisters will uncover secret after secret that exposes them to danger at their Nantucket cottage.

The Lighthouse Inn, Book 2: The Nantucket Historical Society pairs two women together to begin running a defunct inn, not knowing that they're bitter enemies. When they come face-to-face, Julia and Madelynne are horrified and dumbstruck—and bound together by their future commitment and their obstacles in their pasts…

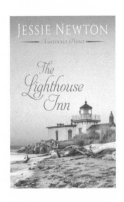

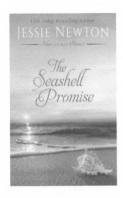

The Seashell Promise, Book 3:
When two sisters arrive at the cottage on Nantucket after their mother's death, they begin down a road filled with the ghosts of their past. And when Tessa finds a final letter addressed only to her in a locked desk drawer, the two sisters will uncover secret after secret that exposes them to danger at their Nantucket cottage.

Books in the Five Island Cove series

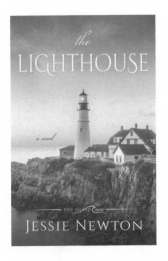

The Lighthouse, Book 1: As these 5 best friends work together to find the truth, they learn to let go of what doesn't matter and cling to what does: faith, family, and most of all, friendship.

Secrets, safety, and sisterhood…it all happens at the lighthouse on Five Island Cove.

The Summer Sand Pact, Book 2: These five best friends made a Summer Sand Pact as teens and have only kept it once or twice— until they reunite decades later and renew their agreement to meet in Five Island Cove every summer.

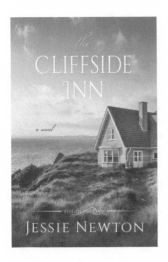

The Cliffside Inn, Book 3:
Spend another month in Five Island Cove and experience an amazing adventure between five best friends, the challenges they face, the secrets threatening to come between them, and their undying support of each other.

Christmas at the Cove, Book 4: Secrets are never discovered during the holidays, right? That's what these five best friends are banking on as they gather once again to Five Island Cove for what they hope will be a Christmas to remember.

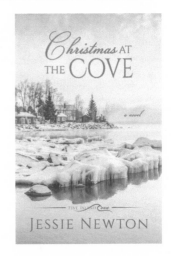

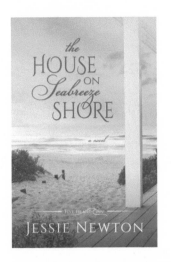

The House on Seabreeze Shore, Book 5: Your next trip to Five Island Cove...this time to face a fresh future and leave all the secrets and fears in the past. Join best friends, old and new, as they learn about themselves, strengthen their bonds of friendship, and learn what it truly means to thrive.

Four Weddings and a Baby, Book 6: When disaster strikes, whose wedding will be postponed? Whose dreams will be underwater?

And there's a baby coming too... Best friends, old and new, must learn to work together to clean up after a natural disaster that leaves bouquets and altars, bassinets and baby blankets, in a soggy heap.

The Seafaring Girls, Book 7: Journey to Five Island Cove for a roaring good time with friends old and new, their sons and daughters, and all their new husbands as they navigate the heartaches and celebrations of life and love.

But when someone returns to the Cove that no one ever expected to see again, old wounds open just as they'd started to heal. This group of women will be tested again, both on land and at sea, just as they once were as teens.

Rebuilding Friendship Inn, Book 8: Clara Tanner has lost it all. Her husband is accused in one of the biggest heists on the East Coast, and she relocates her family to Five Island Cove—the hometown she hates.

Clara needs all of their help and support in order to rebuild Friendship Inn, and as all the women pitch in, there's so much more getting fixed up, put in place, and restored.

Then a single phone call changes everything.

Will these women in Five Island Cove rally around one another as they've been doing? Or will this finally be the thing that breaks them?

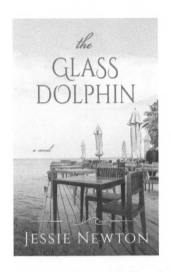

The Glass Dolphin, Book 9: With new friends in Five Island Cove, has the group grown too big? Is there room for all the different personalities, their problems, and their expanding population?

The Bicycle Book Club, Book 10: Summer is upon Five Island Cove, and that means

beach days with friends and family, an explosion of tourism, and summer reading programs! When Tessa decides to look into the past to help shape the future, what she finds in the Five Island Cove library archives could bring them closer together...or splinter them forever.

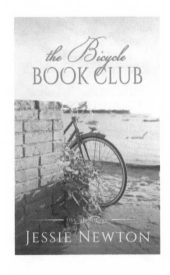

About Jessie

Jessie Newton is a saleswoman during the day and escapes into romance and women's fiction in the evening, usually with a cat and a cup of tea nearby. The Lighthouse is her first women's fiction novel, but she writes as Elana Johnson and Liz Isaacson as well, with over 200 books to all of her names. Find out more at www.feelgoodfictionbooks.com.

Made in United States
Troutdale, OR
06/27/2024

20860512R00249